GEISHA

By Stephen and Ethel Longstreet

THE POLITICIAN

MAN OF MONTMARTRE

By Stephen Longstreet

THE PEDLOCKS

THE BEACH HOUSE

THE LION AT MORNING

THE PROMOTERS

THE BOY IN THE MODEL "T"

GEISHA

A NOVEL

B Y

Stephen and Ethel Longstreet

FUNK & WAGNALLS COMPANY / NEW YORK

Author's Note

Translations from the Japanese texts and poems used were done with the help of Yamamoto Otsuka, to whom we here mark our thanks.

FOR
SHIRLEY BURKE
who helped make
this book
by demanding
we write it

What tends to promote luxury, and to gratify all sensual pleasures, may be had here at as easy a rate as anywhere, the town is a universal theatre of pleasures and diversions. Plays are to be seen daily both in public and private houses. Mountebanks, jugglers who can show some artful tricks, and all rary-shew people, who have either some uncommon or monstrous animal to show, or animals taught to play tricks, resort thither from all parts of the Empire, being sure to get a better penny here than anywhere else . . . Some years ago, our East India Company sent over from Batavia a Casuar—a large bird who would swallow stones and hot coals as a present to the Emperor.

From an early Dutch history of Japan

BOOK ONE

It is important that a lover should know how to make his departure. To begin with, he ought not to be ready to get up, but should need a little coaxing . . . One likes him to behave in such a way that one is sure he is unhappy at going and would stay longer if he possibly could . . . Both lovers should go out together at the double doors, while he tells her how much he dreads the day that is before him and longs for the approach of night . . .

From the Pillow Book of Sei Shonagon

1

Heavy with crests, surrounded by shouting swordsmen, the Tokugawa shoguns—barbarian-destroying generals—ruled the country. The Emperor, a descendant of the sun itself, was powerless; he lived with some placidly loyal nobles in Kyoto. There were five kinds of people in the land: the *daimyo*—lords—the samurai warriors, the farmers, the craftsmen, and the traders and merchants, a new class arising with vulgar cheerfulness. There was order after dreadful epic wars, and a cruel but reasonable justice. The real rulers for the Tokugawa shoguns were the *bakufu*, a military governing council, which used the name of the Emperor as a figurehead while keeping the Emperor as a harmless symbol to be respected. There was no outside contact with a dim world but for some Dutch traders kept on a small island, and all foreign influence was repelled with violence and sealed off. So the samurai and their lords sat content, not realizing that the traders and merchants were slowly acquiring the wealth of the land, along with a growing desire for the pleasures and comforts they could buy. They patronized the artists and the actors who were beginning to mock slyly, with expressionless faces, the iron-armored strutters with their two swords and ribbon-tied top-knots.

The first Tokugawa shogun, in the beginning of their power, had gone to the bare lands near the east coast. Ignoring the older traditions of the city of Kamakura, he built his capital on a reedy marsh where there were no hills, at the site of a tiny village called Edo. A great moat was dug and a stone castle was built within it. And it was not long until there was a business district of Nihonbashi, a grand park at Ueno, shops, theaters and jugglers at Asakusa, the Yosukuni shrine, and beyond the city the gay dissolute streets of the walled Yoshi-wara glorying in well-dressed and pleasure-seeking citizens. Edo quickly became a great city. Rice, pleasure and business were Edo's reason for existence, and the country people said: "A true citizen of Edo never keeps a coin overnight in his pocket."

The gray-green mist of early morning rose reluctantly from the city and from pleasure-tired Yoshiwara, a district known first as Rush Moor, but by a change in the Japanese character reading *Yoshi* it was turned into Joyful. Now the last of the night revelers were moving toward O-mon—the Great Gate where the watchmen stood to prevent escape. They guarded the women, prisoners of over a hundred and fifty brothels and four hundred teahouses, women who were the hundreds of carefully trained geishas and the several thousand courtesans.

Two fat, drunken men with shaved heads, firmly held up by the strong arms of the pleasure house servants, sang loudly to each other:

GEISHA

Ha! *Bon ga kita no ni,*
Now the O'Bon festival has come.
A man without passion in him
Is like a Buddha of wood,
Metal or stone . . .

The head watchman, an old scarred samurai, bowed, for
the drunkards were from the Shogun's castle, as their crested,
now crumpled, robes showed. "Shall I get you a public palanquin, honorable gentlemen?"

One of the drunkards blinked like a red-eyed hawk, and
pulled at his swords with hands now too feeble to obey him.
"Get away, you filth, you're all after money, all you courtesans, guides, servants . . ."

The gray-haired head watchman, his face scarred with
sword wounds, was an old *ronin*—an outlaw samurai whose
lord had been killed in battle—and he bristled at the common
insult, but the more sober of the two revelers tossed him some
coins and pulled his companion into a public litter. The old
ronin stood growling, looking at the coins in his heavy four-
fingered hand. He cursed. "And I used to follow a great
daimyo, a lord who wouldn't let these perfumed *wakashu*
sleep even with his horses."

The sun rose higher. The long rows of teahouses and pleasure houses were silent after a night of music, dancing, food,
and refined and detailed debauchery. The only things that
seemed alive were the wood and charcoal fires lit by some
early risers, a cat moving with disdainful dignity between
puddles, a servant running with a covered tray from some eating place. Otherwise the floating world of Joyful Moor slept,
weary, drugged by *sake* and other bought pleasures. Along
the main center street, the Nakanocho, flowering cherry trees

scented the morning. The bright blossoms were already falling from the trees, trees that never bore fruit. Behind the high
fences that separated the establishments the nodding fawn-pink
and peach-pink blossoms contrasted brightly with the weathered timber.

Four Fingers, the old *ronin* at the O-Mon gate, had stopped
his growling. He looked once at the sky, now a robin-egg blue,
and went to the gate shelter and poured himself a small cup of
strong green tea. He drank it frowning. He was getting old and
there was no future in guarding the O-Mon; soon he would be
discarded and would die in some hovel down by the rice wharfs,
like the artists who drew the pictures that were cut on cherry-
wood blocks, printed on mulberry paper, and sold in the shops
for a few cents, fifteen to twenty *momme*, each. "Ah, we eat
each other, and the gods eat us. The tea is poor and weak this
morning."

There was shouting out by the gate and Four Fingers gulped
his scalding tea and ran out. A wrinkled, thin-legged man in
his forties, but looking much older, with a *sake*-blossom nose,
a mouth lacking teeth, and a head that was quite bald, was
wrestling one of the guards.

Four Fingers pulled off the brawler and smiled at him.
"Now, Kitagawa, you go sleep off last night. You've got a
nose full."

The wrinkled man grinned, showing the places where teeth
were lacking. "Old Four Fingers, you battered pot, I must
paint you. I'll make you young again, make you handsome, take
off the wounds. I, Kitagawa Utamaro, can do it. And I'll give

you beautiful women, on paper. . . I'm sorry, old friend—
that's all I can afford, drawing paper."

"That's enough for us. Now roll along home."

The artist staggered off and Four Fingers grinned through
his scar tissue. "He's happy. Wine and the *yujo*—the women—
what else does a man, or an artist, need?"

Inside the pleasure houses the fusty smell of sleep was pre-
dominant, even over the smoke of an orgy and the odor of last
night's food. In one house a girl had a dream still in motion. She
imagined she was Shizuka, the concubine of the great warrior
Minamoto during the Kamakura period, hundreds of years before. The dream became the novel she had been reading before
she had fallen asleep . . . and as Shizuka she ran away with
the warrior's brother, the young ardent Yoshitsune . . .

"Now after great hardships, after a desperate fight with bandits, completely tired out and broken of heart, they had no
choice but to part from each other, at least for the time being.
They hoped that they would meet again soon. But alas! Only
the Sun God knew. It was to be the eternal separation.

"Now, Yoshitsune, caressing Shizuka as dearly as he could, explained to her in a pathetic tone how they were placed in a dangerous situation and persuaded her to go back where she would
be in safety. Buried in showering tears, she expressed her sorrow
in a denial to be separated from him until death would take her
away. Although she reluctantly obeyed him at the end and took
a saddest farewell, passionately did she wish that she could fly
over him as he disappeared amidst the fast rising fog, but she
was not a bird . . ."

Suddenly the dream and the novel ended. The girl was awake

and in her room at the Kataya teahouse in the Yoshiwara pleasure district of Edo. She was O-Kita Mitsu, a young and beautiful geisha, not any legend out of a fashionable novel. She was not a character in a foolish love story haunted by the ghosts from old *Otsu-e* pictures. One used to bring back these pictures from the village of Otsu, and now these pictures were being replaced by the *ukiyo-e* prints of the pleasure world, the floating world. How true the legend is—one can change the past by what one thinks of it.

O-Kita opened her eyes to a morning sun that felt like warm milk as it came through the paper panels. She became aware of the high wooden pillow she slept on, with the half circle cut into it so she would not disturb her elaborate hairdress. She kicked her naked heels on the softly colored sleeping pad, yawned and stretched her small delicate arms out of her sleeping robe, and then sat up abruptly; the dream had fled completely and she had gray lead in her heart. She was the most wanted geisha in the Yoshiwara but like a few thousand other women she was a prisoner here. Some of them had been sold as children by their parents, some kidnapped, some sentenced here by judges, and she even knew several sold here by husbands or sent in as orphans by greedy relatives.

She shouted, "Neko! Oshaku!"

A blank paper panel slid soundlessly open and Neko—Cat— came in rubbing sleep from her small eyes. She was eight years old, and still plump with baby fat, and now puffy with sleep.

"Neko, why isn't the tea ready?"

"It's warming. Oshaku is fanning the charcoal."

"You're not maids; you're country clods." Then, feeling sorry, O-Kita smiled and waved an arm, remembering how the little Cat had wept every night for weeks when she first came to the Kataya teahouse, at the age of five, sold by her own father. "One speck of dust in the tea and I'll have you flogged with a straw by the door porter," she warned lightly.

The little apprentice geisha went out quietly. O-Kita looked at herself in a Chinese mirror. At twenty her smooth face showed no sign of the years of singing and dancing, playing the *samisen* and *koto*, reciting poems, jollying the rich fatties, patting the old boys, and being witty with the actors and artists, and people from the castles of the Shogun. O-Kita herself had been four when she was brought to the teahouse, sold by a man who had kidnapped her from somewhere up north near Nagano. He looked like a Fukusuke dwarf, they told her later. She hadn't cried; she just bit to the bone the arm of the woman who bought her. Later she quickly learned her skills and became an apt pupil and a house favorite.

At fourteen she had already been famous, but she wasn't spoiled. Yet what had she to show for all the years, all the long nights of entertaining with wit and music? This room, that red chest of costumes, two *samisen* with catskin heads, two dozen books and gold coins worth ten *koku*—and a *koku* could buy five bushels of rice; also a chest containing the prints the artists had given her instead of pay for her amusing talk and music. On the wall hung a painting of Goro, the wild hero of myth, sharpening his arrow; she owned a six-panel screen by Sesshu showing in soft grays and dense blacks the ravines and the sharp pines, the winding river like apple peelings, the little boats of the fishermen, the cruel crags touching rain clouds. The screen was a subtly beautiful thing, telling of the hardness of existence, and the passing forms of nature ever renewing themselves. Hokusai, her greatest admirer among the artists, would stand in front of the screen and sigh.

9

"It's nothing, O-Kita, but black ink on light gray paper, and yet it's everything, everything. How can anyone say it all better than this screen? Play me a sad song of women and men and love, O-Kita. Let's forget for an hour that we hunt all our lives for the things we missed in childhood."

Usually Hokusai was more fun.

O-Kita didn't often play and sing for the artists; they were poor in their tattered gray robes, always hungry, begging their publishers for a few *sen*. O-Kita looked away from the tall gray screen and its bewitching landscape. It was for solitary hours when she could stare at it uninterrupted and feel a glow, like being one with Kwannon, the Goddess of Mercy, who was actually a man but worshipped as of neither sex. O-Kita, waiting for her morning tea, remembered Kwannon had gone down to Hell to call on Amida for compassion for the damned, and a rain of lotus petals fell and Hell was broken open, and the damned all escaped. But such easy solutions were only in stories; in life one didn't escape, not even from morning tedium and melancholia. "Oshaku, tea!"

Oshaku came in with the tea service. She was twelve and already a woman, and she would be a dancer as soon as her training was over. Oshaku was over-refined, and the other apprentices made fun of her, but she would just lift her dark head higher and tilt her curved little nose at the ceiling, ignoring them. Cat followed Oshaku into the room, carrying the charcoal glowing in its container of hard-baked clay. She was bubbling over with some morning gossip, but she waited, seated on her haunches in anticipation, until Oshaku had properly served the geisha her morning tea.

Oshaku placed a spoonful of powdered tea into the simple white bowl and poured the steaming water over it. With a small whisk she beat the tea for a moment, then bowed low and handed the bowl of tea to O-Kita.

O-Kita raised the bowl level with her eyebrows, lowered it and sipped. "Well, Cat, what low talk is driving you fit to bursting? Some tasty bit of gossip, I'm sure."

Oshaku said, "I don't see why you permit her to spread gossip."

Cat grinned. "I don't spread it, I just invent it, usually. But, O-Kita, this isn't gossip. It's true! There is a packet with the great seal of the castle on it. It came this morning by a servant wearing the crest of the Shogun. It has your name on it!"

O-Kita looked up and handed the cup to Oshaku. "Is this more of your invention?"

"No, no! I swear to it by Kwannon herself! It's for you, and Madame Hairy Lip said you must be bathed and dressed in ceremonial robes to get it from Madame Hairy Lip herself."

O-Kita waved off the fresh cup of tea. She began to fling off her sleeping robe. "Come on, get my bathing things, and bring the scent the lord from Fukui gave me."

"The rich farmer who fell into the fire?"

"You know which bottle."

O-Kita tried not to show her excitement. Twice as a young dancer she had been asked to entertain at the great stone castle of the Tokugawa Shogun. But never since she had become a famous geisha had she gone through the Nijubashi—the double bridge—and walked past the white towers to entertain the guests of the Shogun Iyenari Tokugawa.

In the steaming heat of the bathhouse O-Kita stood slim and naked while the two young maids, naked also, poured cleaning water over her shoulders, flat belly, and shapely legs. Her skin was marvelously golden and a young poet had written a poem

11

to it. He had killed himself, not because of the owner of the skin, but because of his gambling debts, playing *goban* for high stakes.

"What an honor, a call to the castle," shouted Cat, pouring hot water from a cedar bucket. She had a child's big stomach, round and firm, and her skin was the color of those brown-amber plums that came from Kochi. "A bigger honor than ever came to this house. The Shogun is wonderful, just a year as ruler. He always looks so pale and bored when they carry him through the town, I wonder what he wants?"

"It's his seraglio," chattered Oshaku wisely. "It contains over fifty women. Such a task for a man who married a daughter of the Shimazus of Satsuna—of the Fujiwara house, too. None of the Tokugawas ever have enough women."

"What other sport is there for shoguns?"

"Look who's talking," said O-Kita, slapping Cat's little rump with a wet towel. "Now, let's soak in the hot water."

The three girls stood in the large hot water tank, the near-boiling water up to their necks. It was an almost unbearable pleasure.

O-Kita wiped her brow with a dry towel and said, "We're wasting our time guessing. They just need someone to play the *samisen* or the *koto*. The nobles of the house of Hitotsubashi must be coming to visit the castle."

Cat shook her head. "Stingy, that's what the Hitotsubashi are. They pay the rate for service, and give you a cage of *hotaru* as a gift, as if fireflies had any practical value."

The steamy atmosphere of the bathhouse was invaded by shrill cries. Naked girls and some wearing only a brief under-garment began to circle the hot pool, all excited by news of the message for O-Kita from the castle.

"One of the princes must be in love with you," said a fat girl.

"It's the young Shogun himself. He must have been here the other night, his face hidden under one of those straw baskets the priests wear when they go to the courtesans."

"Oh, no! They've found out that O-Kita is really a princess kidnapped from Osaka castle."

O-Kita, ignoring the shrill giggling, smiled and stepped gracefully from the bath, her pearly skin steaming, the beautiful curves of her body relaxed. She said, "Listen to the young crows shout that they never eat rice because it gets between their teeth."

Cat stuck out her behind, closed her eyes and said, "And the trapped fox says 'People who eat meat disgust me.' You all wish you got messages from the castle."

With dignity, O-Kita and the two young girls, wrapping themselves in their bathing robes, left the bathhouse, now an animated scene of two dozen girls and women bathing, steaming and scrubbing themselves in an atmosphere of wet wood and hot brass.

Madame Kataya was the tenth of her family to run the Kataya teahouse. And legend had it that the first Kataya had been among those who, almost two hundred years before, had petitioned the Shogun to establish the Yoshiwara pleasure district. The present Madame Kataya, a lean old biddy with sharp eyes, sat this morning on a red Chinese chair, pinching tenderly the cheek of her favorite girl apprentice with much affection, feeding the greedy little mouth sweet rice cakes. Madame Kataya remembered when O-Kita had been her favorite, at just this age, and she rubbed her fingers together and dismissed the child. "Go and practice the tea ceremony, Jita."

She looked at the table where lay the crested, silk-wrapped message tied at both ends and fastened with the castle seal. She warmed her thin bones in the glory of her house receiving this wonderful honor and thoughtfully rubbed the down on her upper lip that had given her the name the girls never used to her face. She stared at the old *kakemono* painting hanging on the wall. It was a religious text of remarkable calligraphy of the Shin-shu sect of Buddha, whose founder discouraged celibacy among priests and preached that all men are the same. A good thing too, mused Madame Hairy Lip, or there would be a great deal less business in the pleasure houses.

O-Kita came in. Her hair was done in the *tsub-ushi-shimada,* the most elaborate of the geisha styles. Her neck and face were freshly powdered an even, lusterless white, and her eyes were made up. She bowed low and stood waiting, her hands in the sleeves of her ceremonial kimono of gold, red and pale blue. The sash was very wide and the color a deep purple; the bow was tied in back, indicating that O-Kita was a geisha and not a courtesan; the courtesans all wore the bow tied in front. Madame Hairy Lip's trained gaze went down to O-Kita's white socks that were divided at the big toe, and to the polished wood sandal-like shoes.

Her old voice said, "You expect to walk to the castle, O-Kita?"

O-Kita kept her head down, staring at her reflection in the table. Too many thumps on the face had taught her long ago not to answer the old hag in kind. "I have dressed to do honor to the house of Kataya. My poor rags distress you?"

Madame Hairy Lip made a harumping sound in her ancient windpipes and took up the message from the Shogun's castle.

"They'll do."

She broke the seals and removed a scroll of smooth paper that crackled as she unrolled it. She read it while she fingered her upper lip. Then she looked up at the expressionless geisha.

"You have been requested to go to the Shogun's castle and take your musical instruments, your bedding and your maids with you. Your best robes, of course. I don't have to tell you I'll skin you like a fish for pickling if you misbehave, or steal, or insult a guest. Don't glare. I know your foul temper. As for your morals, that's your own affair. But respect your duties as a great geisha." Madame Hairy Lip remembered how much she had loved O-Kita once; she put her arms around her and said softly into her ear, "For you are a great geisha, more beautiful, more witty, more graceful than any I have known. Even as great as the Gi-o of legend, who long ago was loved by Kiyomori himself. They will come for you when it gets dark. And remember not to scratch your head."

O-Kita felt numb with wonder, and remembered the blows and caresses Madame Hairy Lip had once given her. Times do change. She bowed and went to her room to set her maids packing for the visit to the castle. She refused to talk about it and slapped Cat when the child got too excited and vocal.

O-Kita sat down on a *tatami*—floor mat—and thought over her situation calmly. She was no fool, and she had no illusions left. She had grown up in the teahouses, in this woman-trap, this vice section, and she knew intimately the gloss of pleasure and the gayness of its brothels. She could thank some gods that she had enough talent to be a geisha, and not to be condemned to the ranks of the low prostitutes who lived and died in the

Yoshiwara, doomed to hopeless slavery and a ghastly destiny. What had kept O-Kita from going to drink, to debauchery, as so many geishas did, was her temper and her personal pride. She had taken what she had to take, but she kept herself privately on the alert against fuller exploitation and disease; she was not one to wallow in the vice around her. There were things to regret in her life: humiliations, defeats, moments of horror she did not want to recall; but as a realist she knew she had survived, and survival was everything in this place, this city, this world. One could so easily become *baka, kuso*—a fool and dung. Years ago she had dropped a coin between the stone foxes that guard the temple of the god Inari, who brought rich husbands to girls, but now she no longer wasted money on such dreams. She would be free some day, but she would not be a diseased drab stinking from raw fish and pickled horseradish, or gesturing lewdly through the grills for the attention of the drunken louts and their ideas of pleasure.

There were thousands of women here. Very few escaped, but she would. She would be free from the whole miserable system of slavery, enforced services, the ritual obedience to the great and the rich who lived off them. All of this she would escape, she told herself; but it was hard to believe sometimes. There was so much tradition piled up behind this dreadful life. There was so much tradition behind everything. Hokusai was right when he said to her, "The dead, my dear O-Kita, are the real rulers of Japan."

What would come of her visit to the castle? If the fruit be bitter, or if it be sweet, the first bite tells.

2

The large man in the enclosed space of the palanquin was unused to riding in a litter on a country road. His breakfast of rice gruel and green tea taken an hour ago at Kyoto rode uneasy in his stomach, and he cursed Ebisu, one of the seven gods of luck, and the ceremonial robe he wore. He could see dimly through the fine yellow silk curtains and hear the slap of the sandaled feet of the four men who moved quickly, despite the heavy weight of the palanquin on their strong brown shoulders. He could hear the shrill shouts of the servants of Lord Ito Kojin crying out, "Bow down! Bow down!" as they passed a group of farm people standing in a field near the road in the early morning sun. The straw and unpainted timber sides of the simple huts in the village were set in an irregular pattern along the sides of the Tokaido Road, the great road with fifty-three way stations that ran from Kyoto to the capitol at Edo.

The large man was young; he was over six feet tall, too tall for the crowded interior of the richly-decorated palanquin made for a much smaller man. He had a pink skin that had reddened in the sun but never tanned, and yellow corn-colored hair with a slight wave to it fell over one of his very blue eyes. The procession he was part of was past the village now, rolling along at what he suspected was a good four miles to the hour. He put his head to one side and looked out through a slit in the canary yellow curtains. The four shouters up front were strutting along, followed by the two fat servants of Lord Ito Kojin carrying their plumed warning staffs of office, and behind them came the dozen samurai—those who serve, he remembered, translating from the Japanese automatically. The samurai always amused him, these bully boys, bare-kneed, in heavy leggings and flopping sandals treading the earth grandly, proud of their gay coats, their crab-like armor, and the two swords pushed with patterned care through the belts around their hips. They had a professional walk, a cock-on-the-dung-heap attitude, he decided, the way they would cut the air with a swagger, peering out from under their big round hats of straw, with war-like grimaces, with mask-like features so well reproduced in the woodcut prints he liked to collect.

The samurai of the period of the Tokugawa dictatorship were as dangerous as they looked. There was nothing to prevent their cutting down any peasant or merchant whom they met; in fact, this right was theirs to keep them fierce and strong, ready for service to their lord, their *daimyo*.

Behind the sword carriers came servants in the livery of Lord Ito Kojin, bearing his colorful seal crest on their gray garments. They carried the bedding, the boxes of personal gear and clothing, the portable shrines, the hundred other items small and large of travel and ritual that these people set so much store by. The large man in the palanquin figured they had three hundred miles to go yet and he moaned, rubbing his wide shoulders free of a new cramp.

Lord Ito Kojin was a *daimyo*—great name—and a *hatamoto*— a banner knight—of the Tokugawas. He was one of the feudal barons of these tea green islands, and he traveled today just ahead of the large man in his own palanquin, not bothered by the swaying, or the two dozen other servants with their tall piles of boxes and bundles, the banners, or the men leading the graceful overbred horses. Looking the other way, the large man saw a long line of more samurai bringing up the rear, with servants carrying the warning plumes and the last shouter warning the village they had just passed, "Bow down! Bow down!" and not to dare to lift their dusty heads until the procession was out of sight.

The large man with the yellow hair wiped his face with the back of a big long-fingered hand—an unexpectedly graceful hand, and shouted, "Kibi! Kibi! Foxy!"

The curtain on one side was pulled open and a very thin, very dark little man with a witty fox-like face looked in, and said in a crisp level English, "You ride much easy, Heacock Sir?"

"Talk Japanese, you grinning little varmint. How the devil am I going to improve my Japanese?"

The interpreter, Kibi Jizo—called Foxy by the large man— made a droll mouth and rolled his head from side to side. "And how, honorable foreign devil, am I going to earn my dismal bowl of rice if I do not interpret?"

"*Sake wa nome, nome,*" said Daniel Heacock. He spoke Japanese the way he had learned it during four years as doctor to the Dutch traders on the island of Deshima off the Japanese coast, the only place in Japan where outsiders were permitted.

"Sorry, but no wine," answered Foxy in Japanese, running alongside the palanquin. "We'll have some *sake* soon when we stop to change to the traveling clothes. It's a hard trip now, but if you like great beauty you will see much of it from here on."

"I'm going to ride a horse from now on, Foxy."

Foxy smiled again, showed a tip of his tongue, and shook his head. "Oh, Heacock Sir, that is against the orders of Prince Kwammu Taira who says the foreign devil is not to be shown to the people. This is a most secret mission, and for you they have broken the regulation of the Tokugawa Shogunate permitting none of your people to travel in Nippon."

Answering in English, the thoroughly shaken traveler said, "A hell of a lot they care what they permit when they need my services. I'm a damn fool to have come, to have let Lord Ito talk me into this."

Foxy's face went expressionless at the mention of the lord, and he fell back out of sight with a hiss of respect. The large man reached behind him for a set of yellow Chinese saddlebags and took out a small thick notebook of sewed rice sheets bound in boards, and a slender stoneware bottle. He pulled the cork out of the bottle and swallowed, with a grunt of pleasure, a mouthful of good Holland gin. Sighing he drove the cork back into the bottle and picked up the notebook. It had been begun earnestly as the sort of travel journal so popular in Western countries at that time, but he had been very careless about keeping it up to date. He flipped its thin strong pages and peered at his irregular small handwriting. Perhaps he should give up pen and ink and use a brush in that beautiful calligraphy the Japanese marked down as writing; his prose might be more interesting.

JOURNAL OF DOCTOR DANIEL HEACOCK
1794 A.D.

"April 18th. The men at the Dutch factory at Deshima are against this trip."

He looked up from the journal. What was he doing here? So far from New England, where he had been born, orphaned early, and sent around among the relations to be raised and educated? It had been a good boyhood, and he relished the memory of it now as the litter jogged past a tiled temple and the strange smells and odd sounds of the procession came to him. He could not fully believe he was here and not still the parentless boy who had been sent to be with a family going downhill. But before that the family had been big and sprawling, and rather careless with its health and itching for money, like any other family. They had been there a long time. When Daniel came to know what was around him, he understood that they were all New England farmers—working, horse trading, and combing out their pride with the long hair of their women; the women were very proud of their long hair. Daniel could remember it all when he wanted to, even in the midst of such strange surroundings: the big house full of oak panels and furniture in good Colonial taste, and solid comforts, and layers and layers of old wallpaper that seemed to be the only thing that held all the family histories together.

Uncle Ben put up hard cider and Aunt Rose sipped wine and they went to the Cape in the summer and Daniel played on the shore, stepping on the crackling seaweed pods and getting sand in his hair, while far out at sea he watched the ships that passed all the time. In the late fall they had clambakes, and the lobsters tasted wonderful, and the jelly they made down in the old kitchen smelled so it took months to get the grape odor out of the bed linen. Everyone liked Daniel and a mean-eyed pony came one spring and had to be sold after he had kicked Daniel in the head. Daniel was unconscious for two days . . .

The little face of Foxy the interpreter broke in on Daniel's memories. "Heacock Sir, that statue by the road is of Daikoku, god of wealth. The *daimyo* who owns this land is worth ten thousand *koku* a year. He is of the Tendai sect of Buddha, and he has his own Noh theater to dance and give plays."

"Tell the carriers to go easy. They're breaking my back."

The little interpreter disappeared.

Alone again, Daniel picked up the thread of memory. He certainly hadn't planned anything like this when he was a boy and went hunting with old Doctor Wells. Doc Wells loved dogs and hunting guns until he had an accident crossing a wall and they buried what the shotgun had spared.

Daniel used to lie in the clover field behind his Aunt Rose's house, smelling the hairy-legged bees at work and the reek of Cape Cod sea kelp from the ocean front and listening to the click of glasses and the card players in the hot afternoon, talking of minor scandals. Later the smell of horses would mingle with the sound of approaching hoofs, and that meant that the uncles were back from the farms or shipyards, biting the necks of good cheroots. Supper was laid in the big dining room and everyone ate a lot, comfortable in their shirtsleeves, and the elders picked their teeth behind snowy napkins. There was early Country Gentleman corn and wedges of juicy red watermelon, and the good Spode china cups were filled with coffee that had been brewed in a big white pot.

Daniel grew with the smell of sea and the scent of meadow grass. When he went to the city of Boston and sniffed it he didn't like it. But the sailing ship trips to Europe later with his uncles were very fine, smelling of new leather luggage and tar and sailor's sweat.

GEISHA

His boyhood was spent in the apple orchard or the dusty barn, and on the road the huckleberry pickers took. He could still remember the pain in his heart when a younger aunt died (the one who wore her hair longest and had white arms and put body powder on her shoulders). He recalled even today the stiffness of starched little girls at dancing classes, and walking across the meadows where the cows were.

He could even feel the ache of the groin in swimming when he dove deep down into the cold blue, and the world was a dull roar far away and they made him dry his hair in a rough towel. They made him play games and remember English kings, with dates.

Going to Europe to study medicine, with Doctor Wells's old medical cases and books, and learning the surgeon's art in the dirty halls of the hospitals. The great London doctors, out of prints by Hogarth, in their big wigs and with gold-headed canes, pointing out the parts of a disemboweled human body laid open on a table—some highwayman just cut down at Tyburn—and everyone holding sweet herbs to their noses to keep out the smell. And the howling of the charity wards and the dull knives of the drunken surgeons. A world good to escape from, to leave and go home.

He could remember back where it had always seemed just right before it all became all wrong. He never forgot the family at the Cape even when he was gone from them and only came back for a week or two every few years. The old house was older and they no longer bothered to paste back the wallpaper that hung from the corners of rooms in which tired voices spoke of the wealth they would have had if they had only held onto the farmland. Uncle Luke was very old just before he died. Aunt Rose was the only one who had any money now, and she did

things for poor children, bringing them in small groups to the
sea in summer, where their skins looked white on the churning
surf and their scabby bodies were piled with sand. They dug
desperately in the packed wet shore with thin fingers as if they
hoped in desperate agony to dig in for the winter before the time
came for them to go back to the city slums.

Winter was the best in those early years, Daniel felt. The
crackle of sleet on the roof, the ice on the dogwood limbs, and
the deep snow sprinkled with crystals, and the chilled breath of
running along the cold, cold seashore. Everything was gray
and white and the sea was all black and just before dark the
lost birds would fall against the house and he used to go out
and bring them in and thaw them out next to the stove.

The stored apples in the cellar used to smell like sweet mold,
and the books were all soggy and hateful to the touch. The
street lights were strung beads then and he took farm girls out
to the meadows and wooded lanes and fumbled and ached and
made a damn fool of himself; and when he fell in love she was
married and he grew to hate and admire her and he laughed
when she sent him a Christmas present, a banjo he never learned
to play.

"Sh'taniro! Sh'taniro! Shantu!" shouted the advance guard
of Lord Ito's procession as they moved up the Tokaido road
to Edo.

Daniel picked up the journal, his litter shaking rhythmically
as the road wound around great silent stones planted on a terrace like flowers. He was still uncomfortable, but he was on his
way, even in this insufferable, abominable method of travel. He
had come a long way from a New England world and certainly

he had never planned to be here in his later twenties (in two years he would be thirty and already the blond hair was thinning at his temples).

He had lost all capacity to resist the currents of his life. He knew he was belligerent toward respectability. The dream of a calm existence, doctoring in some New England village, was lost too; he could never go back home to practice the medical knowledge learned so hard in cold, damp London. Circumstances always conspire against us, he told himself, and pity for one's fate is a dangerous Christian virtue. The first seizure, the first falling down, the coma and catalepsy, the horror of the gasping attack were still vivid in his mind.

The awareness of the disease had at first destroyed Daniel's will to live. But Doctor Rush, in Philadelphia, had said to him, "Epilepsy, my boy, is something a man can survive. As a medical man yourself, Daniel, you know the Greeks thought it was a divine disease, and at least one of the great philosophers had seizures. Besides, these attacks may be months, even years apart . . . Oh, come now, face up to it—of course you can practice medicine. What is your specialty? Oh, surgery? Well, hmmm, let's go down to the River House and have some fall cider. No, no, a drink now and then soothes you. Twenty-two, are you? A mere minor. When you're an old whale like I am you'll realize the nonsense of any fundamental certainty to anything, even a disease. You'll survive."

Doctor Rush had been right. He had not fully atrophied into bitterness, but he had developed an urge to run away, to travel; he had never gone back to the Cape. Just written a long, maudlin letter and taken a tea ship to China . . . Canton. Dirty, wonderful, stinking, exciting Canton. He had had on the average only two bad seizures a year. He had written some poems. And then he wandered to the Dutch preserve of Deshima, a tiny island in the harbor at Nagasaki. And here he was even able to practice a little medicine, although the sturdily healthy European merchants were rather dull patients. While he was there he had treated one lovely and frail Japanese woman. She had died, but her husband was impressed with his medical skill, and a few months later asked Daniel to start on this secret journey to use his healing magic on a mysterious but supremely important Japanese patient.

When he started on this trip into the interior of Japan, forbidden to all other Westerners, he wrote in his journal:

"A surgeon in Asia at least doesn't have to be perfect. Not by a long shot across the bows. The Dutch are fat and greedy, but good sorts, and their ills come from their gluttony at tables and excesses in bed with the teahouse girls. They say I am a fool to go to Edo on this thing. But four years of being locked up as they are on their damn crowded island is enough. Besides I like what I see over here and I want to find out who makes these wonderful woodcut prints and find more of the early ones. The artists Maronobu, Kiyomasu, Kiyonobu, Kiyohiro. Like all collectors I am a fool, and as a doctor I suppose I look forward to a challenge to my skill beyond whittling at the sore behinds of these Dutchmen, or giving them stomach drenches that would kill most mules back in the colonies."

He flipped the pages and reached to extract the cork of the gin bottle again.

"May 2. I like to think I am the only white man now on the mainland of Nippon. And most likely I am. They do not want us here and except for the Dutch merchants and traders cooped up on that stinking island across from Nagasaki they want no contact with the outer world or us, and I can't blame them. It's a very beautiful land and tomorrow we begin the long trip to Edo. I have brought two sets of surgical instruments, one still packed in flannel as it came from Amsterdam. I have performed the operation four times, and only lost that old man in Calcutta when his heart gave out. I hope, by Butsudo, that the sick man in Edo has a good strong heart and isn't a palace dandy or worn out by the geishas and the courtesans . . ."

The large man was aware suddenly that the swaying of the palanquin had stopped, that the shouts of "Bow down! Bow down!" were being repeated. He looked out. They were in the shade of great pine trees. He saw the courtyard of an inn—a *tsukiyana*—in a hilly garden. A row of inn servants, men and women, were kneeling almost prone on the ground, while the samurai ran about scowling, stuck full of swords, resembling, Daniel decided, nothing so much as his Aunt Rose's pin cushions. He threw his sandaled feet out of the litter and his body followed, and he stood stretching his aching joints in the white sunlight, glad to be on steady ground, unaware that in native dress and with yellow hair and blue eyes, his six feet two inches looked like the devil Emma-O—the regent of Hell—to everyone.

A fat man and a thin man rose to their knees among the inn servants but kept their heads down. Lord Ito Kojin's chief servant stepped forward, legs apart, his wide belly held up with dignity, and he was barking orders to the inn's owner. Some of the prone servants were looking up with terror at the large yellow-haired man and they were beginning to shake. Daniel Heacock turned to find the palanquin of Lord Ito being set down beside his. The bowing that was expected for such a great feudal lord took place and Lord Ito came gracefully out into the sun wearing splendidly colored ceremonial robes in which gold and red predominated. He paid no attention to the prone servants and bowing attendants or to Foxy, the kneeling interpreter. Daniel lowered his head, but that was as far as he would debase himself before this lord of the *hatamoto* class. He liked Lord Ito; he was a charming young man, with very handsome features and very dark eyes, and his mouth had a humorous curve.

"Heacock Sir, you look bone weary."

The little interpreter, still kneeling in the inn courtyard, did not look up as he spoke. Daniel Heacock answered in Japanese. "My behind is in distress, my guts are full of wind and there are wild voices in my ears."

Foxy the interpreter retranslated the word for guts. The Lord Ito laughed, his shaved head and black topknot hair shaking. He made a rapid gesture with his arms inside his great colored sleeves. "We shall change all that. We rest here and change into travel clothes for the hard road, I regret, ahead of us. We cannot spend the night here at the first station. The matter at Edo is most urgent." He pressed Daniel Heacock's arm through both their robes. "And grave, most grave."

More servants were lifting their heads to stare at the yellow-haired giant. Several of the samurai made growling sounds and reached for swords, or fingered their ornate iron sword guards called *tsuba*. Foxy, with a serene eye and wary gait, collected their baggage.

Seated on mats inside the cool scented comfort of the inn, under the great cedar beams, they had water poured over their hands from gourds. They then dried their hands with towels handed them by kneeling servant girls. Daniel was not hungry, and he could not honestly say he liked Japanese food, not after the saffron-colored curries of India and the really delectable cooking, Cantonese and Mandarin, of China. In many ways, he had decided, the Japanese were behind the Chinese. But they had a greater vitality, more curiosity and a clever ability to create new art. They were fiery and warlike and as alert to the power of cruelty as to the brawling gusto of living. Proud of his skill with chopsticks, he helped himself to *sashimi to kyuri*, thoroughly enjoying the cucumbers and raw fish in lime juice.

He refused the *kamo no koma-giri*—chopped duck croquettes would not travel well in the jolting litter.

Lord Ito smiled at Daniel. "You begin properly by not over-eating. It's not good to fill up like a bag of hay. The *sake* isn't bad; it's Nigori *sake* from Akita."

Daniel took the offered white bowl of warm rice wine and took a deep swallow. Everyone laughed as he smiled; it was not the mild Seishu *sake* he was used to, but contained at least twenty percent alcohol.

"Lord Ito, you're so right. This isn't bad at all."

The warm wet napkins came around with the golden limes, and Lord Ito, at ease on his haunches, said, "We will rest and change from our ceremonial robes to travel clothes. An hour enough, Heacock Sir?"

"I'll be ready." It was difficult getting up. He'd never learn to be comfortable in that squatting position.

He followed a little maid in white socks and a dark blue sash into a small mat-floored room where sleeping pads were laid out. The gray paper walls closed in on him. One red lacquered tray on the mats held a rough spreckled stone, a twig of olive green pine, a lotus flower and several small smooth blue pebbles. There was nothing else in the room. He lay down on the sleeping pads and put his hands behind his head and stared at the roof rafters. He felt a kind of floating sensation, almost an elation that had no connection with reality, no bonds; he existed in a kind of strange infinity. With intense reluctance he admitted to himself that the early symptoms of a major attack of his illness were appearing. It was eight months since his last seizure, and he had been able several times since to fight off another one with the pipe. But there was no time to smoke now—certainly not here and now, on a one-hour stop—and the gear was packed away in his trunk. He clenched his fists and said in a rasping whisper, "No, no."

He tried to focus his eyes again on the rafters; a very slim elegant Japanese rat with a curled brown tail ran by overhead; he had no idea whether it was an hallucination or a real creature. In panic, laughing extravagantly, he began to recite the native festivals and holidays: "Shihohai, Ehonairi, Hatsuni, Kazizome, Hatsuyume . . ."

He was aware that Foxy had come silently into the room and was staring down at him. The little man grinned and held up a sheet of paper on which was a colored woodcut of an actor playing a woman's part. "Very fine print I bought for you from one of the merchants stopping here from Edo."

Daniel, sweating, sat up and took the print, trying to focus his vision. "Toshusai Sharaku ga, it's signed. Who is he? I never saw any prints by him." He held his breath and then began to breathe slowly. "What an odd way of drawing. But marvelous, Foxy, marvelous." In focusing on the print he began to recover from the feeling of detachment, of floating.

"Must be a new man. The Fuji-and-ivy seal is the mark of the publisher Tsutaya Jusaburo. A sly fellow."

Daniel was engrossed in the print. It was a remarkably simple thing, rose and tan tones, just a head against a neutral background. It had a wonderful freshness and vigor, and was an ironic comment on the actors who played women's parts. His fears and apprehension faded away. "He must be a very new man. I've never head of him. But he's a master, a real master."

Foxy nodded. "You better change now into traveling clothes. The Lord Ito is already changed. I'll get your bag."

Daniel hunted in his sleeve for one of the dark brown Java cigars the Dutch liked and put it in his mouth. Foxy came back with his traveling bag and began to take out Daniel's gray traveling clothes. A little maid glided in, as if on wheels, with a small clay pot of glowing charcoal on which a cup of *sake* was warming. Foxy extracted one live coal from the pot with small tongs and held it to the end of the big man's cigar. Daniel puffed it alive and put the woodcut print on the floor. He began to disrobe.

"We must find out about him in Edo, this Sharaku. Maybe I can meet him."

Foxy handed him the cup of *sake* and Daniel drained it and stood still while the little man in genial efficiency danced around him, winding the sash around Daniel's travel robe. "You sound better, Heacock Sir, much better now. When we get to Edo we will go to the Yoshiwara and pick out the best geishas to entertain you and the most wonderful courtesans. Oh, we'll make a night of it—lots of nights of it."

Daniel looked at the little man, grinned and answered in English, "You little swab, you think you know how to cheer me up?"

Foxy answered back in the same language, "We make one hell of a time of it, eh?"

Outside, the clear sound of the procession reforming, the clatter of the warriors' armor, the contralto of the maids' voices, and the neighing of horses announced they were ready to move on. Daniel, fully recovered now from his introspection and skepticism, felt exhilarated from the *sake*, pleased with the new print. The dark shadow of the personal horror was for the moment brushed away.

3

The loud-voiced peddler of red peppers and calendars, a tall man for a Japanese, was in the prime of life, but already his face, long and of rough features with large onyx-textured eyes, showed the hunger and the turmoil of a hard life made harder by some struggle toward self-realization.

"Who will buy my fine red peppers?" he shouted in a voice husky and loud. "Who will buy my peppers red and strong? Who wants a calendar? Who wants to figure back to the Year of the Hare, or ahead to the Year of the Tiger?"

There were other hawkers, offering dried fish, noodles, paper umbrellas, singing birds, beancurd-rice candy, fortunes, hair oil, pickles, lamps, and trays of carved wood, all crying out their wares. The peddler of red peppers and calendars cried the loudest, rattling his basket of peppers and pushing his tray of calendars violently into the stomachs of passersby. Incense sellers, letter writers, friers of cuttlefish in sesame oil did business, but not he.

"Follow the holiday dates from Sho the first month to Ju Oni Gwatsu the twelfth. Red peppers to make the mouth water! Months to make love, or plant, or go on a long trip to a shrine!"

The streets of Chuo-ku, the central ward, were only a tenth of the city, but here all the business was done. The rest of Edo held temples, parks, and homes of the lords and samurai. Here along the Sumida River's muddy banks, past the Nihonbashi bridge and right up to the Shogun's castle, life fought and shouted, pushed and remained excited. Rice warehouses, the street of brightly colored theater fronts, the shops of the print publishers, all proclaimed their offerings boldly in large painted letters. In the dry parts of the river bed, crossed by the moon bridge, archery targets were set up, and by the canal the acid smell of the city jail promised punishment for wrong-doers. The pepper peddler ignored it all; men carrying rice sacks, racks of paper dragons, piles of theatrical robes, pails of sea-life packed in dripping seaweeds, pungent pickles and the angry spit of crabs clashing their green stone armor together in baskets.

The red pepper and calendar peddler suddenly turned his back to the crowded street and stood facing a doorway. A large prosperous citizen, followed by two servants carrying a large carp and wrapped packages, approached. The citizen recognized the big thin back of the peddler.

"Hokusai!" he said cheerfully, slapping the peddler's back and spinning him around. "What kind of game is this?"

The peddler rolled his dark eyes, laughing, facing his disgrace. "Kiyonaga, you see before you the result of almost forty years of earnest work, study, great industry and talent. Will you buy a red pepper?"

The well-dressed man shook his head and made a hissing sound of pity. "My dear Hokusai, you are the greatest draftsman in Japan. Your prints once sold in every shop. What devil demon brought you down to offering housewives bargains in overripe trash?"

"Hunger, frustration, bad luck; but mostly hunger. I tell you, full integrity is too hard. Sometimes I eat my stock in trade, and usually I sleep in the gutter. So now I must yell peppers and calendars. Would you like a set of dates for your theater posters? You were clever to give up print-making for posters. At least you can rest on your behind, paint brush in hand, and dream up adventures. But a print artist has to degrade his conscience into shapes for popular appeal, or else he must try to sell things no one seems to want."

The poster painter laughed and rocked back and forth in feigned shock. "We have to bend our talents a bit in the wind too when we sell posters." He turned to the servants. "Take these things home." He also took the tray of calendars, the basket of red peppers. "And *this* too. *Yoroshiu*—everything is all right."

Hokusai stood very still, entertained by his friend but weak from hunger, trying to be expressionless. His stomach rumbled, his hunger ached in every fiber of him. Kiyonaga took his arm. "I know of a lord who needs an artist. After all, why not you?"

"Why not?" said the hungry artist.

"Come along and we can discuss it. There's a good little eating place up the street."

The eating place had a huge painting for a sign: a thin man wrestling with a huge white radish, and animals grating giant turnips. Inside, the print artist and the poster painter sat on mats before the low teak table. The food came and the hungry man ate. The raw thin slices of fish, the *soba* buckwheat noodles, the salted pressed pickles—everything was eaten quickly with fingers or chopsticks. Hokusai kept looking up over the bowls at his friend and, swallowing and sweating, puffing and moaning with pleasure, at last he pushed aside the container that had once held *yakimona*—fish and fowl boiled together. Carefully, with the damp warm napkin the waitress handed him, he wiped his eyes, mouth, jowls, cleaned his hands, sat back, burped politely and sighed. "Ah, I tell you, Kiyonaga, when you have been too long without love and food, a hungry man can't be trusted not to choose his belly first."

The poster painter smiled. "You are still in love with O-Kita?"

"I admit it. Amorous episodes aren't improvised only by your theater friends. Yes, I'm still in love, but what chance does a beggar stand with the most popular geisha in Edo? I ask you, can I give her bolts of silk, deep sea pearls, chests of musk and other scents for the secret corners of her body, rare screens painted by the great masters of the past?"

"But you can give her the fever of your love."

The artist was sketching the body of a woman in spilled sauce on the table top. He looked up smiling. "That's fine for plays, but in real life a girl has to think of her future, her old age, and put something by."

"I am sorry for you; envious, too. It's a sweet poison, love."

"I amuse her when I can afford a robe clean enough to visit her, and bring a gift of a little pine tree in an old bronze pot. She enjoys my silly sketches of old men wrestling foolishly with young girls. But that is all. It's sad, isn't it? All the time we spend longing."

Kiyonaga's face became serious as he nodded. "Yes. All the energy we expend on love, on women, on four legs on a sleeping mat. I tell you frankly, Hokusai, I'm really happy to be getting old enough not to feel the itch of desire too often. It's like being unchained from a devil clawing out your vitals."

"You don't, I see, know O-Kita Mitsu." He motioned to the waitress. "My friend will stand me treat to a bowl of Shochu *sake*."

"No, no, not that stuff distilled from the dregs. It's pure fire. Two bowls of good Seishu."

The little waitress padded out of the room in her white-stockinged feet.

The artist rubbed out the drawing of the geisha on the table top. "Now tell me, what lord needs an artist?"

"Lord Ito Kojin is coming to Edo, from Kyoto. There is something mysterious about this trip. You understand. Prince Kwammu Taira is going to give a series of parties, and Lord Ito Kojin, to repay favors, will have to open his house and give parties in return. I know his steward and his house in Edo badly needs doing over. It hasn't been lived in for five years. There was a nice little fire last month that burned off the old roof. There's room for lots of new wall paintings, hanging pictures, and even a few screens. I know you work quickly."

"Quickly?" The artist was relaxing, eyes closed. "Like lightning when I'm hungry. All those empty walls. A painter dreams of walls to cover. When I'm weak with hunger I dream of a wall a mile high and ten miles long and I'm painting on it with a broom the size of a water buffalo's head . . . the wildest pictures, of men at play, at war, making love, eating giant fruits and vegetables. And over it the great cone of the mountain . . . Fuji." He looked out to the busy street, not noticing the little waitress who had come back and was silently pouring warm *sake* into two little cups. "You can't see it from here. My grandfather remembered when it erupted and Edo, seventy-five miles away, was six inches deep in volcanic ash. It's the only reality for me, that mountain Fujiyama. Kiyonaga, everything else is for the moment or, like knitting with water, it slips away, blurs and vanishes. Only Fuji exists."

The poster man touched the brooding Hokusai's arm. "Listen, here is some money. Have you a home?"

"No. Someone loaned me some money on it, and I lost the house." He drained the *sake* and helped himself to some more.

"You support too many people. Give away, lend, and when you begin to spend there's no stopping you."

"Yes. You wouldn't believe how many books I illustrated last year, how many woodblock prints I cut. They pay so little. The money just went. Then suddenly there is a slowing up of the print publishers' demands and I'm out on the street."

"Here is some money. It's for you alone. Get to a bathhouse. Have your head shaved properly, and buy a good black hemp robe. Eat till your skin is stretched tight and it shines. What else do you need?"

"I haven't any brushes or ink stones, or any paper."

"All right. But be presentable, and be at Lord Ito Kojin's house tomorrow at noon. It's north of the Shogun's castle, along the river. Anybody will tell you which one is Lord Ito's. It has a red gate behind a statue of Junishi, one of the seven gods of luck, and he's seated on his tortoise."

"No wonder he's so slow to reach me." Hokusai was pleasantly dizzy with food and warm *sake*. "Tell me, have you seen the Shogun passing by in procession lately? There is a rumor that he is dead up there in the castle."

"Something is happening, I don't know what. Many of the lords have been called to Edo. No, I haven't seen the Shogun. But, Hokusai, let me warn you. Don't get mixed up in anything. The Tokugawa Shogunate is here to stay. If there is something stirring up there at the castle it's a good turn for you. The lords all need pictures for their homes and they'll try to out-feed and out-entertain each other while they sit and watch each other for the next move. If anything is wrong with the Shogun, you can be sure that everybody is jockeying for position."

"It's intriguing. The stuff to make picture histories of."

Kiyonaga stood up and clapped his hands for the tally. "We artists are the historians of our society. But only as bystanders or observers, remember that."

"That's my trouble," said Hokusai. "I can't stand with my hands clasped together on the side of the road. Listen, maybe they are going to bring back the Emperor from Kyoto and make him the real ruler again. Maybe we'll have a civil war. What pictures to paint, what times to live in! It's good to be alive and fed."

The waitress listened, and looked at them so hard her eyes crossed.

Kiyonaga warned again, "Just keep out of trouble. And be at Lord Ito's at noon." Hokusai remembered his manners and added an old politeness, *"Arigato gozai masu.* I thank you with all my heart. I am too unworthy."

The poster painter eyed his friend, wondering what demon drove him, what destiny awaited him. They had been print makers together, he the older man, and this vital amusing fellow. Born Ise, called Tetsuzo, always changing his name. Hokusai was a new one; before that he had signed himself Sori. And before that others as he threw off the styles of the Kano and Tosa schools of art. He mocked himself as the peasant of Katsushika, where he had been born outside of Efi in Shimofusa province. A drifting boy adopted by a family of mirror makers for the Shogun's court, he worked as a wood engraver, then in a circulating library where he studied earnestly the book illustrations, and at nineteen became a pupil of the great Katsukawa Shunsho. The poster painter sighed. Shunsho, the master of so many of them, had died the year before; already they were debasing his style.

Restless Hokusai had followed and studied so many artists, looking for something he couldn't seem to find. Illustrating books, making actor prints. Even the Dutch devils and their Western art attracted him with those copper engravings that were filtering into Japan. Scientific perspective, shading in the round, realistic representation. It had ruined a lot of the young artists. But Hokusai had swallowed it all, digested some of it, threw up what he couldn't use, and gone on. A shabby, wild young man, too much in a hurry, too much on the run. Never stopping to stay with a style that could be a success with the print publishers. Not worrying much over tomorrow. He did *surimonos*—those fanciful greeting cards printed in detailed care—in a way no one had done them before. Then, worn out, dissatisfied, he turned to landscape painting before bringing that too into the prints. Close to forty, he was still full of promise, and still an apprentice in many ways.

The poster painter wiped his mouth carefully. Hokusai needed help, not just food, but it wouldn't have any lasting affect on him. He would only squander whatever money he earned. Tomorrow and the day after he'd be back desperately peddling paper umbrellas or overripe fruit, and sleeping in the streets.

"Luck go with you, Hokusai."

"Kiyonaga, I could cry with thanks, but I'm too full to be that grateful."

The two friends parted. The successful theater painter went home to a fine house and a waiting family, to his collection of Chinese porcelains, old screens and scrolls, and masks from the Noh dramas. The artist Hokusai went to find a street corner barber to shave him in the proper fashion. Later he soaked deeply in the steaming water of a bathhouse, puffing and spewing like a fountain and making everyone laugh at his antics. He put on an undergarment with a black silk neckband, and an unlined robe of a subdued cockscomb red. A fine dark brown silk crepe obi sash finished off the costume, redeeming him into society.

It was dark when he reached the streets, beautiful with lanterns. The moon was a silver sliver. When he got to the teahouse of Madame Hairy Lip he gave the door porter a small coin and joked with the bowing little maid.

When Madame Hairy Lip herself stood in front of him he made a mock curtsey and with an ironic gesture of his arms, said, "You shine to me like the eyes of a tiger."

"Don't give me the salty side of your tongue. Where did you steal those clothes?" She ran a finger expertly over the edge of the robe. "Weren't you peddling cat meat as rabbit just yesterday?"

"No, just cut-up old grandmothers as shark meat. Is O-Kita engaged tonight?"

Madame Hairy Lip made a tight purse of her loose mouth and rolled her head proudly. "She has no time to play for poverty-stricken artists, I can tell you that."

"I'll wait. Maybe I can draw funny pictures for the party. I have no pride. I enjoy laughing and scratching during these parties while your geishas entertain. You know, I could become a male geisha myself, a *hokan*, if I didn't have such a mad itch to draw all the time."

"Not in my house. Besides, O-Kita isn't here." Madame Hairy Lip tried to expand her lean body and thin bones like a blowfish. "She's been summoned to entertain at the Shogun's castle. And she may be there for several days."

The artist handed the old woman a coin. "Brew a vat of green tea and jump in. I shall be back."

"I doubt if there will be room for you here. You don't think O-Kita is going to waste time with a mere artist after entertaining the lords and princes for the Shogun."

Hokusai smiled crookedly and waggled his hand under his chin like a billy goat's whiskers. "You're a lovable woman, pure gold, with a heart as big as a pickling tub."

Turning on his heels like a Kabuki actor, he left.

The night had turned very black like the inner skin of a blue plum, and the Yoshiwara was filling up. Men with baskets over their heads to hide their identity were slipping from house to house to inspect the courtesans behind their wooden grills. Girls from the teahouses were guiding merrymakers to some particularly popular beauty. Wrestlers, actors and gamblers strutted in doorways. Geishas on their high clogs followed by their servant girls carrying robes and musical instrument cases were hurrying along to entertain impatient guests. Lanterns were lit and strung to sway in a slight breeze, and the cherry blossoms fell from potted trees like pink snow into the street and onto the robes of the pleasure-bound citizens.

Hokusai wandered out of the O-Mon gate and down to the

river bank, smelling the night odors, the damp earth, the little enclosed gardens where water fell musically and the black bamboos seemed to grow before one's eyes. The world was evil and beautiful, cruel and gay.

He went to a supply shop that he knew was open late and bought brushes and ink stones and rolls of paper, carefully inspecting the thin paper for strength and color in the light of the big rapeseed oil lamps. Satisfied, burdened with packages, he went back down to the river bank and rented a room in a disreputable house where they knew him. Here he lived precariously among professional gamblers (hard-eyed men tattooed from head to toe), palanquin porters, *sumo* wrestlers (giants of over six feet with great tun bellies), shoddy actors of women's parts, horse gelders, jugglers, and animal trainers of mangy monkeys and smelly dogs. Here existed odd people of all kinds, filling the house that leaned at a dangerous angle on its rotting piles over the muddy river edge. Hokusai knew most of the tenants; he liked movement and noise around him. Dirt and smell never destroyed form and composition.

In his small square room with its gray paper walls he lit two large *andon*—paper floor lamps. When the rushweed wicks were burning seed oil, he laid out the low drawing platform on the floor, set out his brushes, his blue-green water jar and his ink stones. He rolled up his sleeves and squatted low over the sheet of paper on the board. He had cut himself off from the noise of blows, impolite sounds, laughter and curses that filled the house. He was a man transformed. The clown, the ironic spectator was gone. He was serious; he seemed to be in a trance. He breathed with a slightly open mouth. After grinding some fine dark ink and mixing it with a few drops of water in a small tray, he dipped a thick brush that came to a needle-sharp point into the fluid. Hokusai began to draw rapidly, with a direct unerring sureness and almost unbelievable speed.

Lines black-rich and sooty became thick or thin, broken or curving almost endlessly, all coming from the controlled brush. He used the point or the rough sides of the bunched hairs, he twisted and turned the tool for the effects he wanted. Now his whole world was one of marks, of shapes that were the symbols of his dreadful, wonderful passion for drawing, that drug that dominated his life.

He was sketching ideas that had come to him for the walls of Lord Ito's house. He was drawing O-Kita as the fabulous To-yotama Hime, the legendary daughter of Ryujin, the Dragon King of the Sea. Hokusai was fascinated by the intricate drama of moving water, drawing its waves, its spume and spindrift with skill, making of the wild sea foam little fingers clawing at the hulls of scurrying fishing boats. O-Kita-Hime he drew first as a dragon, as the exciting story of his childhood had it; then he transformed her on a new sheet of paper into the beautiful woman creature from the sea. He covered many sheets of the soft paper, showing her married to a Mikoto-Hokusai whom he mocked and gave features like his own. He drew almost breathlessly their lovemaking, their byplay, man and woman, the games of half-gods and demons and mortal man in lusty marriage. Oh, if the walls of Lord Ito were only large and if there were enough of them this could be expanded in size to a great cycle of paintings! He put an extra drive into the drawings as the night grew cooler and the noises of the riverfront became lower in pitch, punctured often with a blow or a scream. He painted with a swiftly darting brush the dream, the hunt of every man for perfect love, love unobtainable so far, love insatiable. The drawings came hot and direct with no smudge or fault from his fingertips, fingers that learned from his mind and marrow. Now the lovers had consummated the best part of their duties to life. O-Kita-Hime and Mikoto-Hokusai as dragon princess and legendary folk hero faced each other, O-Kita-Hime big with child. The artist painted the scene where she gave her husband warning not to follow to watch the child arrive. She was going to the feather-thatched hut to bear their child. In birth pangs she saw her husband disobeying her, coming to watch her. Now, almost too fast to follow, Hokusai drew the last sheet as O-Kita-Hime in anger turned herself again into a dragon, returning with her newborn child to the deep sea. So ends all love, say the poets, after the first madness of perfect ecstasy.

The artist dropped the brush. The rapeseed oil in a lamp bubbled and sent up a plume of twisting smoke. Hokusai looked at the drawings scattered across the mats on the floor. Tired as he was, cramped from squatting in one position, he was elated at his work. The images of O-Kita-Hime as the sea dragon plunging into the sea . . . of the lover-husband, Mikoto-Hokusai, standing sadly on the shore, were, the artist knew, marvelously drawn with an economy of line and a sureness of touch crisper and more emotional than anything he had yet set down. Yes, even better than the Edo Hakkei—the set of prints of the eight views of Edo. Lifting a small brush, dipping it in the ink, he quickly signed the sheet of paper before him in a new way: *Gwakyojin Hokusai—A-man-mad-about-drawing Hokusai.*

He blew out the *andon* lamps. A pleasant weariness filled him. He sank down on the sleeping pads and a few fleeting unidentified images passed as he fell asleep without dreaming.

4

"It is morning—we wait for Lord Ito to give the word to start.

"Sentiment is often the first refuge of a man writing of himself. Ideas and memories haunt him like things that walk at night. This writing, beyond its basic purpose to pass time, is one man's hope of holding in his hand all that was once so intangible, those crazy things that have flowed through his fingertips, almost before he could think them out.

"Will I reach Edo alive? Does it matter? But I'm pleased to be away from the Dutchmen and their tiny island of isolation.

"I am aware of strong influences driving me on and on. It would be nonsense to say I have not lived hard and been touched by some of what I liked or disliked. In the world of a misfit like myself the temptations and achievements, as I see them, are not hard to dredge up. I hope to write here an honest journal of things seen in a land I love. May I live here till I die. My Aunt's Bible relished a good bereavement. Death and love are old themes. I may be near death, but love I hope to taste again.

"The weather in my mind, the state of my health, the function of my glands, the bread I eat, the native wine and Dutch gin I drink (or don't), all go into the making of this journal, along with all of my personal, obstinate characteristics.

"The servants, porters and soldiers are shouting outside—perhaps we march soon. It is a fine morning and the landscape excites me. Lord Ito is becoming a fine traveling companion.

"I'd like now to be like those expert doctors, masters in the forming and designing of thought and philosophies, who can write smoothly on the history and process of man.

> "All, all of a piece throughout!
> Thy Chase has a Beast in View;
> Thy Wars brought nothing about;
> Thy Lovers were all untrue.
> 'Tis well an Old Age is out,
> And time to begin a New. . . .

"The lines of the poem have been running through my mind all morning. Perhaps now that I put them down I can forget them and write more of this journey.

"I have not yet recorded that when Lord Ito asked me to go to Edo on this mission he offered me a small bag of gold coins. We faced each other, he in his brocaded robe, the expression of his face set in that bland pattern that passes among these people for the proper way to carry on this kind of meeting. I would have gone for nothing, but I took the money with, I fear, a kind of greed, because I have formed the mad (if not mad at least foolish) idea that I can settle somewhere along the coast, serving as a doctor to the local people. I would like nothing better after this mission is done; I want neither fame nor great wealth. Just to mellow away, like a Chinese sage on his mountain top.

"This is all nonsense. Every man dreams of escaping himself . . . The procession's drums are beating out front. Foxy has just come in to grab the saddlebags. He says it is a very hard day ahead. And there is danger from bandits, or something like bandits. He has taken my ship's cutlass from its canvas bag and put it with its wooden sheath under the saddlebags."

The ceremonial robes were gone and Lord Ito raised his hand, as if in benediction, giving the signal to start. The procession was dressed in more comfortable gray and black for the tortuous journey over rough trails. Daniel had discovered there were no roads, in the Western sense, to Edo—just paths. The swaying of his litter commenced again and went on for hours, but he was, although not used to it, at least accepting it, and while he was often on the threshold of being ill, he managed to remain more or less in control of his stomach.

Foxy ran up to the side of the litter. "We are going first to Otsu, a little village where the road takes two paths. But first come many small villages."

"I feel so divided in here, Foxy, I can send half of me up one road, and half up the other."

"Very beautiful lake, Lake Biwa. Very blue," added Foxy.

"Color doesn't interest me. Are we climbing?"

"Low mountains. You are lucky you're not walking."

Daniel stuck his head out past a curtain. They were moving slowly up among the low clinging hills, and ahead he heard the warning cries of the Lord Ito's servants shouting: "Bow down! Bow down!" and "*Sh'tamiso*—down on your knees!"

They were in a mountain pass and the village of Oiwake clung to its sides. They went on slowly to another row of houses called Otani, and now Daniel could see Otsu itself where they would stop for the night. Beyond the village he saw the blue expanse of Lake Biwa, a blue that took his breath away and made him wonder at the inexhaustible variety of life.

Daniel held on as the litter began to descend in bumps toward the lake. Foxy came up again to the curtain. "Famous eight views of the lake here. Fine temple nearby at Mii."

"I just want to sit on the ground. Tomorrow I'm riding a horse."

"No, no, you're not supposed to leave the palanquin."

Daniel fell back into the hot interior of the palanquin and cursed the foolishness that deadening boredom at the Dutch trading island had made him accept this whole crazy adventure. It had been bad enough to be cooped up four years on a Japanese island that wasn't four hundred feet in either direction, and overcrowded at that, with fat Dutchmen and native servants and too much bookkeeping and ledger marking. But now when he knew he was the only white man in Japan proper, and not a minister plenipotentiary of any foreign power, a fear like one of his seizures suddenly gripped Daniel and he looked out at the blue lake to cheer himself up. He leaped out of the litter and felt the suffering in his legs and arms pin-prick in cruel pain as his pent-up blood ran freely again in his limbs. Foxy came up past the panting bearers carrying the procession's household goods. "Oh, well, Heacock Sir, if you are out, come and we'll buy you some *Otsu-e*—Otsu pictures."

"Are they woodblock prints?"

"No, no. You'll see."

Peasants in rice-straw coats stared as they walked into the village past bells tied to the branches of ginkgo trees.

The procession of heralds, grooms, cooks and staff bearers went by and Daniel found himself facing a small open shop. A sign hung over it: a painting of a fat red Buddhist god. It was powerfully and simply drawn. Daniel and Foxy went into the shop. An expressionless shopkeeper with a dark saturnine face did not appear to be at all shocked by the appearance of the big blond man. Stacks of large paintings on brown paper were piled on clean mats, paintings in deep earth colors streaked with white. They must have been produced at great speed, Daniel thought, for the artist had blocked in hands, feet, faces, with rough squares and circles, and finished it all off with fast black lines that added features and details.

Foxy slapped a pile of paintings. "Once these were all religious subjects and people took them home from the temple. But now some are most amusing, no?"

"Who paints them?" Daniel asked the shop owner.

The owner, leaning against a tooled mahogany casket, staring politely at the big man, said, "My own family, for many generations, have worked on the *Otsu-e*."

Foxy said, "You hang one upside down for luck, then the baby doesn't need carrying all night. This one can keep off robbers, they claim."

Daniel chose three wonderful paintings—a devil beating a drum, and a god of long life having his high head shaved by a barber climbing the head on a long ladder, and a hunter with a hawk on his wrist. Then he added a slender girl dancing with a bunch of wisteria blossoms.

"Can we buy these?"

Foxy threw some coins to the shop owner. "That's why they are here. Let's get back to the procession or the Lord Ito will cut off my ears."

They started for the door. Suddenly, the little shop was filled with samurai in their creaking armor, menacing them. Foxy said

softly in English, "It seems you shouldn't have left the palanquin, Heacock Sir. Scowl back at them."

Daniel, gripping the paintings in one hand, stared about him,
trying to out-grimace the samurai. Then, roaring a shout, he
pushed his way between the two largest and most furious of
them, and walked out into the late afternoon sun. Foxy, eyes
down and grinning, managed to follow him quickly. The clanging samurai turned to come after them as they walked down to
the camp that was being set up near an inn by the lake.

The little inn, a resthouse reserved for nobles, was bright with
orange lights coming from behind its sliding shoji panels. Servants, sheltering baggage and animals for the night, bustled
among the great pines rooted in the well-trod level ground. The
brimming deep blue lake had a background of black mountains
that seemed to be cut from thin black iron sheets and pasted
into the landscape. Small horses, neighing, trailed scarlet silk saddle cloths through the camp.

Daniel entered the main room of the resthouse. Lord Ito,
seated on clean straw mats, was drinking tea, and his servants
were busy around him. He motioned Daniel to his side. "I don't
suppose I can keep you hidden even from the *oni*—evil spirits?"

"No, I'm too big. And tomorrow I want to ride one of those
fine horses."

The Lord Ito sighed. "I wish someone else had been chosen
to bring you to Edo." He laughed and patted Daniel's arm.
"But I find you a great deal of a man for one who is an outsider." He clapped his hands and Daniel was served tea. "Wait
till you see the Idzu peninsula and the Gorges of Amagi. They
frighten people."

"I wonder why I came. You've told me very little about my
mission, Lord Ito."

"Soon we shall eat and settle for the night and you'll feel better."

Daniel realized that for the first time they were speaking Japanese together without an interpreter. He felt better and more comfortable as he swallowed the hot tea. Lord Ito was a likable fellow, aware of his high rank, but human nevertheless. The soft wind coming in over the lake and the pines was melancholy and yet restful, and Daniel was happy to be in the warm interior of the well-lighted inn waiting for his supper. It was a moment relatively free of doubt. He had again the gift of hope—it had been missing from his life a long time.

"Tell me, Lord Ito, just a little more of what is ahead of me."

Lord Ito waved his attendants out of earshot and brought his slender hands out of his sleeves, spreading out his fingers. He looked handsome in the yellow lantern light.

"You must understand when I came to you I had good reason to believe you were a great doctor. We too have our great doctors, but your people go boldly inside the body and know secrets we do not know. Secrets about what is inside us. The auguries were excellent and in your favor when we came to you."

"Surgery has come a long way," said Daniel proudly, "since it was in the hands of our barbers."

"The devils who form stones inside of people are very evil and they cause much pain. We never cut for such stones. All this you know. You want to know whom you are to open and relieve of stones in the bladder, but I am only permitted now to say it is a personage of great importance, and this you already know."

"Is it a man?"

"Ah, here is food," said Lord Ito, as bowing servants began to set down small colorful bowls of eggshell-thin flowered porcelain. They also brought small pans to set over charcoal fires, and they cooked dishes of beautiful vegetables cut and arranged in charming patterns on small lacquered trays. Daniel took out his chopstick case and sighed; as pretty as everything looked he still missed the wonderful tasty food of China. Clever and artistic as the people of Japan were, they had never developed a cuisine like the Chinese. . . .

Lord Ito skillfully, as his retinue of servants sat around *hiba-chi*—fire boxes—watching in the background, moved shredded fish to his mouth with carved ivory chopsticks. "You have been buying some of the crossroad paintings, I hear. Don't waste your time. I will get you Kano scrolls in Edo by our best masters."

Daniel gloomily ate his unsatisfactory food. "I like the work of simple people. And your woodblock prints are magnificent. Do you collect them?"

Lord Ito made a small polite laugh that ended in a whistle of exhaled breath. "That trash from the street and the rabble? That's for porters and merchants and the scum in the Yoshi-wara. It is not our true art."

"I can't agree, Lord Ito. It's marvelous art. Maybe it is for the people, but the artists are great men."

Lord Ito looked in amazement at Daniel. "Artists as great men? What odd ideas you have. Artists are just craftsmen, like wood-cutters and good cooks."

Daniel put down his chopsticks and picked up the *sake* cup. He took a long swallow and waited for the warm wine to bite. Suddenly he felt the inn timbers shake. He looked up to find a samurai with a great bleeding gash on his forehead shouting and gesturing to Lord Ito.

From the courtyard and camp came the screaming of tormented horses and the shouting shrillness with which men go into battle. Daniel could make nothing out of the fast chatter of the wounded man bleeding on the clean yellow mats.

Lord Ito rose, pulling at his two swords, his face taut under the shaven forehead. "Do not go out. We have been attacked!"

"By whom?" asked Daniel, leaping up.

A lamp fell from a rafter, spilling fire. Foxy ran up, mouth open, carrying two pistols from Daniel's baggage. Outside a man screamed as his throat was cut. The inn servants were prone on the matting, weeping and shouting strange words. Daniel noticed that their eyes were tightly closed as he ran past them and out onto the porch of the inn, a pistol in each fist.

A dramatic turbulence filled the world. Several of Lord Ito's soldiers were lifting ancient wheel-lock muskets to their shoulders and those that had already fired were enveloped in a thick gray gunpowder smoke. Under the black pines a ring of samurai and soldiers were backed in a semi-circle close to Lord Ito and moving around them were horsemen in red and black armor, swinging their long pointless swords at helmets and padded shoulders. It reminded Daniel of a picture screen he had once seen of two armies facing each other and banging their weapons against the heavy armor protecting heads, bodies and calves.

The noise was dreadful. Every warrior was crying some high-pitched sentence mixed with a kind of braying roar of defiance, as he chopped, skipped and snarled at an enemy. It was no pageant on a screen, Daniel realized as he saw a long spear go completely through a samurai, whose features howled in agony and pain.

The attacking horsemen were passing him now, and Daniel

lifted one heavy pistol (good French steel weapons he had bought in New Orleans) and fired at a head that seemed all teeth and dark red helmet. The firing powder went off and the face dissolved into a red rose of flesh and torn tissue. The heavy lead slug did dreadful damage.

Behind Daniel, Foxy grabbed the empty pistol to reload it; and he handed Daniel his ship's cutlass. "I bring this. Make lots of chops." For the first time Daniel felt fear.

Something sharp and tearing stung his cheek and he felt blood run down into a corner of his mouth. Daniel roared in pain and went forward howling something his grandfather used to shout when angry. "By the god Jehovah and the Continental Congress, you damn helots!"

He fired the other pistol at a bearded face, then reversed the pistol with a toss and hammered its butt into a wide yellow forehead that cracked like eggshell. The horsemen had all stopped their savage attack and were staring at the giant with the yellow hair swinging a heavy cutlass among them.

A horse reared and the rider fell down near Daniel's feet, into the pine needles on the ground. The man on the ground turned like an eel and held up a short sharp knife.

Daniel sidestepped and felt his cutlass cut through armor, through shoulder bone, and catch with a tearing jar in the ribs. He tore the weapon out with some disgust and whirled around. The horsemen were retreating into the dark pines running away from this tall demon. With a shout the servants of Lord Ito ran forward to cut the throats of the wounded on the ground.

A perceptible vitality drained out of Daniel, and the thin acid smell of gunpowder drifted in ribbons among the lower branches of the black trees. Lord Ito, in magenta robe, sword in hand, stood with some of his samurai. On the porch of the inn a lamenting sound died out as everyone watched Daniel walk slowly over to Lord Ito. The blood was still salty in his mouth but he knew it came only from a deep scratch.

"*Yoroshiu,*" said Daniel.

Lord Ito bowed three times. "You are a great warrior, Heacock Sir."

"Maybe I was just angry because they didn't let me finish my *sake,*" Daniel tried to talk lightly. "Who are they? Why did they attack us?"

"They are *ronin*—outlaws, samurai who no longer have masters and hire themselves out for pay to do these things."

"But you're the messenger of the Shogun himself—who would dare attack you?"

Lord Ito handed his sword to a servant carrying a horn lantern and shook his head. "I am most upset and I feel I am unworthy of escorting you to Edo. I have failed to protect you. You are wounded."

Daniel shrugged. These people had, he knew, a habit of being too humble in their pride of duty. "It's just a scratch. Were they after money?"

Lord Ito walked to where one of the dying attackers lay on his back. The man was gasping in his struggle for breath. A spreading area of his chest was wet with blood. The dying man looked up with glazed eyes at the lord and the strange white man and Daniel felt this warrior must already think he was seeing the other world. A retainer grabbed the dying man by his topknot and threw fast barking questions at him.

The dying features vibrated as a shiver of horrible agony and pain ran through the body, and the doctor in Daniel Heacock knew the man's heart could no longer do its work. The man died with one last kick of his bronze-armored feet in the dusty pine needles. The retainer stood up respectfully, not lifting his eyes to Lord Ito as he wiped his thumbs on his sash.

"We shall not know from him who sent him," said Lord Ito dryly. He put an arm on Daniel's. "Let us finish our meal. You have killed men on the Tokaido road."

"Some of your soldiers need medical attention."

"They will be taken care of. Don't pamper soldiers and samurai. Chop stone, but caress silk."

Daniel handed the cutlass and pistol to Foxy, who was grinning with a new respect for his white man. Daniel sat down crosslegged on the porch of the inn and let a small maid shaking in fear wash his cheek and lay clean white paper on the small cut. He begged off eating more food and sent Foxy for a cheroot. He sat smoking it, slowly enjoying the aroma of the good Dutch-cured tobacco.

Under the silent pines it was ink dark now. Fireflies burned holes in the night as men moved slowly scattering fresh, aromatic pine needles over what had been a battle. The dead men had been removed almost at once to some mysterious place. Daniel supposed he had killed two men, or at least maimed them dreadfully, with the cutlass and pistols. He had killed men before, not just those who died on the operating table or later. He had no feelings on that score; he knew too well the senseless butchery of religious wars, and of battles for greed.

But he was affected by the battle he had just taken part in. Was it only because he had figured so prominently in the fighting? As he thought of it, he considered the possibility that his unknown and mysterious mission was the cause of the attack.

What awaited him at the end of his journey, at Edo? Could Lord Ito give him any of the answers?

He was still worried over the symptoms he had felt in himself the day before. He knew a seizure was coming on him. When? A week, a month—he might be able to hold it off for as long as a month, if he were careful. Perhaps he could take one of the inn maids as a bye-wife on the sleeping pads for the night; Foxy could arrange for a bye-wife. But sleeping with a woman when he felt a serious seizure close only brought it on quicker.

More fireflies were dotting the night, the wind in the pines was wilder. From the lake there was the sound of oars and the lament of water fowl. Out of the dark, Lord Ito approached him, dressed now in magnificent red and green, fresh ivory-handled swords in his sash.

"I have disgraced you, myself, the Tokugawa, Heacock Sir, by permitting this thing to happen."

"Lord Ito, you will offend me if you say that again. It is hard for me to express, for I do not speak the language as well as I would like. But I mean it when I say you are a brave man, and the fault is not yours. I know how important it is to keep face in this country. We of the West have a gesture that makes everything right."

"What is that?" asked Lord Ito, looking at Daniel earnestly.

Daniel held out his hand. "We have a custom of shaking hands to show everything is all right."

Lord Ito eagerly grasped the big man's hand. "Like so?"

"Like so," said Daniel. "Now, what do you think is behind the attack on your procession?"

Lord Ito squatted and so did Daniel. "You must know the Tokugawa Shoguns rule fairly and firmly. They are military men. It is not wealth, or a life of ease they want, but to control for the good of Japan. Now a change is coming over the country, and this change is not for the good. The people no longer have respect for the soldiers. The power of money is going to the merchants. And merchants are greedy people; you have just to see their big paunches heavy with all their neighbors that they've eaten."

Lord Ito looked out to the solid forest forms and the dimpling lake in the moonlight. He went on. "There has been a famine for several years. The crops in some parts of the country have been bad. The merchants have been buying up the produce of the land. They have it in their warehouses, and they sell only for outrageous prices. There have been dreadful riots; people are demanding that the merchants distribute the stores."

"That seems only right."

"Yes, if we could control the distribution. But some of our magistrates have been killed. We have tried to control the merchants, but we need them too. They are clever. They have the money, the methods of transportation, the ships. Osaka was burned not long ago, and the revolt spread. There was much bloodshed. The merchants have been warned to change their ways. Now there is talk the merchants will try to bring the Emperor to Edo from Kyoto, and put him back as the only ruler. Then his forces will have to protect them."

"I'm still puzzled about tonight, Lord Ito."

Lord Ito sighed. When he spoke his voice was husky. "If you could be prevented from getting to Edo it would be easier to bring back the Emperor."

"Why?"

"I must now tell you—your actions tonight deserve it. Your patient is the Shogun Iyenari Tokugawa himself. He is dying in agony from the treatment our doctors are giving him."

Daniel whistled. "If he should die, you think it would be easier to bring back the Emperor."

"The merchants think so. And the Shogun's heir is still a child. There will be disorders, and demands for the Emperor will come. You see why I must get you safely to Edo?"

Daniel nodded. He understood fully now the seriousness of his mission—and also what would befall him if he were unsuccessful. He was, however, not too surprised that his patient was the Shogun. From all the secrecy surrounding this journey he knew that his patient would be of very high position. But to Lord Ito he said only, "It's such a pretty land, there is such a love of beauty in everything. And yet, just like the rest of the world, you are a cruel people.

"The wheel turns—and everyone wants to be on top."

There was a scuffle below them and soldiers with torches came up to the porch, roughly pushing a huge ruffian caked with mud and scarred with scratches. His hands were bound behind his back. A samurai shoved the fellow down to his knees in front of Lord Ito. "One of the band that attacked us. Unhorsed. We found him sulking in the little woods beyond the temple."

Prince Ito stood up in his stiff robes and looked down at the prisoner. "Who sent you? Who is it that dares to attack the procession bearing the crest of the Shogun?"

The prisoner made a hard mouth and moved his lips with a ferocious agility. He had, Daniel saw, no hope for mercy. He asked for none. "I am a *ronin*. My master committed hara-kiri at Nikko castle, long ago. That is enough for me to say. I go the way of *Bushido*."

"Is it your wish to die?" asked Lord Ito.

"When I was born I knew that."

"You are an outlaw. But once you were a proud samurai. You expect a good death."

Kneeling, the prisoner looked up, expressionless, his heavy eyelids narrowed to slits, his bruised flesh showing through rents in his armor. "I welcome death. I lower my head. Cut it off properly. I am a gentleman, not a peasant."

Lord Ito said, "There will be no easy death for you. I will strip you naked. I will bring out all the old women from the villages and you will run between them and they will throw dung and stones at you and tear out your eyes and your privates with their iron rakes. And dogs shall eat you while you, defiled as you are, still live."

The *ronin* shook his head as if he didn't understand. "No! That is not honorable, my lord. Even a *ronin* dies by tradition. One strong stroke of the sword. I am no *ketojin*—no hairy rascal." He spat in the direction of Daniel.

Daniel watched the cruel mask Lord Ito's face had become. The *daimyo* said, "On one condition will your head and your body go to Hell properly. Who planned this attack? Who paid for it? Jili, strip him—go rouse out the old women with their dung pots and rakes."

The bound, kneeling figure looked up and gave a hollow deprecatory laugh. "A good death and I tell what I know. Don't be disappointed. What I know is very little."

"Go ahead. I'll judge."

Baring his big yellow teeth the bound man, rolling his head to drive the sweat from his eyes, said, "I was hired by one Unji in Edo at the Brocade Teahouse to gather a band. I know nothing else about him. A dark man named Brother paid us in gold. He said: 'Go to the road and wait. When Lord Ito's procession comes kill the *ketojin*—the foreign devil with the blue eyes and the yellow hair.' We expected no giant, however. I implore now—the sword."

The *ronin*, tired of everything, panting, lowered his head and exposed his heavy powerful neck.

Lord Ito nodded to a huge samurai who lifted his sword high with both hands and brought it down on the neck of the kneeling *ronin* with a grunt of effort.

There was no need for a second blow. The head rolled away. Lord Ito turned and went indoors without saying anything else.

Daniel rose to his feet, unaware that his mouth was open. His throat was very dry and he could not unclasp his fingers; they were balled up into tight fists. Some of the torches began to sputter and go out.

BOOK TWO

The months and days are the travelers of eternity. The years that come and go are also voyagers. Those who float away their lives on boats or who grow old leading horses are forever journeying, and their homes are wherever their travels take them . . . and I too for years past have been stirred, by the sight of a solitary cloud drifting in the wind, to endless thoughts of roaming . . .

From a travel book by Matsura Basho

5

O-Kita, in a petulant silence, stood in the barely perceptible wind of morning on a terrace of the Shogun's castle, looking at a world that was not quite real to her. Somewhere out there were the four concentric circles of moats that protected the palace. Last night she had come here, carried in a *norimon* (a kind of palanquin), past ferocious stone lions. She had been filled with excitement, encased in a transitory moment of wonder, feeling in the presence of something beyond contemplation. But she had not been called on to sing, or recite, or play music, or be witty. She had been assigned a room with her two little maids, and was as forgotten as the dwarf trees and the weathered stone walls and the red lacquer columns of the court-yard paved in yellow tiles.

There was a numb quiet about the Shogun's castle. Some servants moved quickly in the distance, and beyond that the moss-covered stones sloped silently down to the inner green moat. Past that were the parks and the river bank, and beyond it the city.

What was the use of her best robe, the one with iridescent dragonflies, her jasmine scent, her ornate coiffure stuck with jeweled pins? The pleasure and excitement she had felt when she saw the invitation were gone. Something sinister was going on in the Shogun's castle. Why else would no one call on her? Why was she wanted here?

O-Kita fought back tears of disappointment and fear. One is lost in this world and calls it experience, she told herself; life spares only children and the very old.

The sliding *shoji* door behind O-Kita opened and eight-year-old Cat came out, bowing, signs of rice eaten carelessly still on her lips. O-Kita turned away from the view of the court-yard, fully in control of herself now.

Cat bowed again very low and announced, "Prince Kwammu Taira."

O-Kita saw in the doorway an old man, his topknot white, wearing a robe of simple design in kingfisher blue, draped on a thin, wiry, well cared for body. There seemed to be a delicacy about him, she sensed. His bearing suggested that he was fully aware of his identity as a great prince but that he would not force his full power on her. Her training had taught her to quickly judge character. Most of all she was aware of a strain of malice in the old prince as he made a proud, restrained bow to her.

"We are pleased to have such a great geisha with us."

O-Kita put on her profession, like a well tailored robe, and bowed very low, extending her hands wide from the sides of her body. She stood head down in humble dignity. "We are unworthy of such an early visit."

"Yes, yes," said the old prince. "Come here."

She lifted her head and moved gracefully closer to him.

"Shall we sit down?"

O-Kita nodded and they sat on the terrace on mats, facing each other. The old cunning face told her nothing. It was well known, she remembered, that he cared nothing for women. The entire population of the Yoshiwara spoke of his preference for *yaro* and *wakashu* and their disgusting vices.

"O-Kita, these are strange times. Of course all times are strange, but these are strangest."

O-Kita watched the arrogance that now dominated the old face. There was a perceptible vitality in these fashionable old bones. Certainly no senility.

"What can I do to be of service, Prince Taira?"

"We know your teahouse, and your mistress. We can trust you to do a service for us, and you know we can reward and we can punish." He clapped his hands and a castle servant came silently out from behind a screen with a large basket. She put it near O-Kita and went back inside as silently as she had appeared.

The basket contained oranges wrapped in gold leaf, long scrolls of calligraphy to ward off evil spirits, and glazed porcelain vases so scarlet the color seemed almost created by magic.

"Gifts from the Shogun himself."

"What service can I do for all this?"

From somewhere in the castle came the sound of a *shakubachi* —a bamboo flute. Its high pure tones made O-Kita shiver with fear. The prince picked up and balanced a gold-wrapped orange in one hand and did not look at the geisha. "In a few days Lord Ito Kojin and his procession will arrive in Edo. We will arrange for you to entertain where he is present. For some years he has not lived in Edo, but he is a great admirer of geishas. He drinks a lot. We want you to please him by your skills."

"That is my duty, to please."

"There is more." The now tranquil slant-eyed face was staring directly into hers. "We here at the Shogun's castle

67

would like to know whom he has been friendly with these last few years, when he was not in Edo. We would like to know what he talks about in his relaxed moments. And also we must know his feelings about the merchants."

O-Kita lowered her eyes to the matting. So she had been invited to spy within the castle walls. Silently she prayed to the Sixteen Disciples of Buddha—Oh Lord Amida Buddha, protect me from this clever, so clever old man. Aloud she said, "It will be as you wish, Prince Taira, you and the Shogun."

He watched her to see the effect of his words, but her pride and poise did not break under his steady gaze.

"The Shogun is going to make one of his rare appearances outside the castle this afternoon. A little hunt has been arranged and he will stop at the temple of Dempo-ji with his retinue. You will be admitted into the courtyard of the temple and I will arrange for Lord Ito's town steward to meet you. He is a good person to know. He too loves the Shogun. He will give a party later at a teahouse. You will entertain."

The prince suddenly tossed the golden orange at her and she caught it and held it to her stomach, bowing very low, as the prince left.

It was a long time before she dared look up. She had been too long a geisha to be shocked by anything that happened around her, but she was, for all her temper, sensitive to nuances that most women missed. O-Kita was aware she was stepping into some unquiet dark, that she would live the next few days or weeks on pure nervous inspiration. Suddenly she realized that she had crushed the golden orange she gripped and its juices were running down her fingers and onto her robe. The old man with his unsavory words had pushed her face back into the dirt of the Yoshiwara.

The courtyard of the temple of Dempo-ji basked in the afternoon sun like the lizard's back which its roofs resembled. Yellow-robed priests stood in rows. Behind them stood soldiers with matchlock muskets, lances and swords. Many indicative details pointed to this being a special event. Nobles of the court on clogs of cryptomeria wood stood in casual groups talking among themselves. Baskets of offerings—grapes, pears, persimmons, even a brace of golden pheasant with their iridescent three-foot tails—lay before the entrance to the temple.

The painter Hokusai, walking slowly among the splendidly dressed people, knew that although his position in this society had changed overnight, it could change back again to red peppers and calendars the next night. He had spent the morning inspecting the house of Lord Ito, watching the working men finish their repairs and the herd of servants clean the place. The walls were wide and tall, and he had ordered great panels of silk, on which he could paint the series of pictures of the legend he had sketched the night before.

Narrow Eyes, as he had called Lord Ito's steward, had suggested that Hokusai pay his respects to the Shogun at the temple with some feat of painting. "One doesn't see the Shogun much these days. And he might ask you to improvise a painting on the spot. He likes to do that with artists, Prince Taira tells me."

Hokusai had merely nodded and said, "Surroundings do not hinder an artist. I will improvise if he asks me."

Now the artist's eye suddenly caught a cluster of colors in the back of the courtyard where certain less important people had been permitted to enter and stand. Hokusai crossed the worn tiles of the temple courtyard and smiled at O-Kita, who stood expressionless in white porcelain-like powder, her fine robe held by her two little maids as she clicked her fan open. His heart seemed to beat faster, and his love for this geisha made him feel a fool.

"The priests pronounce fine auguries for this visit, O-Kita."

O-Kita made a brisk pettish bow; a great geisha could not show much tolerance for poor artists in public. "You look as if you have won at gambling, Hokusai."

Cat giggled and wiped her smirk into silence with a sleeve. The artist laughed cheerfully and took O-Kita's hand in his. "I have certainly won the pleasure of seeing you today, O-Kita. It's a great scene, isn't it? The people waiting, the thin elongated shadows and the gleam of shiny objects. I tell you I want to jump for paper to draw it all."

"I remember my lessons in art," said O-Kita, touching his arm. She was very fond of Hokusai and knew that if she were not careful she could fall in love with a mere artist, a drifter with no permanent home, a man who got drunk on sweet potato wine and never saved his money. She must not let herself be seduced by art, by its shapes and color. True splendor is only in the heart, she told herself, and the passing pleasures of the flesh build no fortifications against oblivion. Many great geishas had been destroyed by love. She had sworn to herself she would not be, not at least till she was old at thirty; then some fat, prosperous merchant would marry her and she could wrinkle like a prune into a placid old age.

There was shouting. Riders were approaching in the courtyard. O-Kita freed her hand from the artist's grip, and turned toward where the Shogun was riding into the courtyard. She had only seen him twice, both times from a distance. Everyone bowed and went to their knees and bowed again. O-Kita twisted her head to look at the Shogun as two servants passed her, leading his white horse and its brocaded silk gear in a slow dignified walk. The Shogun looked thin and gray. He was a young man, with hollow eyes and a mouth made firm by biting back pain. He sat stiffly in the saddle but bent forward as if to ease some pressure that bit deeply at his dignity and could disgrace him in public if he were not the Shogun. Officials in black silk helped him dismount slowly.

The Shogun Iyenari Tokugawa had ruled Japan for five years. His head was slender, his eyes deep-set and very dark, his bearing cool and precise. He was said to have a good mind, to be interested in the arts, to commission painters, to read books. O-Kita had heard—it was common talk—that he was in-fluenced by his friends—too influenced, perhaps—and that his health was being undermined by his large seraglio of beautiful women who filled many of the apartments of the castle. This was only to be expected at the court, even after his marriage to a daughter of the great Fujiwara house.

Looking at the Shogun walking slowly up the temple steps between the court nobles and the black-robed officials, O-Kita felt the power of the Tokugawas to keep order and offer justice in the land. And they were always respectful to the Emperor, making others respect him, the direct descendant of the Sun.

In their shining brocade robes and creaking basketwork hel-mets, samurai were bowing to the Shogun. Guards, carrying white staves of office, preceded his procession, the saffron-colored robes of the priests making a colored contrast against the weathered cedar wood pillars of the temple entrance.

Cat, from behind O-Kita, said, "Oh, this is so exciting!"

O-Kita too felt the glorious brightness of the day, the excitement of many people in the temple courtyard. She looked around for Hokusai but he was gone, lost in the crowd.

Just below the terrace on which stood *daimyo* and *hatamoto*, the great names and the banner knights of the Tokugawa, the crowd pressed forward. O-Kita was almost overthrown; she grabbed her kingfisher beak combs to keep from losing them in the bustle.

Looking up, pushed close, she paled as she saw Hokusai himself bowing low to the Shogun on the terrace of the temple. He carried himself with proper respect, but with that casual acceptance of any situation that she had so often lectured him against and which spoiled many advantageous circumstances for him.

Cat exclaimed as she clung to the train of O-Kita's robe. "It's the laughable one again, who draws the things that make you laugh."

"He's not making the Shogun laugh," said O-Kita. They were too far away for her to hear what was going on up there on the terrace where Hokusai stood, head down in respect, facing the Shogun, Prince Taira and some court officials. They were, O-Kita knew, the huge court's nobles: knights, hereditary vassals, outside lords, and the counsellors and members of the Shogun's council. O-Kita had never seen together at one time so many of the people who made up the elite group around the Shogun.

And that brazen maker of drawings and woodblock prints was accepting it all as if he had been born in the castle himself. O-Kita blushed for Hokusai, wondering what they were talking about on the temple porch.

"Your name and reputation as a painter are not unknown to me," said the Shogun. Now that he was dismounted the Shogun was not as pale as he had been, and with arms clasped in front of him there was little sign of pain on his face.

The artist said simply, "It is a small thing I do, Your Highness, but if it pleases you I share with you some of the pleasures of my art."

"Is it true that you do amazing things in new ways?"

"I do them my ways, and if they amaze others they often amaze me too."

"We hear," said Prince Taira, lifting his old and clever head, "that Hokusai painted a wall hanging—a *kakemono*—of a frog climbing a large flower leaf, chased by a serpent, and done in a remarkable way, partly without a brush."

The Shogun asked with interest, "Without a brush?"

Hokusai spread his hands by his sides, palms up. "Talk becomes enlarged, and truth is bent a bit in the telling. I have prepared something here today, Your Highness, that will show my foolish art in a new way, as no artists have ever used it. If you would permit and would not be bored . . ."

The Shogun nodded. He seemed in pain again, and he looked at the artist as if wondering at the life of men who could do only those things that pleased them.

Hokusai bowed and went to the temple wall. He looked about him and pulled out from its position a huge door, ten feet tall and six feet wide, covered with a strong white paper. There was a hiss of protest from the priests, but Hokusai ignored them and waved to two boys carrying bundles. One boy handed the artist some brushes and a tray of open pots of paint.

Hokusai put the door flat on the terrace floor. He took up his largest brush and dipped it in a pot of paint. Then he slapped it down with a skill and speed that appeared blurred, into a series of deep blue curving lines that suggested water, and then a winding river on the white surface of the door. The artist handed the brush to one of the boys and motioned the other one forward. The boy, a little shy, held out a small cage of woven moor rushes. From this cage the artist pulled out a protesting red-combed rooster and held it over his head. One of the boys came forward and put down a tray full of bright red paint, the thick paste used to print crests and seals on documents and paintings.

Hokusai, carefully as if performing in a theater, dipped the feet of the worried rooster in the red paint. Carrying the bird, the artist walked to the bottom of the door lying flat on the terrace floor. He put the rooster firmly down on the white paper surface. He patted its tail feathers and the freed fowl ran swiftly across the surface of the door, leaving full and distinct impressions of its inked red feet. Once off the door, the rooster looked foolishly around, arched its neck, opened its yellow beak, lifted its wings and disappeared into the crowd, uttering all the time a half-strangled cry of rage.

Hokusai bowed to the Shogun, who was standing by the pattern of red rooster's feet and blue curving lines. "Your Highness, I offer you the river Tatsuta in the autumn."

"Yes," said the Shogun, smiling for the first time. "This is the Tatsuta river just the way the poets have immortalized it as carrying away on its deep blue waves the fallen red maple leaves of autumn."

Prince Taira nodded. "No tribute can express the wonder of

the court at your imagination and skill. You are a *sensei*—a master."

Even the sour-faced Matsudaira Sadanobu, the powerful administrator of the nation, whose very look often took the place of words and froze most people speechless, said, "Better than a juggling trick at the theater."

The Shogun nodded. "I like imagination of this kind. I like any man who has courage to do things a new way."

Hokusai bowed very low at this praise. "Your warm words are my reward, Your Highness."

The Shogun was already moving down the steps to his waiting escort.

Prince Taira said to the artist, "The Shogun is going back to the castle. You have pleased him. Some of us are going to the Ginkgo teahouse to drink *sake* and listen to the geishas play and talk. Bring the door and sign it for the Shogun's collection."

Hokusai bowed again, not too deeply, and lowered his eyes. He had certainly made all their eyes pop out on stems today.

Pleased, he turned to the two boys standing behind him, rubbing their noses and kicking each other slyly in the shins. "The painting goes to the Ginkgo teahouse, and don't wipe your damn noses on those robes. I'll be along soon. If you need help to carry things, hire some porters."

The boys nodded as Hokusai threw some coins at them. He went into the temple smelling musty from its grease, cedar wood, and dying flowers.

The elation of his public performance had left Hokusai. He always enjoyed amazing people like this, but deep down he knew it was a buffoon's way of bringing forward his claims as an artist with imagination. He was getting on in years, he mused in the dark temple; he had done so little of what he had hoped. At forty, would he still be hungry most of the time; at fifty, would people collect his work; at sixty would they say Hokusai was a most amazing fellow, and what a delightful draftsman? At seventy, perhaps, would he have perfected his art so that between him and his visions there would be a perfect coordination of seeing, remembering and projecting with brush and paint; and at eighty, would they . . . he broke off the daydream, like dropping a clay pot, and focused on a scene before him.

Against the back of the temple wall was a great screen, very old, with figures of gods and demons, symbols of faith, and the fading forms of misty mountains and the rocky atmospheres of the world. Several people stood before the screen pushing between their teeth slips of paper on which were written prayers. The mouths of the people were chewing up the prayers; most of them with their eyes closed. When someone had a good pulpy prayer, he removed it from his mouth with his fingers and threw it onto the screen. To one side stood O-Kita, earnestly chewing on a prayer paper.

From the side the artist watched her, her beautiful little eyelids closed. The artist watched as she took the wet wad of prayer paper from her mouth and threw it at the screen. It did not stick to the surface of the screen as so many did. It fell to the floor. The gods had refused O-Kita's prayer. She went out slowly into the sunlight where her two little maids waited for her. Hokusai wondered what her refused prayer had been.

6

In the morning most of Lord Ito's retainers arose stiff from
the fight of the night before. Some showed wounds, bandaged
arms and lacerated heads.

Lord Ito looked up at Daniel when he heard his request and
answered his question. "You want to ride and not be carried?
I can't refuse, not after the help you gave in the attack last
night. But you will not go too far ahead. There may be other
bands who want to kill you, for assassins have an uncommend-
able tenacity."

"You believe the man's story?"

"It is consistent with other stories I have heard. There is
much plotting going on. Soon there may be great changes."

"I'll stay in the procession. I have no interest in politics. A
plague on all politicians."

Lord Ito smiled. "Go and choose any horse—even my favorite."

Daniel went to the horse lines where the smell of fresh
droppings, hay, and oiled horse gear all brought back memories
of the green acres in the Berkshires and on the Cape where his
boyhood summers had been lived on farms full of active
animals. Daniel picked out a beautiful solid little horse with

plump buttocks and slim black legs, and a hide of gray dappled with black markings as interesting as the writing on an old scroll. The saddle was of soft red leather. When Daniel came near, the horse smelled him and the creature pulled back his ears and showed strong stained teeth. But once in the saddle Daniel controlled the horse's head and mouth by a cross lock of the reins that a jockey in London had shown him. The horse understood the situation and accepted it.

It was much better riding than being carried and Daniel inhaled the fresh air and sunlight. When they came to a village and a headman bearing gifts came out to stare at the yellow-haired giant on the horse, the villagers were kneeling to the procession heads down. So they went on for several days more, resting or eating or sleeping at the over fifty stations on the Tokaido road. Lord Ito came to Daniel one night as he sat brooding and said, "You ride well."

"I try—the horse is a good one."

When they rested or stopped to boil tea Foxy read to Daniel. He had brought some novels along. One was *The Man Who Spent his Life in Love*. It was a work of *ukiyo-zoshi*—demimonde fiction. The author was Ihara Saikaku, and the novel was written a hundred years earlier but was still popular.

Foxy explained, "It expresses the idea that the two great interests of the pleasure or floating world are love and money. Anyone, the author claims, who becomes very successful in accomplishing these two things, he is called a *tsujin*, what you call in your language an expert."

"Not very romantic, Foxy."

Daniel was making progress in reading Japanese, but not

enough to read an involved fast-moving novel. So during tea
and rest periods Foxy read from *Koshoku ichidai otoko—The
Man Who Spent his Life in Love*.

" 'When I was asked,' " he read, " 'what type of woman I
would like to hold in my arms, I see a woman who is between
fifteen and eighteen years of age. Her face has the look of
poise, is smoothly rounded and the color of pale pearl-pink
cherry blossoms. The features permit no single flaw, the eyes
are not narrow, the brows, thick, do not grow close together,
the nose is so straight, the mouth so small, the teeth white and
regular. The ears are charmingly long with the most delicate
rims and stand away from the hair so that one can see where
they join the head. The dark thick hair grows naturally on the
forehead and there is no trace of any artificiality . . .' "

Daniel said, "The hero sounds as if he's buying a horse, not
describing the girl of his dreams."

Foxy wet a finger, turned a page and went on reading. " 'Her
hair falls down like water over a slender neck. Her fingers are
pliant, long, thin-nailed. Her feet should not cover eight copper
coins laid in a row. The big toes curl upward, the bottoms of
her feet are translucently delicate. Her body is neither larger
nor smaller than what a man desires, and her hips must be firm,
not given to shaking flesh, and her buttocks hard, full and
round.' "

Daniel chewed a leaf and looked up at the sky between the
trees. "He's not describing any real woman; he's just describing a doll, a toy."

Foxy read on. " 'She must be an expert in those special arts
expected of women, ignorant of nothing, and there must not
be a single mole on her entire body.' "

"He's so wrong," said Daniel, taking the book from Foxy's

hand and throwing it down. "A mole properly placed gives a girl character, makes her an individual, an entity as a personality. Agreed, Foxy?"

"If you say so, Heacock Sir, but I'm sorry you do not like my novel. There were some very interesting developments on a personal level later on."

Traveling was harder now; the narrow trails went up the sides of mountains, through fern forests, past noisy waterfalls and great trees full of shrill birds. Always the turning and twisting of the trail followed as best it could landscapes not interested in letting man pass by. Sometimes they met porters carrying bales or loads balanced on bamboo poles. The almost naked porters trotted along, heads down, strong brown legs climbing or descending the trail, a pace they would keep up all day on a bowl of rice, a bit of fish, some twists of root, a white radish or a yam.

Once they met a party of plump merchants on good horses, protected by hired soldiers with rusting matchlocks that could no longer be fired. The merchants gave way and waited while Lord Ito's procession passed them on a narrow trail, but they showed little respect; laughing and chewing on sunflower seeds and spitting vulgarly, aware of the power of the purse.

Near dusk one night they came across a band of men with wild hair and hawk's eyes, men in torn and dirty robes, with worn polished arms and brown fists. There were a dozen of them, all hairy and white-toothed like wolves. They were bandits and outlaws but they did not attack. The procession of Lord Ito was too big and strong. The outlaws stood on a ridge above the procession passing below and Daniel saw among them a tall girl with wild, uncombed hair, and wearing a man's sword belt. There was nothing of the polite city girl or the humble town woman about her wind-blown beauty. Then the outlaws were gone and Daniel decided he was thinking too much about women and he would not let Foxy read so many popular novels to him. He could practice his reading of Japanese on philosophy, or something else dull. So that night Foxy read from Tama Kushige: " 'All things in life—great and small, their very existence in the universe, even man himself and his actions—are due to the spirits of the gods and their disposition of things. In general, there are various kinds of gods . . .' " By this time Daniel was already fast asleep.

Daniel enjoyed riding the small strong horse, riding hard down a curved trail and then waiting until the procession re-formed and they slowly went up into cheek-touching clouds. He was always charmed by the lakes and waterfalls. Sometimes it rained, great slanting ink lines of water, just as Daniel had seen it in the prints he had bought. Nature seemed to be following art. But real rain was uncomfortable, and the big hats and the umbrellas and the rice-straw coats worn by the peasants did not keep it out. When the procession halted they sat around smoking fires that refused to burst into warming drying flames, or lay in some station on the Tokaido road listening to the rain slip with a gurgle down the roof and beat into the ground or drip drip around them in a chill dampness that bit the bone. The blinking red eyes in the pot of charcoal gave off only an illusion of warmth.

And after the rain there was mud, and when the sun came out everything steamed, and when everything was dried out one tired and sweated and drank too much water. Daniel was becoming depressed as he felt, small symptom by small symptom, a seizure growing on him. He still had no idea of how close the seizure might be; he knew only that it approached. He wondered whether he should tell someone how to treat him if he had an attack. Knowledge of his infirmity might, he realized, lessen Lord Ito's confidence in him, and make more perilous his mission. He decided to say nothing for the time being.

When they came near the town of Shizuoka, Lord Ito said to Daniel, "I must reward certain of the samurai who best fought off the bandits. Have you ever seen the Chinkina danced?"

"No, I can't say I ever have," Daniel answered, wary.

"It is for rough men and men whose sensibilities have become jaded. We will hold a Chinkina dance when we get to Shizuoka. I must attend, as the lord of my men, and you must come—forgive me—for it is given in your honor."

"Why in my honor?"

"To my samurai, you were the hero of the fight. It was your help with your fire weapons and your odd sword, that turned the tide."

Daniel smiled. "On those terms of flattery I'll gladly come. But I don't make speeches."

"We don't make speeches at these things. Just a little drunken bragging. And you don't have to orgy, or you can orgy; that is up to you. In this country it is seemly and proper to get drunk and to orgy after battle."

"Thank you, Lord Ito."

It was already dark when, after a hard day's travel, they came to the town. At the inn Foxy dressed Daniel in a good robe of powerful reds and much gold. "My advice is don't drink all the

sake in sight, Heacock Sir. Don't pay any attention to the boast-
ing of the samurai. The women are there for their skill in
pleasure. And don't be surprised at anything."

"Who dance the Chinkina?"

"Low class courtesans or geishas in these unimportant towns.
But they think like all public women, low or high. To make you
happy, to be rewarded."

The party was held in the biggest teahouse in Shizuoka. It
was run by a middle-aged woman who was called O-Roma—
Miss Pony, as Daniel translated it. It was the usual country teahouse with its bowing maids, the ritual of removing shoes, clean
rooms and sliding screens and the smell of body powder, intimate female life and the scene of damp gardens outside its
windows.

Lord Ito and ten of his samurai, and Daniel, were bowed into
a long room and seated at low tables. Food appeared, tea was
served, and many white jars of *sake* were opened. Daniel ate
little, and drank carefully but often as the samurai offered
toasts and bragged loudly.

It was quite warm in the room but no one pushed open
any of the windows. Behind a curtain a drum began to beat.
The samurai began to chant. Daniel's head was fuzzy and he
regretted having drunk so much *sake*.

"*Chinkina, chinkina, hai!*" shouted the samurai.

The curtains opened and Miss Pony was behind it, beating on
a small lap drum. One of her girls was plucking on a samisen.
The music was, to Daniel's ears, the usual Japanese scale, too
shrill and very odd, but there was a beat of sensuality to it.

Lord Ito made some jest and the samurai all laughed; a great
lord's humor is always gut-busting, Daniel remembered.

Ten girls appeared, almost rolling into the room with their

mincing walk. They were fully dressed in ceremonial robes, and on their faces and necks was the liquid porcelain powder of their public trade. Daniel did not feel they were women at all, but more like dolls dressed for some holiday. Certainly this was not his idea of Venus Aphrodite; to want a woman a man had to isolate her from other women, to see her as an individual. He refilled his *sake* cup and watched an unresisting maid coyly scream as a samurai grabbed at her.

The dancing girls were moving now in a slow swaying that seemed to have little violent effort to it and not much suggestion. Suddenly the music stopped. All the girls froze into position. Only one girl, too late, made a final gesture. She was still moving after the others were still. Everyone laughed. The samurai began to shout words that to Daniel had no meaning. The girl who had failed to stop in time began to untie her sash. Expressionless, she dropped the sash on the floor. The music began and Daniel waited; again it stopped. Another loser lost her sash. He understood the game now. He gulped his *sake* and wished he was back at the inn; this was a foolish game. A girl lost her kimona, then her undershift and stood staring half naked at the men. The steam of excited breath, spilled *sake*, and the close odor of the dancers filled the room. Daniel opened a window screen a few inches. When he looked back a short girl was pulling off her underpants exposing raddled flesh, flabby thighs.

The dancers no longer looked alike. Their bodies with no powder on them were yellow and brown, mottled, and oddly shaved. Sweat ran between their breasts. Some were still young—only ten or twelve—and had small budding breasts. Two were older and their breasts sagged obscenely. The game went on and the samurai slapped each other across the table, broke *sake* cups gleefully and shouted like animals in rut, showing their yellow teeth. They twisted their hair from their eyes with oily fingers, making grunting sounds that Daniel supposed were words.

Daniel saw Lord Ito sitting calmly, drinking little. The tallest girl was naked now. Her legs were bowed, her arms too thin. Her breath came with some difficulty from a chest Daniel suspected of being tubercular. Daniel wondered if she were too ill to go on. A small girl was becoming animated as she clung to her one remaining shred of attire. Then this too fell. The women no longer looked like dolls. They looked hungry, or amused. And one seemed drugged by the music as she gestured in a frenzy and pranced about, legs apart, with large hips and flopping breasts, coming nearer to the table.

The gestures no longer could be called a dance or even a game. It was obscenity, vulgar without being enticing, sexual without being graceful. And to a New Englander like Daniel sinning must at least be graceful. It was a poor thing, and yet only Lord Ito and Daniel seemed to know it.

The samurai were stumbling to their feet, joining the dancers, beginning to get rid of their swords, dropping their robes. Big in chest, short in legs but powerful in the arms, their heated faces turkey-red, they were mauling the shrill animated girls. The drum went on with its booming leer. Some of the lamps were blown out. The goat smell, the lust grew. Daniel knew that even he would be roused to an animal level if he stayed. He did not want to stay. He was not revolted at the idea of an orgy, for he had been around too much in his life to feel superior to this, and the power of shock had long since gone out of him. But a feeling of disgust for the greedy sensuality, the sordid lasciviousness of this group, overcame him.

He rose to escape, and saw that Lord Ito was already gone. Two little maids clung to Daniel's arm as he tried to leave. "*Iya! Iya!*—don't, don't!" they screamed, spit and *sake* spraying from their drunken little mouths.

Daniel pushed them off and thought: love enters the body through the nostrils; it doesn't smell very appealing here tonight. He stepped over couples rolling on the mats in shameless frenzy. With drunken fumbling shouts, the orgy continued.

Daniel tripped over a *hibachi* full of dead coals and found at last the place where they had left their shoes. He put his own on and plunged into the garden full of frogs grunting like lovers. He got to the street, thinking of the bitter weight of time lived and wasted. And he thought of the sea which could always cleanse his disgust. He thought of tangerine skins and pebbles among the starfish, silk froth on waves, and a night walk soft and dusty as moths. From behind him came the shrill cries of drunken men and women at their ultimate games. Daniel felt lost. Foxy came up to him from behind a hedge. "I didn't think you'd stay, Heacock Sir. Love is like a liquid—if it doesn't pour, it isn't there."

"Damn you," said Daniel in English, wiping his wet face with his best robe's sleeve. "You and your rotten native sayings. This rotten country, its rotten habits, its rotten women. What the hell am I doing here? And . . . what . . . is . . . here . . . ?"

Foxy realized his master was drunker than he looked. Politely, by one arm, he led Daniel back to the inn.

It was one of the mornings Daniel did not want to wake up to. Usually he bounced up. He felt moored now, like a deep-rooted tree, in some troubled nightmare. He tore himself free and came half awake and stirred, his mouth tasting sour and sorrowful. Through his half-lifted eyelids he saw the white sun bleaching the inn, and he lay there tasting the stale bitterness in himself. It was minutes before he moved at all, and then he rolled over with a groan and shut his eyes tight and tried to drown out all thinking and feeling. He failed and sat up trying to fight off his demon so urgent and insistent. He was still close to disgust in memory of the night before.

He was sitting there too miserable even to reach for the *sake* bottle when there was a knock on the door and Foxy came in. His eyes were bloodshot and his unshaven face had a stubble on it.

"I worried all night, Heacock Sir. You were ill. You screamed in sleep."

"Don't listen."

"We start soon."

"I'll be ready."

He needed an instrument of annihilation or escape. He had to stop thinking of the sordid scene of the night before. He thought of a print of a geisha girl by Utamaro. He rebuilt it from memory. The face was of real poetry. She turned and the range of her flesh tones, the carefully sure beauty of a body moving was like something no other great painter had yet caught. She was dancing to the sound of waves and music blended perfectly, and the grace of it and the clean firm sureness of it was something so real and yet so far off that he could not believe it. A slim young girl, real, alive, and breathing, a kind of goddess, with something added that at the moment he

could not put into words. He thought of the liquid flow of
battered Greek marbles, of tall trees bending in a misty wind.
The image leaped before his eyes, a transfiguration, a thing of
some soft and poetic passion far from the everyday reality of
Woman.

She turned now and the face filled the room, filled the throb-
bing atmosphere, filled it with a shape that, in its dark eyes, the
tilt of neck and head, the rhythm of surface, was the very mystery of existence. The very substance of flesh and love and the
fleeing moments of life. The tragic awe of beauty is here . . .

Then came a flood of brightness that stabbed the eyeballs,
and the lights went up and only the mood remained in the common little room of stained boards.

Daniel shook himself; this vision was a sure sign of a seizure
coming soon.

7

There was nothing in Doctor Daniel Heacock's stout oak chest with its brass-bound hinges that could help him ease his own illness. Not antimony, mercury, cathartate, nor Peruvian bark. It was something completely unrelated to all the simple things the London doctors had lectured him on; it was not in any way like jaundice, scurvy, worms, flux, palsy, vapors or rheumatism. He had at first hunted desperately in his edition of the *London Pharmacopœia*, and dosed himself with drinks of saffron root, of buckthorn; he even tried the old wives' remedies of sorrel, goose fat, and bloodroot. And he knew he was a fool. He was scientist enough to know there were some things man could not understand.

He read again and again the text on the nerves, written by Doctor Barner who had made some stab at the problem. But the words of the text were bitter for him to read: "In all derangement of the nervous power we must admit a fluid in the medullary substance of the brain and nerves . . . perhaps some organic lesions of the brain itself . . . As for treatment when the worst is present, the kindest is often the straitjacket, shaving and blistering, a purge with soluble tartar, clay cupping, snow packs . . . in the end one must admit to a mystery, for

89

all cures are only found in the causes. . ." Finally Daniel had flung the book away, never to open it again.

How much better were those who died quickly of the throat-sickness, or those who got the smallpox and were saved from the oozy pustules by scratching in the arm with the dried lymph of the pox itself. He could almost envy the subject, so stiff and beyond everything but the last indignity of the dissecting table. Even those who died of the other forms of pox were better off—they got anodynes for pain, and in the end eternal peace. To be healthy as he was and yet live for the seizures that came every handful of months was black horror. Only the pipe was an escape, and the pipe made everything indifferent in its escape. He could not remain active and a physician and surgeon with the pipe.

Daniel sent Foxy to ask Lord Ito to visit him. The young lord came and Daniel asked him to sit down.

· "I am low in spirit, Lord Ito. It's a personal thing—an illness I have carried with me for many years. I will explain it to you."

"You want a woman perhaps? These inn maids are not like the best-smelling courtesans of the Yoshiwara in Edo, but they have a certain skill and charm. I understand why the Chinkina dancers disgusted you. They are for boors and soldiers."

"Women bring on my illness quicker." Daniel looked up and shook his head. "Don't worry, Lord Ito, it doesn't interfere with my surgery. It happens only once or twice a year and is over in a matter of moments."

Lord Ito looked at Daniel, slowly tracing in his mind what these hints could mean. "When a mad fox bites a farmer, the farmer becomes first numb, then foams at the mouth, then must

90

be tied down. You have not been bitten by a mad fox, Heacock Sir?"

"No. Have you ever seen a man fall down and his mouth talk madly, yet no sense comes from him, and you have to hold his tongue so he will not choke?"

"That is the sacred illness, and the priests say it is the soul struggling with the flesh. Such people are held in honor among us."

Daniel said sadly, "You may so honor me. We call it epilepsy. Nothing of it is understood in my country. Maybe your priests are wiser. Now I have told you. If I fall down in this manner, put a guard around me to shield me from the view of the people. Put something like a stick between my teeth so I can breathe and I do not swallow my tongue."

The two men sat in the presence of something beyond contemplation, staring at each other. Lord Ito said, "I knew you were not just like most men, and this divine thing you suffer bears me out. Also I think when you reach Edo, and see the castle of the Shogun, your mood will be lighter. Good night."

"Good night, Lord Ito."

Daniel listened to the night sounds of the inn after Lord Ito had gone. He went to his saddlebags lying in a corner and deep down in one he found a long flat Chinese box. It was of black wood bound in silver bands on which were engraved dragons, scaly and curling their tails into their own mouths as their bodies went completely around the box. Daniel did not open it. He took up his journal and wrote:

"When I fear a seizure I am incapable of leading a decent

life. Nights are haunted by nightmares. At times I suffer terribly from mystic horror—a most excruciating fear.

"Such a spell might be followed by a convulsion, and then hypochondriasis, lethargy, weakness and impotence. Before a seizure my melancholy and irritation increase; I become morose and quarrelsome; at times I throw myself at people and yell at them. I hear voices, visions go past me as if in a dream or delirium, or else I experience a poignant, unbearable blissfulness.

"After a convulsion I am overcome with depression and anguish. I feel like a criminal, with an unknown guilt. I can be quarrelsome and insulting. Then afterwards . . ."

He lay the journal aside and pulled a floor lantern closer. He opened the flat dragon-decorated box and took out the outfit for smoking. This could calm him, and often had postponed an attack for a few months. But it had its own perceptible grip on him. He held up the *yeng-tsiang* pipe of orange wood in his hands. He had bought it several years ago in Peking where he had first smoked opium. He lit the small lamp and from a metal box took up a pill of *gow hop*. He rolled it smooth between his thumb and first finger, thinking all the time of the deficiency that made him so unadaptable to normal life. He then put the pill on a *yen hauch* needle and held it in the blue flame coming from the perforated glass of the globe of the *ken-ten* lamp. The pill cooked and sizzled and with the *tsha* knife Daniel carefully placed the pill in the bowl of the pipe. He took three long pulls of the opium, then sighed in sadness and lay down on his sleeping pad and took three more pulls. He began to drift placidly into peace and quiet, the menace of the imminent seizure now gone. A smile came to the sleeper's face. In the sweet strong smell of the room he slept in a world beyond reproach and demands.

Some days later the procession of Lord Ito came at last, slowly, to the outskirts of Edo and stopped to reorganize itself and change into ceremonial robes. Heads were shaved, and horses were curried and brushed. Daniel stood by the side of the road looking up at the dazzling cone of Fujiyama, and at the villages, their feet in water, like a floating necklace around its base. Lord Ito, his topknot freshly tied, his best robe rustling, came and stood by Daniel's side.

"*Irrassbai*—welcome to Edo. Once this east coast was all reeds and wilderness. But the first Tokugawa Shogun built his capital here at Edo, and now we citizens of the place dream of it when we are not at home."

"You've been away a long time."

"There was trouble." Lord Ito frowned. "Hypocrites were in power and I was foolish and had ideals. But my story would bore you."

Daniel knew it wouldn't and that Lord Ito was not in the mood to talk about it. "Have you had any news of the sick man, Lord Ito?"

"No. We'll know more when we enter the grounds of the Shogun's castle. I regret that you must give up your horse and get back into the palanquin for the trip through the city."

"I suppose it's best," said Daniel, stretching. "But it's not comfortable."

"If the vulgar population of the city saw you they'd crowd so they'd collapse the bridges. They'd mob the castle gates.

However the curtain silk of your palanquin is thin and you will be able to see much of Edo as we pass."

Daniel looked off to the huddle of the city and beyond it to the curving bay, black with ships riding at anchor, and that special blue Japanese sky that was now scrubbed clean after a rain. It had rained hard all night; a bone-breaking rain, Foxy had called it.

There was a jumble of high-pitched shouting from the head of the procession. All were now in festive attire, the same costumes they had left Kyoto in and then packed away for the duration of the rough trip. The samurai were strutting in polished splendor and tightening their sword sashes, the bearers were adjusting their loads on the bamboo yokes. The ghost-thin smoke from a roadside fire made a brown ribbon tying earth and sky together as some servants had a last cup of tea before entering the great city of the Tokugawas: Edo, on its reedy marsh, with its curving bay set under the great mountain so steady and solitary on the horizon. Daniel could understand the touchy dignity of these people. It fitted their landscape.

Daniel got into the palanquin. It seemed more cramped than ever after the freedom of horseback riding. Foxy adjusted the curtains and looked at Daniel. "You would like a cup of tea?"

"No," said Daniel. "I just want to stop traveling."

"Be very careful, Heacock Sir. At the castle there is always some intrigue and I have only a little idea of why you are here."

In English Daniel said, "Like hell you have. Hand me my bags." He took out the stoneware bottle of Dutch gin and took a long pull. He pointed a finger at the little man. "Foxy, my own true friend, you can't get anything as strong as this. Here, have a swig."

The interpreter winked, wiped the neck of the bottle on the sleeve of his robe and took a swallow. He puffed, panted, beat his chest politely with two fingers and allowed a tear to drop out of the corners of his slant eyes. "Blow the man down," he said softly in his precise English while he struggled for breath.

The procession started with shouting and the banging of ceremonial staffs. The sound of cymbals began to clatter and Daniel looked out at the outskirts of the city—houses and temples built of wood and of colored timbers, with trellised doorways, moon gates, and closed shutters. Some people were bowing, and officials with tall metal staffs containing iron rings now surrounded Lord Ito as he passed on his horse.

Suddenly a guard of horsemen joined the procession—men wearing huge basketwork helmets and shaking lances, controlling their horses with great skill. More people were bowing as the procession, at a steady three miles an hour, moved towards the city. Daniel looked out for Foxy, but the little man had run ahead and Daniel had no idea what section they were passing through. He suspected that the basket-helmeted horsemen were a police escort.

Foxy came back, smiling. "Now we shall have no trouble getting through the street gates. The head of every street, every square in Edo, has a gate across it and sometimes a procession must pay dearly to get them all open."

"Who are the people in the basket helmets?"

"Police officials. They'll keep the gates open."

"Gates across streets?"

"Oh, yes," said Foxy and ran off again. The procession went

on slowly. Now Daniel saw they were at the great gates of the city itself, painted red with large gold letters. Once past them there was nothing, Daniel saw, but the usual plain houses of the oriental towns he had seen before. People did not display their wealth on the outside in this part of the world, and one could agree with their caution. One of Daniel's legs was asleep and he had bumped his head peering out. He took another swig from the gin bottle; he felt his heart thumping and he knew he was worried and even frightened of what lay ahead.

People stood, heads bowed down, staring sideways. The procession of Lord Ito was a good half-mile long, and very impressive. It was a silent crowd. Daniel observed them carefully; he noticed that their city faces were pleasure-marked, work-scarred, often wise and rather cunning. They paid no attention to the servants crying out and soldiers shouting, *"Sh'taniro! Sh'taniro!"* There was no kneeling, there were no faces in the dust here. The cry changed to, *"Shatu! Shatu!* Keep back! Keep back!"* as the silent watchers came closer to the procession, causing the formation to break up from time to time.

Every hundred yards there was a gate across the street and it would swing open as the procession came up to it. Daniel saw Lord Ito and his retinue ride proudly ahead, heads high. The pungent smell of the city came to Daniel's nose, the odor of people actively living, their flavor and leavings, their food and spices, the smell of markets and little gardens. Daniel liked it. It had personality, this odor; it was the smell of a city not ashamed or backward, but rather forward; even too bold and gamey perhaps, but full of fun and a desire for pleasure. Daniel laughed; he was making things up, and he reached for the gin bottle. There was just one good drink left—and then it was empty, and the rest of the bottles were packed somewhere with his baggage.

They were crossing steep moon bridges of wood, and far ahead a great yellow-roofed castle swam in the sky. The procession moved with a precise skill through the streets, but Daniel had lost all sense of direction. Now a new pace and rhythm began to take over the procession and the bearers of the palanquin took it up and made a humming sound as the litter swayed and the speed of the procession increased with a kind of firm military stomp. The streets were packed with watchers and the cry of "*Shatu!*" was like the echo of a cracking whip.

The horses were trotting rapidly, and soldiers ran beside them hanging on to the red leather reins. Everything that could jingle, jingled, and whatever could rattle, rattled, including the iron crab-like armor of the samurai. These military figures were twirling their mustaches into warlike scrolls and stamping their shin-guarded legs like dancers heavy as bears.

Below his litter appeared the dark green slime of moat water. Then Daniel saw the sloping walls of an embankment made of huge gray stones placed carefully together to fit perfectly.

He leaned far out to see better. A castle sat on this stone foundation and then he was in a courtyard, a huge courtyard surrounded on every side by terraces, wide porches, and lofty buildings ending in the curve-hipped roofs that were proper for castles.

The procession stopped. As the palanquin was set down Daniel felt lightheaded from the gin. He laughed and put his feet down on the courtyard stones and stood up in the strong light, weaving just a little on his feet.

People were bowing and staring at him and saying, *"Yoro-shiu."* Lord Ito was bowing to court officials in black silk and they were bowing back and Daniel, smiling, bowed too, just to keep in the spirit of things.

Foxy was at his elbow. "You'll be housed in the east wing, Heacock Sir. Just bow and walk. The baggage will follow. *We* are drunk?"

"I am—you're not. This the Shogun's castle?"

"Oh, yes. We are in, and how we shall get out, *that* is another problem."

"I see your point, Foxy. Drunk or sober, I see it. Yes."

Daniel frowned and followed the kow-towing officials and Lord Ito into a small building that he supposed you could call a little palace. It was marvelously fitted and made of wood and tiles and screens and flagstones. It even had a private little stream beside it, and a garden all rocks and moss, with plantings very graceful and yet so simple.

Inside the little palace the red ceiling beams shone and the low teak furniture and vases and comfortable yellow mats suggested it would be an easy place to live in. Servants were prone on the matting, not daring to lift their heads to look at the yellow-haired blue-eyed giant.

Foxy, very snooty, went among them thumping each on the back of the head with his white-socked big toe, sending them about their business.

Everyone else sat on low cushions and waited, for this was a land of ceremony.

Tea came, and rice cakes. Lord Ito sat cross-legged at the low table with Daniel and the court officials, and everyone was very ceremonial. Daniel looked up at a six-panel screen showing a battle between demons and men, everyone slashing boldly in red and gold, and fragments of people and demons scattered artistically across the eight golden panels. He wondered if it was painted by Sanraku Kano, and if he could carry it off; he realized he was still drunk.

Lord Ito said, one hand on Daniel's knee, "You are tired. I know I am. The greeting, as is only proper, has been official and very fine." He waited for Foxy to translate.

"How official?" asked Daniel after Foxy had translated it into English. If Lord Ito wanted to pretend that Daniel couldn't speak or understand Japanese, Daniel was willing to play along.

Lord Ito, lifting a porcelain teacup even with his eyebrows and then lowering it to sip slowly, said, "You will find, Heacock Sir, your interest in our insects and birds well rewarded. Your mission will show many new splendid specimens."

The officials all nodded while Foxy rapidly translated.

Daniel tried to hide his amazement at this new description of his "mission." "Of course, Lord Ito. Insects and birds."

Daniel rose as they all rose, and bowed as they bowed. Then the sliding doors closed and he was alone with Foxy and a warming *hibachi* box of glowing charcoal. Foxy took the teacup from Daniel's hand. "We better speak the English, Heacock Sir, ah so, much the better for us here. Walls have the eyes and the ears, yes? So."

"What the hell's the matter? I'm not here to collect goddamned bugs and birds or such nonsense."

"Lord Ito whispered to me at the door—quickly, tell the white doctor to be patient. There is trouble in the palace."

"Maybe the Shogun is dead?"

Foxy shook his head. "There is no way of knowing. Now you rest till we are called?"

"Is all my baggage here?"

Foxy nodded and looked around at the black and white walls that closed them in. "You rest. But please, keep the head most very clear, eh?" Foxy's English broke down when he was excited.

Daniel said, "What's biting you, Foxy? What's eating you?"

"I do not like it here much. Not at all. And so you keep head so very clear. You no smoke the *yeng-tsiang* pipe and *gow-hop* pill, eh?"

Foxy was not even looking at him. He was examining a finger as if he hadn't ever seen it before. Daniel said harshly: "All right, get out."

JOURNAL OF DOCTOR DANIEL HEACOCK

"I need several pipes—but I don't dare with the task ahead of me. I can only sit cross-legged on the floor and brood.

"When we're very young we think all our passions, tensions, desires, are eternal—but like leaves on a river it all must sometime float out to the sea. You can't ever go back to the past, because the past isn't there. Only an idea has a being and an existence. A thoughtful man must find, not only the reality, but the secret inner form of things. And here in this country everything is hidden in legend and symbol. Everything has a new kind of being here.

"Perhaps I shouldn't have written this as soon as I got to Edo. But I've studied their art, their music, their language, so that I am like an outsider who stands looking in, and because his vision is fresh, sees more than one who has been here since birth. I am most likely wrong. What are they striving for? Simple things, but never foolish ones, their sages say. Anybody can be a physical hero, a blustering samurai. Unflinching stupidity, clare-colored blood spilled like steers' gore, intricate sexual encounters in strange places. It's a fraud. Any cow in a butcher's yard can die bravely. And make a heroic face at the world as it gets its throat cut. It's harder to live, harder to think, harder never to pose as a brave man. I'm getting sleepy. I can hear a stream falling over rocks nearby . . ."

8

Lord Ito had sent a messenger to Daniel in the afternoon. "I am giving a party tonight. It is urgent that you attend."

Daniel had wondered about this invitation. Would his patient be among the guests? It wasn't likely. He decided the ways of these people were strange; he could only wait and see.

At dusk, when the great mountain faded haughtily into the night, the party began in the house of Lord Ito. The palanquins had come and deposited the important guests from the castle and the town. The geishas, with picturesque fragility, had come with their music cases and their little maids, some of them from the castle, some from the teahouses. The *toro* lanterns, symbols of the soul of Tamagiku, a legendary courtesan, had been set up in the garden, and at the sliding screens one could glimpse the gaiety and hear the music behind all that was going on.

On the street outside stood a peddler of fireflies, with his little cages of glowing insects. "Famine in the north and they play their games."

A fat citizen smiled. "They'll open plenty of *haku cho*—

white porcelain *sake* bottles, three pints to a bottle, and that's
good for my business."

A group of painted men out of some volatile bizarre world
appeared and ran into the house; they were the *hokan*, male
singers and dancers who would perform such buffoonery and,
if the party went that way, the *suteleko*, an erotic pantomime
dance of great adroitness.

The firefly peddler asked, "Have they sent for the courtesans
yet?"

"Not yet," said the *sake* merchant. "But O-Kita is here tonight—really the most marvelous geisha in all Edo. Ah, I wish I
could afford to have her entertain my guests every night."

"This Lord Ito Kojin, I hear he was outlawed once. What
has he been up to?"

"Not outlawed. Some scandal at the castle."

A turbulence of mist, damp as rain, filled the street as several
jogoku—unlicensed prostitutes—came up, arm in arm, chattering
and laughing. Lord Ito's servants chased them off, and frowned
on the people watching from the street and moved them back.
From the house came the clear music of O-Kita playing her
samisen with a plaintive touch, poignant with promise and
possibility.

A man got out of a litter, tossed a coin to the bearers, and
went up to Lord Ito's door. He had several rolls of paper under
one arm and he faced a servant boldly. "I am Hokusai. Get out
of my way."

The servant looked over his shoulder and Narrow Eyes,
Lord Ito's steward, nodded. The artist came in after slipping off
his clogs.

"They started early." The steward slapped the cheek of a maid carrying in a tray of cakes. "Keep the tray level." He turned to Hokusai. "It is a very lively affair. But you will be amazed at the white man. High as a tower, hair the color, so help me, of beach sand, eyes, honestly, it's frightening, like a spoonful of blue lake water."

"Ah, he must be Dutch. I've seen their engravings, printed from copper sheets. Is he an artist?"

"That I don't know. You've brought some amusing scrolls to show the guests?"

"Naturally," said the artist, trying to peer around a corner into the large well-lit room where the party was going on. His quickening pleasure was like provocative music. "That's what you asked for."

"Go in, Hokusai, and sit in the back. Lord Ito will tell you with a gesture when to show your scrolls. If they want courtesans early, you'll be out of luck."

The artist, fingers twitching with joy, went quickly to an opening in the sliding walls and inched through. In the party room he sat down cross-legged in the shadows. Low tables of wine and food stood around. A row of geishas and dancers sat in a semi-circle, and in their midst O-Kita was singing the poem by Basho she had once sung for Hokusai:

> "*Koyotaki ya*
> *Nami ni chiri naki*
> *Natsu no tsuki* . . .

> "In clear waterfalls swims
> On the immaculate waves
> The summer moon."

Around three sides of the large room sat Lord Ito, his retinue, and invited court and city guests. Some were already heated by wine, some were still eating. Many were listening, and among them there was the wonderful monster himself, splendidly obscene as to hair and eyes and size.

Hokusai examined him—what a creation, transcending nature! He was nothing like the fat Dutchmen in their baggy pants and wide brimmed hats that Hokusai had seen in the copper engravings. This man with his huge shoulders, powerful arms, the solid narrow face with its strong nose and wide blue eyes, was like a new kind of dragon from some ancient scroll come alive. It sat now, arms folded, looking intensely at O-Kita, listening to her just as if it understood what she was singing.

> "*Shimokyo!*
> On the piled high snow
> The night rain."

Hokusai examined the strange features, the way the eyes and the nose made up a face so daringly ugly and un-Japanese. He began to put away in memory the crisp slight curl to the yellow hair, the hard thin mouth with a suggestion of sensuality in the lower lip, the jutting cleft chin and the cords of muscle in the powerful neck.

Now the white man was looking back at the artist as if he had felt his close scrutiny. Hokusai smiled boldly and held up a wine cup. The creature also lifted a *sake* cup and took a big swallow. Hokusai liked a creature who could drink, and he too sipped. When his eyes came back again on the monster, he was watching O-Kita once more, swallowing her radiance as she swayed sinuously in ripples of silk. Hokusai supposed he had a normal man's desires, reproduced like any animal, and made love intricately. He imagined mating images of these great blonde things and he cursed again that he could not have ink and brush now to draw it.

> "In the cold evening
> I got lumbago
> And went home."

There was laughter at this sudden ironic turn in the music and words. O-Kita, who seemed to draw sustenance from some secret strength, lowered her head in this room given over to the essence of pleasure. She sat expressionless under her white powder, aware of the stare of the creature. Lord Ito nodded to her to go on and O-Kita began to sing the poem written about the O-Mon gate, the only entrance and exit to the Yoshiwara.

> "Dream of spring
> When the streets
> Are scattering
> Cherry blossoms
>
> "The warnings
> Of autumn come
> When lanterns
> Light the streets."

Somehow she knew the white giant understood what she was singing, this marvelously large object that was a man such as she had never seen or imagined before. He frightened her, too, the way a bear would, suddenly met on one's path for the first time. And like a bear whose sleek coat and great waddling dignity would impress one, this man too, for all his frightening

size and uncouth stare, was something different and vital. She
certainly would have been fearful of going near him or touching him, and across the mats of the large room, and despite the
strident chatter of guests, she could not overlook his turbulent
presence any more than one could overlook a mountain.

He was untrained in polite matters. He stared frankly at her,
a look plaintive without melancholy, with the enjoyment her
singing gave him. He moved on the mat; no one had told him
it was not the proper way to show respect. He looked big
enough to see his reflection in the sky.

Two of the *hokan* dancers leaped into the center of the room
and began the wild crude dancing for which they were noted.
It would grow more and more obscene. More *sake* bottles
would be opened and warmed. Soberness was transcended. The
drinking was justified by tradition. And soon they would send
for the courtesans and she, O-Kita, would bow and go out and
Narrow Eyes would slip her and the other geishas their tips and
back she would go to the castle in a petulant and moody un-
easiness.

She saw Hokusai seated in a corner, patiently, and perhaps
futilely, waiting to be asked to show his work. He was dipping
his finger in a sauce from a fish dish and drawing something
on the back of a scroll. Compared to the barbarian with his
yellow shock of hair and huge frame Hokusai suddenly seemed
to O-Kita, for the first time, neat and respectable, a gentleman
of sorts. The dancers were expanding their low gestures and
several guests were drunk and pawing the matting. A sediment
of wisdom called doubt made O-Kita wonder if life held only
this exhilaration without true gratification.

It was not right in front of a stranger, and when O-Kita
looked over at the creature he was partly obscured by Lord

Ito, who was whispering to him. So he could understand civilized talk, perhaps like a dog or horse, she reasoned, that responded with some sort of understanding to words.

Daniel had been careful not to have too much to drink. He still wondered about Lord Ito's reason for the party, and for inviting him.

He had been very excited by O-Kita's singing. He understood most of the words of her songs and was amazed at how fragile Japanese poetry was compared to his favorite, Andrew Marvell, or even John Donne and certain of the Restoration poets with their wonderful love poetry. O-Kita herself made his chest pound from her tangible radiance. Such perfect beauty was shocking in a public entertainer. He had, of course, none of the prejudices about oriental women that most Westerners had; he had lived too long in China, and elsewhere, and known too many kinds of women to feel there was any reason to compare her with the pale women of his youth. (We never—he had heard—love the same love twice.) There was nothing as perfect as O-Kita in the United States or Europe. Or had his standards changed? Had he become a victim to this part of the world, rather than its objective viewer and bystander? She sat now, head down, while the dancers grew more vulgar.

Lord Ito moved toward him, and said into his ear, in an almost inaudible whisper, "We'll slip away now. For you to examine the Shogun. I have sent for the courtesans for my guests and no one will pay us too much attention. It's an unworthy party I've given, but it will throw the Shogun's enemy off our track."

"No, it's a good party," said Daniel. "I'm very impressed. But I'll need my instruments."

"I sent your interpreter to get them. Come."

Daniel rose and followed Lord Ito behind a screen and through a low door as the courtesans entered, the large bows on their kimono sashes tied in front. He looked around as he left, but the beautiful geisha was gone. Outside a smoky tranquil rain fell.

The palanquins were waiting behind the house and Daniel crowded himself into one. The bearers splashed off into the night, rushed on their way with shouts and growls from behind. A light rain spattered gently on the curved roof over Daniel's head as he swayed and bounced. Now he understood Lord Ito's message. He was about to take the first step toward accomplishing his mission. But his mind did not dwell on what was in store for him at the palace. He thought of the beautiful geisha he had just seen; she was already a half-obliterated illusion, like his vision of the Utamaro print. No, her exquisite delicacy lingered with him still, and he wondered why she had so touched him. He had never been ineffectual and inarticulate with women, and of professional women he knew a great deal. They had no repugnance for him; rather they had a very definite charm. Still none had ever affected him as immediately as this graceful singer and her delicate beauty.

He held on to the side of the palanquin, frowning. It must be his illness growing stronger. Almost always in the last few years some adventure with a woman had brought on a great seizure. Damn it, he had not come here to count an array of calamities.

He frowned in angry dissatisfaction, sensing some final disaster. He should never have come to Edo.

Even as he thought this, the muddy tramp of the carriers took the litter across the bridge to the Shogun's castle, their accelerated breathing making a gray smoke in the deep green falling rain. Their pace was increasing again and more shouts behind drove them on into the great courtyard where pitch torches blazed near some of the castle doorways.

Daniel got out of his palanquin into the center of a black pandemonium of guards and castle servants. Lord Ito came up and took him by the arm, leading him quickly down echoing hallways, preceded by two men in palace armor carrying lances and lanterns. The walls shed fear over Daniel's shoulder, a fear as vague as music heard far off over water.

They entered a large audience chamber filled with incense. Many columns, great logs unpolished and uncolored, supported a ceiling of gold and colors bright and carefully applied.

In the room were many men with their heads down in respect; many were kneeling. Lord Ito threw himself to the floor and Daniel bowed toward what looked like a dais. On it sat a pale young man with very sad eyes. He was gripping the arms on his chair as if in fear or pain; certainly he was in some intolerable agony of spirit.

Daniel looked over the officials and court nobles in their little lacquer-colored caps, brocaded coats, and trousers of heavy yellow silk. Their sleeves and trousers were six or eight feet long, so they moved with difficulty, neither feet nor hands showing. Daniel had heard this court dress was first used in some ancient time to prevent assassination and make escape difficult.

The figure on the dais stirred. Daniel studied the face, the yellow robe embroidered with flowers, and the great S-shaped cap that pressed on the almost gray brow now bathed in shiny sweat.

Suddenly Daniel realized this was his patient.

Lord Ito was saying to a very old man, "Prince Kwammu Taira, may I present the foreigner, Heacock Sir? He is studying our birds and insects, by the honorable permission of our great Shogun."

The old prince nodded and clicked open his fan. His bright black eyes looked up at the tall blond man whose head was bowed a bit as he examined the chamber.

The prince spoke very low. "The Shogun permits the visit, and now ends the audience."

The figure on the dais had said nothing.

A bamboo curtain came down in front of the dais. The old prince looked like an old cat. His somnolent eyes did not blink.

Daniel felt Lord Ito pull him around and he was led not the way he had come, but down a hall draped in yellow and red and past great multi-paneled screens painted with battles and mountains and bridges and rivers.

He found himself in a small, plain room with scarlet carved dragons set into a wall; he recognized old Chinese work. On a pile of very ornate sleeping pads lay the Shogun, still in yellow, biting his lower lip. Two old men with thin white beards were wiping his face and giving him a milky-looking drink from a small blue bowl. The Shogun's face showed a mixture, Daniel thought, of hope, fear, and pain.

111

Lord Ito knelt and bowed to the ruler. "No one has followed us here, Your Highness."

Daniel was aware of Foxy's wiry little body prone on his stomach, kow-towing in the direction of the Shogun.

The Shogun lifted his head and nodded. His voice was thin and high, yet not weak. "This is the wise doctor?"

Lord Ito nodded. "He has treated other men most successfully for the stones of the bladder, Your Highness."

"Have him approach," said the Shogun.

Foxy lifted his head two inches off the floor and said in English, "The great Shogun asks you to come to him. You should first bow to the floor."

"Not on your Aunt Minnie."

Daniel walked to the Shogun and knelt by his side. He took one thin damp hand and felt the pulse. There was a hiss of shock and anger from the two old men but Daniel ignored them. The pulse was strong and steady, but fast.

In English he said, without turning around, "I want to make a full physical examination of His Highness. Who are these two old bluffers with the chin whiskers?"

Foxy's voice whispered to Lord Ito and then said loudly, "You may proceed as you want. The old lads are the great herb doctors, Pi and Mo. Lord Ito says they are frauds and very greedy."

"Have the Shogun's clothes taken off, and get all the lamps over here. Did you bring my medical case?"

"It's all here."

Daniel was aware that behind the sliding screens were guards and other people of the court. The room was overheated from the many lanterns. Daniel carefully opened his old medical case of battered rosewood and its lining of faded red velvet. It had been made in Italy and the instruments were German, Dutch and English manufacture. Some Daniel had designed himself, and these were powerful, cruel-looking things, expertly put together.

Daniel uncovered the Shogun, who lay nude before him. The mighty Tokugawa ruler was a thin delicate young man, a little underweight, and his legs were slightly bowed and bent. The eyes, sharp and deep purple-black in the light, looked up at Daniel with a fatalistic respect.

"Explain, Foxy, that I am going to feel his abdomen, pressing here and there. If I hurt him he is to make a sound. If it is very painful he's to groan. Get the hell off your knees and come up here and help me. Tell them you're a devil doctor yourself and my best and wisest assistant."

While Foxy blandly translated, Daniel took out some very thin steel probes, one of which had a scored end like a file. He handed the probe to Foxy; then he knelt down and began to feel the Shogun's stomach, groin and sides, his fingers moving slowly down to the pubic area. The Shogun sighed and moaned from time to time. The two old men just stared with outraged amazement. Lord Ito followed carefully every pressure and push Daniel made on the yielding flesh under his fingers.

Daniel nodded. "The Shogun most certainly has a bladder infection. The tenderness extends all across the symphysis pubis and groin. I am going to push a probe up through his urethra into the bladder, to see if I can feel the stones and try to estimate how many, and their size. I will have to change his position a bit to get the probe up there without hurting him too much."

Daniel picked up a probe and coated it with olive oil from a small bottle. "It will not hurt very much if the Shogun doesn't move." An almost imperceptible shiver ran through the Shogun as he saw the instrument being prepared.

Five minutes later Daniel was wiping his face and fingers on a damp towel. The Shogun, his whole body trembling, was being given some of the milky mixture again, the two old men salving him for indignities inflicted. Daniel carefully wiped the probe and replaced it in its red velvet groove in the case.

Daniel said, "There are, I think, two stones present in the bladder, one smooth, like an egg, and I should guess as large as a garden bean. The other is ragged and rough, the size of a cherry pit. I am, of course, working in the dark, testing with the probe, but I can feel and even hear stones with the rough end of my probe."

"Can you get them out?" asked Lord Ito through Foxy.

"Not without cutting through the urethral orifice. They are too large to pass alone."

"Pi and Mo say they can dissolve them with their special tiger-tooth powder and meiji root."

"How long have they been trying?" asked Daniel.

"Four months."

"Stones can't be dissolved. They can, if reached, sometimes be cut out. It's complex but I've done it four times, as you know. There are certain tissues and glands to avoid; like the prostate, the ejaculatory duct. I make a direct attack into the bladder, grasp the stones, sew up the bladder and the muscles and tissues, and then I put a drain in."

Daniel watched the Shogun as he listened intently to Foxy translate. The young ruler bit his lower lip with his long teeth and closed his eyes. Then he said very low, as if finally exhausted, "Will the pains go? Will everything be as before?"

Daniel frowned. It would, if he succeeded. He looked at Lord Ito. Had Lord Ito told the Shogun that of four such operations he had succeeded three times and failed once? But Lord Ito's face for the first time since Daniel had met him was set in a mask of oriental expressionlessness. The truth came down on Daniel like a box: he was alone in this adventure, dreadfully alone.

Aloud he said, "If there are no complications everything will be as before."

The Shogun said something very low; Daniel looked inquiringly at Foxy. Foxy said, avoiding Daniel's eyes, "The Shogun wants to know if this will interfere with his going to dally and mount his women, and mar the excitement of the pleasure peak, as he calls it."

Daniel scowled. "Damn it, how can he think of women the way he feels? No, don't translate that. Just say everything will be as before." Daniel put his hand on the Shogun's hot brow, and then took his pulse once again.

Lord Ito asked, "You can perform it now?"

Daniel turned in shocked amazement. "No, I can't do it now! The Shogun has a bladder infection, there is pus, he's running a temperature and his pulse is fast. We've got to bring his fever down first and wait for the infection to subside. I'm not cutting into swollen and angry tissue. Put him on a bland diet. Not much walking, and certainly no riding. If the fever and infection go in the next few days I'll operate if I decide there is a chance."

Daniel looked hard at Lord Ito, who said, "The Shogun says you may go."

Angry at this abrupt dismissal, Daniel strode out of the

room without a bow, followed by Foxy lugging the medical case.

JOURNAL OF DOCTOR DANIEL HEACOCK

"I am writing in rage—never have I seen such rudeness! And these people pride themselves on their politeness, with all the precise forms of court etiquette observed by the book! Just imagine any physician in England or the States being sent off in such a fashion! I am furious! What a fool I was ever to get involved in any of this.

"And those two old savages—what an insult to have them watching every move I make! I wouldn't mind having a doctor who knew something about medicine watching me—he might even be useful as an operating assistant when the time comes. In fact, now that I think of it, he could be very useful in case this illness of mine should come upon me at a bad moment. Damn it, I wish I *did* have a capable assistant around.

"It would be good to have someone to talk to, also—to discuss the case with, and to share my anger, and perhaps to escape with if the going gets rough. There is far too much stealth and secrecy around here for my blood, too many music hall soldiers and guards. An entourage like Lord Ito's could start a riot all by itself, and with so many factions at court, each with its own little army, there could be quite a conflagration if any of these puppets should take it into his pretty head to act on his own.

"This room is too small for my anger. I'm going out for a walk—the rain will cool me off."

9

Alone in a litter on her way back to the castle, O-Kita took stock of herself. She was healthy and alert to all the normal sensual appetites, and she knew that Heacock Sir had more than just appealed to her. But there was a great deal about him she couldn't comprehend. And while she realized that it took courage for him to be in Edo, away from his own people, she wondered if she wanted any personal involvement with him. Besides, there was Hokusai.

She knew that she withheld the center of herself from every relationship she had had so far. No momentary joy ever overcame her disillusionment with life. Supreme and sacred moments, culminations in ecstasy, even love, usually left her dazed and mortified.

She accepted the facts of her external world and didn't brood. She liked people—sometimes even those who were bad for her. She believed in work and did her job, and she found that she was still capable of pity and mercy. She did not feel herself any kind of a sacred vessel, but she suspected her worth. And, knowing her value, she felt deep depression when she was not being appreciated for it.

"*Ashibiki no*
Yamadori no o no

"The pheasant on the mountain
Where my steps are slow.

"*Shidari o no*
Naga nagashi yo wo
Hitori ka mo nemu

"Fans out his tail.
And in the long night
I sleep alone . . ."

O-Kita put down the book of poems. It was late. The party, her part of it, had been over hours ago. Seated on a low mat in a room of the Shogun's castle she could not sleep. The poem of Hitomaro was one of her favorites. She had pursued poetry since childhood. And as she grew older and illusions snapped like threads around her, she more and more turned to the words and images the poets and artists brought to her.

Will he always love me
I ask his heart,
At dawn my ideas
Hang in disorder
With my hair.

There had been a time, years ago, when the lines meant something personal to O-Kita. *Will he always love me.* He had loved her for several months. She was still in her teens then, and he was Lord Sosei. O-Kita had been asked to entertain at a party given by some northern *daimyo* who were making gifts to the Shogun. Lord Sosei had come with them—a farm boy unused to the city ways of Edo, and he had fallen in love with her. He was the first man who had ever shown her any real personal kindness. His country earnestness, his dark purple eyes and innocent mouth made the way he leaned toward her and touched her the act of a puppy. It had first of all, the town said, been a fine geisha romance. Then it became sad and heavy when Lord Sosei was called home to the north. To Lake Towads, where he told O-Kita life was lived in mist and under dripping fir trees and in the caves of demons. And when the snows came they all went out in furs and killed bears with spears and made fires on blue frozen lakes and cooked the meat to share the vitality and strength of the bear god. Lord Sosei had wanted O-Kita to come with him. He had wanted to marry her. When the family of the love-crazy lord asked the son to submit to the family command and leave the girl, he refused and began to drink in the dives of Edo. The Shogun himself then ordered Lord Sosei to return home, and the unhappy youth struck the captain of the guards wearing the crest of the Shogun.

When he was sober again the farm boy's face was stern. He held O-Kita close against his body a long time, and then sent her away to the market to buy some nonsense for a parting gift while he packed for the journey home. When she was gone Lord Sosei dressed all in white and made the proper prayer and the offering to a small Shinto shrine. Then he knelt down and wrapped in cloth the hilt and swordguard of the shorter of his two samurai swords. The vulgar called the rite *hara-kiri*, but in the warriors' code it was called *seppuku*. He did it properly, piercing the abdominal wall on the left just under the bottom rib and drawing the sword all the way across, then a sharp angle turn and a pull upward of razor keen steel . . . By that time, O-Kita hoped when she thought of it, he was already beyond feeling, beyond pain and life; this poor ungainly farm boy who happened to be born a foolish lord who fell in love with a geisha and disobeyed the Shogun.

> And you think
> How long the night
> When you are alone
> And weeping.

O-Kita must have been out of her mind with grief for several weeks after Lord Sosei's ashes were sent home. But she swallowed the herbal brews they gave her, and twice they prevented her from walking into a deep green pool, with flowers of mourning in her hair. After that she became the favorite of the fat rice merchant Buson, and then there were others. But the image of the simple boy remained a long time. It was a popular geisha romance. Once there had been a street song about it, a banal one, and she now wondered if her youthful folly was finally obliterated.

She had not given her favors to any man for some time now. She was contented in her fame as a singer and entertainer—as the best known geisha in her trade. A gray numbness had descended on her of late. The artist Hokusai amused her and she knew he loved her; perhaps if he were cleaner, not always laughing like a fish barrow porter with a flea in his shirt, more respectful of custom and manners, she would have held his head between her breasts. But she had been raised properly, trained to value decorum and tradition; she could not stomach radical ideas or boorish street manners. She might as well think of falling in love with that blond creature at the party as Hokusai.

With a shock O-Kita realized she *had* been thinking of the strange large man since the party; he had been in the back of her mind, lurking there, hunting for ways to take over her sleepless thoughts, and now he had. She gripped the Magatama —the necklace of sacred stones of rock crystal, jasper and agate, around her throat.

She wondered why he fascinated her. Perhaps in his own country he would be called beautiful. There they might think tall men with powerful shoulders and long regular features were handsome. Were the women, O-Kita wondered, so tall and blonde too? He fascinated her like a fabled monster. Some over-powering memory of a fairy tale out of her childhood . . . when she lived in the bed of Madame Hairy Lip as a favorite and where, if she was a respectful dutiful girl, fairy tales were read to her . . . Was it from there she remembered dimly the story of a strange god who came sailing across the dimpling green sea on a giant ginkgo leaf? His eyes were stone blue and his strength and height were beyond all men. He freed a peasant girl on her way to a lord's harem against her will, and they went off on his great ginkgo leaf which leapt from the water and sailed the windy skies and they lived together in tree tops, in love, until the winter came with snow like thick fur and they fell down to earth changed into two red leaves; fell to the soft snow-covered ground having completed their destiny; and by spring were crumpled away.

Whenever O-Kita was unhappy in her childhood she would close her eyes and dream of this fairy tale and go off with her dream lover, a leaf god, who was described in the story as looking a great deal like the creature who had sat and stared at her tonight as she sang. It was a fearful idea to think that through some pernicious guile of the gods she could be attracted to things of this sort.

She knew now why she had been asked to come to the castle. She did not mind being a spy—it was honorable to serve those in power, and they would pay the Kataya teahouse well for her services. But there was so little she could learn. As an entertainer at such parties she could only see the guests at a distance. No men would ever discuss important affairs in her presence. But she would try to be useful to those who had brought her here.

She looked into her bronze mirror and felt the need for fresh air. The rain was still falling gently but she flung aside the sliding *shoji* wall. She looked out and almost screamed; on the castle terrace walk, before her room, stood the creature himself. Some outlandish oilskin cape-coat hung around his shoulders, and the face and hair were damp with drizzle.

O-Kita stood petrified, too well trained to scream, too startled to try and explain this to herself. It was a dream, she hoped, and if she stood very still in the cold dampness, just inside the wall, the dream would turn into another corner of her mind and bring out another less frightening image, a less audacious manifestation of her secret self.

The strange creature spoke Japanese with a slow colloquial politeness as he asked, "I have frightened you?"

The mannered answer to such a situation had been taught her, a kind of hypocrisy and unctuousness, an "Oh no, I am unworthy of feeling frightened in my smallness and unimportance." Instead O-Kita said, "Just a little."

"Don't be frightened. My name is Daniel Heacock. I'm a guest here at the castle. I saw you at Lord Ito's party."

"Yes," she recovered enough to nod brightly. "It would be hard to miss you, Heacock Sir. I am O-Kita Mitsu."

"I'm sorry I had to rush away. Lord Ito had something he wanted to show me."

"You didn't go back for the courtesans?" She gave the question a transient unimportance.

He looked at her. He was wet from his walk in the rain. He saw the book in her hand. "No, I was in no mood for courtesans. What are you reading? I can read a little, but it's very difficult. Not at all like my language."

She stood open-mouthed. "You mean you too can make writing? I thought only the civilized world, we and the Chinese, could make writing."

He smiled. "Look, O-Kita, could I step in a minute and dry myself? I've been sort of upset and I've been walking the terrace to cool off. I'm cold now."

O-Kita bowed politely and stepped back, and Daniel came in through the *shoji*. He stepped out of his sandals and stood very still while she got a towel from a chest and he dried himself slowly after getting out of his oilskin.

"I'm sorry to bother you, O-Kita. But I need human company, just someone to listen to me. On nights like this I remember my grandfather standing on his porch, listening to dogs bark in the next county. He was a little mad too."

O-Kita said, "Will you sit down? If you want tea I will wake my maids."

"No, don't wake anyone. What are you reading?"

"This is a book of love poems. They have love in your country?" She giggled and covered her mouth. "They must have or where would they get giants like you?"

He laughed too. "Read me a love poem. Are the best love poems sad in your country too?"

"Very sad. No one writes well of happy love affairs. This is by Lady Izumi Shikibu.

"When I no longer exist
Will I remember
Beyond this world
Our last time together?"

"Is the lady alive?"

"Oh no, she lived a long time ago."

"Then she knows now, doesn't she, if she remembers?"

O-Kita closed the book. "Are all men like you where you come from?"

"The United States of America? Do you mean in Boston or New Orleans?"

"I am a very ignorant girl."

"A very beautiful one." He said it low and she was surprised at his delicate reticence.

O-Kita said proudly, "Oh yes, that is why I am a very fine geisha. Are the geishas beautiful in your land?"

"No. In fact we don't have geishas." The big man laughed. "I can't imagine a geisha mincing down Boston Common."

"Then who entertains at the parties before the courtesans come in? You do have courtesans?"

He laughed again. "How can I explain to you things you wouldn't understand? Through fear and guilt of sinning, the people could not accept what you here know simply as pleasure of mind and body." He laughed suddenly. "I'm not free of it all myself. Feeling guilt for something you know does no harm is a bad thing, O-Kita. I was told I was conceived in original

sin and I grew up a contradiction between a lost past and inten-
tions of a future in exile . . . I'd like to see you again."

"You can give a party and Lord Ito can hire me again."

"No, no. I hate these parties, and sitting cross-legged, and
that insipid hot wine. I don't suppose you've ever drunk gin?"

"Gin, Heacock Sir?"

"Never mind. Could you show me Edo, the theaters, the art
shops? I want very much to see everything in the town."

"I am here as the guest of the Shogun. I do not think I can
go out of the castle. But I have a friend, an artist Hokusai. He
will be happy to show you Edo."

"Hokusai! The famous woodcut artist who makes the
ukiyo-e prints of the pleasure world?"

O-Kita giggled again. "Hokusai famous? Oh no, these
shabby artists who make the prints—they are not the famous
artists who make the screens and scrolls for the palaces and
castles."

Daniel asked, "Will you come with me and introduce me to
Hokusai? I am a friend of Lord Ito's, and he will do me certain
favors."

O-Kita looked directly into the amazing blue eyes to explain what she thought he did not understand. "A geisha is not
a courtesan. She does not have to sleep with anyone she does
not desire. I say this badly, I know. I mean to provoke no
anger. I should like to go with you and Hokusai to the theater
or out on the river . . . I am most confused." She bent her
head.

Daniel took her hand in his in a silence broken only by the
rain and her breathing. "I understand. You are a lady to me."

"My confusion shames me," she said falling into formula
after a vacuous quiet.

"My clumsiness brought it on. It's unforgivable. Is that the proper answer?"

She nodded, smiled, and he let go of her hand. She said with spirit, "I am not frightened any longer."

"Good. And don't let me play on your sympathies, O-Kita. It's true I'm far from home. But I have no desire to go home, ever. I am not too unhappy a man, but I don't have much to be happy about. I am lonely. Very lonely in a beautiful land."

"No land, of course, is as large or beautiful as Japan."

Daniel looked at her and shook his head. "The world exists only in our eyes. So no lessons. My visit here will last some time. I would be honored to meet Hokusai, and have you and him as my guests in Edo. I better go now." He started to say something about this visit blemishing her reputation, but decided this would be wrong. He stood up.

"The guards will be changing soon," she said. "Perhaps you should not be seen honoring a mere geisha."

"You know better than that." He looked at her closely, pressed her shoulder with a large hand, and went out dragging his oilskin cape after him. The rain had fallen away to a lazy lisp. O-Kita stood in the cold dampness of the open *shoji* panel and slowly slid it shut. She was shaking in some deeply felt emotional grip, as if approaching the peak of love, and to her horror and amazement, and then pleasure, she came to a climax of ecstasy and she sank down on her sleeping mats panting with the unbelievable intensity of the release.

Back in his castle quarters, his mind drenched with images of his visit to O-Kita, Daniel Heacock, reminded again of the important purpose of his journey, could not sleep. His rancor at the way he was dismissed from the Shogun's presence after the examination returned. The rain had stopped and a soggy moon, waterlogged and green, had come out. There was dripping from the castle roof, and a smell of wet ground that gave Daniel a sense of the earth.

Foxy sat over the charcoal fire pot watching Daniel, so there was no chance to get out the pipe and smoke a pill or two. It would be wrong, of course, to get on the pipe while this whole confusing matter of the Shogun's operation was still unsettled. He would be a fool to operate. The stones might be larger than he had estimated; there could be complications: tumors, hardenings, tearing, other damage already done. He knew his life was in danger if he failed. The wisest thing would be to say the operation was impossible and leave Edo.

There was also that oath taken to Hippocrates that he would serve mankind. Daniel stood up, laughed and cracked his knuckles. Service to mankind or not, what really excited him was the memory of the geisha, O-Kita. He must be getting soft in the head to let a woman distract him at such a crucial time.

Foxy looked up from blowing into the charcoal pot. In English he asked, "You can't sleep, Heacock Sir?"

"No, I can't. When I examined the Shogun they treated me as if I were a farm boy in dirty boots. But if they want my services they'd better mend their manners or I'll be out of sight before they can say Robinson Crusoe."

Foxy picked his English words with care, each precisely pronounced. "This is the way the Shogun's palace is. But you can't run. They are at all the rat holes and tunnels that lead back to the Dutch. So we stay; we eat their clams and rice and say how excellent."

"Why does Lord Ito act as if I don't understand any Japanese?"

"He is your friend. He doesn't want certain men to know you understand so much. He is very frightened of what is going on here, I think."

Daniel asked truculently, "I suppose *you* know what is going on here?"

"Some, some little few facts. Yes."

"Don't go humble on me, you little fox." Daniel grinned. "You know what I mean. I'm not going to beg for information."

Foxy shivered, his intuition sharpened by some fear, and he warmed his hands over the *hibachi*. "Lord Ito feels maybe he has walked into a trap. Bang, the log falls, his neck breaks. And maybe our necks too."

"What kind of trap?"

"Don't know. How many nobles in this palace are loyal to the Shogun? All? It looks so, no? Yes. But what if there is a powerful party inside the castle, eh? That wants to bring back the Emperor? All of this getting you here is then only a better plan to kill the Shogun?"

"I wouldn't kill the Shogun."

"But he *may* die?"

Daniel, aware of the barbarity that paraded beside him in all the inanities of this civilization, nodded.

Foxy continued. "If the Shogun does not die from his illness or your operation he may be helped into death by others, and you may be blamed. I, a wild fellow—an *abaremono*—would die with you."

"Is there any real proof there is a plot? Damn it, you people always——"

"As you may have guessed, I am also Lord Ito's agent. It seems that old Prince Kwammu Taira and his friends at court have been accepting large gifts from the rice merchants."

"Who is this old prince?"

"Oh, he is very important. He has much wealth and many retainers. And he does not very much like the Shogun. He never has. When the Shogun is well—that will be the end of Prince Taira's game. But for now, the Prince is acting on an empty stage, and no one is there to tell him to get off. Anyway, he is protecting the merchants, who hold back food in their warehouses, while much famine exists in the north and the west. The Shogun is against the merchants. He wants the supplies distributed at the old prices——"

"I'm not mixing in any of this. I'm here as a doctor. Go to bed, Foxy. I want to do some reading." He felt an oppression in his heart, felt alerted to some peculiar awareness he could not admit to the Fox. "The operation is all I'm interested in, and seeing some of the sights of the city."

After Foxy was gone, Daniel took out several books from a leather trunk. One was a small calf-bound volume, already very old and much shaken in its binding. It was the first book he had bought in England as a young medical student, and as he opened it he saw his callow youthful signature, put down with underscored flourishes. *Daniel Putnam Heacock*, December 11, 1783.

The book was: *The Apologie and Treatise of Ambroise Paré, Translated out of Latine and compared with the French by Th. Johnson . . . printed by Th. Cotes and R. Young, Anno. 1634.* It was a little book that had traveled with Daniel a long time. It had actually been written by the great surgeon almost a hundred years before it was put into English. Yet it made more sense than a great deal of texts written subsequently. (Somewhere among the accordion-folded shadows of the castle someone is playing soft music; is it O-Kita?)

Daniel leafed to a section with a turned-down page and began to read with a scowling concentration words that he had read and reread more times than he could remember:

How to cut men for the taking out of the stone in the bladder.

Seeing wee cannot otherwise help such men as have stones in their bladders, we must come to the extreme remedy, to wit, cutting . . . Now the cure is thus to be performed; the patient shall be placed upon a firm table or bench with a cloth many times doubled under his buttocks, and a pillow under his loynes and back, so that he may lie halfe upright with his thighs lifted up, and his legs and heels drawn back to his buttocks.

Then shall his feet be bound with a ligature of three fingers breadth cast around his ankles, and with the heads thereof being drawn upward to his neck and cast about it, and so brought downewards, both his hands shall bee bound to his knees.

. . . It is fit you have foure strong men at hand . . . that he may neither move his limmes . . . Then the Surgeon shall thrust into the urinary passage, even to the bladder, a silver or iron hollow probe, annoynted with oyle, and opened or slit on the outside, that the point of the knife may enter thereinto, and it may guide the hand of the workman, and keep the knife from piercing any farther into the bodies lying thereunder . . .

(The anatomy of lovers is not medical. The brevity and wonder of it, O-Kita, is only an illusion, not a body.)

. . . and also he who standeth on the patient's left side shall with his left hand gently lift up his Cods, that so in the free

and open space of the left side of the *perinaeum*, the Surgeon
may have the more liberty to make the incision . . . But in making this incision, the Surgeon must be carefull that he hurt not
the seame of the *perinaeum* and fundament . . .

(The castle guards are moving around outside. O-Kita sleeps,
or maybe not. Is she reading too? I'm a damn fool. It's all un-
motivated, accidental.)

. . . The wound must be made the space of two fingers from
the fundament . . . so that it may be the more easily restored
afterwards. Neither must the incision thus made exceed the
bigness of one's thumbe. Then presently put into the wound
some one of the silver instruments called by the name of
Guides, for that they serve as guides to the other instruments
which are to be put into the bladder.

(Squawky morning birds are already sounding. And the act
of love is a cry of strangulation. I mustn't think of O-Kita.)

It will be also necessary for the Surgeon to put another
instrument called the Ducks bill into the bladder . . . and di-
late in so turning it every way to enlarge the wound . . . the
largeness of the stone require dilatation. The stone may be
sought and taken hold of with these instruments. Neither shall
the stone be suddenly plucked out, but easily . . . and at the
length gently drawn forth . . . if other stones remain behinde,
they shall bee drawne forth . . . the end of the instrument hol-
lowed like a scoop, or spoone, shall be thrust into the bladder,
and therewith you shall gather together and take out what
gravell and the like refuse as shall be there, for that they may
yeeld matter for another stone.

(How long has it been since ecstasy and exhilaration brought
me gratification? What enormous confidence I once had in the
power of love. I can't read any more. *Namu Amida Butsu*, as
the Buddhists pray, let me sleep.)

BOOK THREE

I play on a sixteen stringed koto, but I neglect to care for it in rainy weather . . . A pair of big book cases have in them all the books they can hold. In one of them are placed old poems and romances. They are the homes of worms which come frightening us when we turn the pages, so none ever wish to read them . . .

From the Diary of Murasaki Shikibu

10

O-Kita slept, not dreaming at all. When the day came clear and bright she still slept, not waking till quite late. Then she suddenly sat up, in a panic for a moment, remembering her strange visitor of the night before.

She decided she must make known to herself just what this thing with Heacock Sir would lead to. She felt she had been wrong about love—it was in real life different from ideas she had once had about it. There had been a great deal that bore a superficial resemblance to love on her horizon, but she wanted something beyond the horizon. If there was anything there. She no longer knew. Most of the so-called love around her was reduced to the status of a disease, thriving on hurry, jealousy, and snobbery. Truth, faith, in anything seemed a crime . . .

She couldn't say her life wasn't entertaining. Fancy eating places with important men. Everybody liked her. She had wit and courage. She knew she looked beautiful. Her lovely robes; her small hands and tiny feet. She wore her hair fashionably. But she knew something was lacking. Should she let this man into her life?

It was almost indecent, this sudden surrendering of her nerve ends to the pleasure of thinking of love, thinking of Heacock

Sir, of the grim humor of his smile. She was sure he felt the attraction.

She got up and walked around the room and then sat down and stared at the moths battering the screens. The total surrender of love, that physical opening of the gates, frightened her now. She was, she knew, the kind who could never be merely possessed by an emotion, but obsessed. For her, true love must be a necessity, never a mere expedient. And now she felt she had lost all power of volition before Heacock Sir's strange masculine power. She should hate him for being a male. Maybe she would when she got to know him better, but she doubted it.

Anyway, she had promised to introduce Hokusai to Heacock Sir.

One of the publishers of the woodblock prints called *ukiyo-e* —pictures of the floating or passing world—was Tsutaya Jusaburo, called Tsuta-ju for short. He was a round butterball of a man always in a sweating hurry, always talking very fast, ready with a joke or a dirty remark to keep you off guard, always telling about something he believed in with a shrill high voice. His business ability, his good taste, his generosity were well known. His print shop was not one of the biggest ones; it was just a square box-like shop stuck in next to the Miyako-za Kabuki theater, hung with woodcut prints shaking cheek to cheek in the breeze. The doors were removed daily so one could walk into the shop itself almost as part of the street. The remaining three walls were hung with colored woodcut prints. Piles of prints were on low tables with volumes of love poems and novels illustrated with delightful or gory scenes. In the back room there were more bundles of prints tied with ribbons. An assistant trimmed prints with a sharp tool. An engraver made some last-minute changes on the block of cherry wood before him. A printer, his arms covered with red and blue dye to the knuckles, shook his head over a proof sheet of damp mulberry-pulp paper, pointing out where the cutter had failed to correctly match the color blocks. And always Tsuta-ju himself, standing between some of his hired help, about to fight, shout or strike a blow, or running forward into the shop to bow to some samurai wanting a set of prints of the Forty-seven Ronin, or an erotic series on the art of love. Although samurai were forbidden to go to the common people's print shops, because prints were thought to be a dangerous influence, these military men remained steady customers.

Tsuta-ju was not a very successful print publisher compared to the men who published the more classical and popular artists. But he had an eye for design, an enthusiasm for his work. He had discovered the great Utamaro, and now he had a new young man whose prints caused the publisher's fat face to break into a close-eyed smile of satisfaction, excitement and pleasure. "Ah, how can you find anyone as great, as new, as different, as amazing, as Toshusai Sharaku!"

But the housewives, the courtesans, the geishas, the actors, the professional gamblers, and merchants who bought a print, or half a dozen, at ten to sixteen *momme* each, were not impressed with this newcomer. Most customers ignored the startling Sharaku prints: the large heads of actors, the twisted bodies of dramatic action, in scenes from great plays. They bought more pallid pictures: cheerful children, or the long graceful sensuality of Harunobu or Utamaro, or the three sheet series' by Shunsho and Kiyonaga of parties on the river while fireworks went off overhead, or scenes of clashing warriors by Sukenobu, Moronabu.

Tsuta-ju stood this morning in his shop, holding his round stomach with both hands, rocking on his white-socked heels. He faced a thin handsome young man who had the deep eyes of a mystic, a poet, or perhaps a madman.

"Am I sad, am I depressed, do I lament out loud? I tell you you're a fool," said the publisher. "A few months, a few dozen prints, and you're ready to give up. So what if that old drunk and lecher Utamaro says your portraits depict the least attraction of human traits? He never buys prints."

"He's a great man, a great artist, Tsuta-ju."

The fat man, as if trying to alleviate annoyance, lifted fingers to slap his just-shaved poll and shook his topknot. Then he spit in disgust out into the street. "He's jealous of you. Keep making prints. What future is there for you as a Noh dancer in the suite of a Lord of Awa? A horse-turd has more fun, a pig in a basket sees more."

"Lord Hachisuka Haruteru keeps a fine troupe of Noh dancers in the best Awa traditions. And we dancers eat, we have a roof, we get some fame and applause. It isn't so bad to be a Noh dancer."

"That's all old kimona trade. The Kabuki theater is what people want now. Listen to the damn drumming next door and the roaring of the customers. And who's captured it all, all the faces of the actors, the action of the plays? You! Why Hokusai said just the other day, 'This Jurobei, or Sharaku, or whatever he wants to call himself, is the greatest woodcut artist since the great Masonobu.' Do I lie to you often?"

The young man laughed in hollow mocking tones, moving his trained dancer's body skillfully, making no unnecessary or ungraceful gesture. "Hokusai? He's out peddling dog meat for a living. He's a fine one to talk of great printmakers."

The publisher sighed, belched, and nodded, after intense concentration. "It's true nobody knows how great the print artists are, those who make the pictures. But our Hokusai has had a fine turn of luck. He asked me to have you here this morning. That's why I sent for you. He had a collector who wants to meet you. Yes, *you*."

Sharaku shook his head and tied and retied the sash of his worn robe. His deep despondency could not be shaken. "No. I can get several days' work in a dance being held at a wedding in Honshu. And from there I'm going to rejoin the Noh dancers at Awa."

"How sad. In pleasure and pain I felt we were partners," the publisher said, speaking to his rain-stained ceiling. "I should have become a rice weigher as my father wanted, or a horse gelder, a trade my uncle would have taught me. When artists fail you it's time to admit the ultimate futility of human effort."

The handsome young dancer looked down at his worn white socks, at the chipped clogs he was wearing and his skin turned a deep brown-pink as he stumbled over some words. "I haven't had a room for two days and I owe the paper man for drawing materials . . . You see." He seemed unable to go on, tears of frustration in his eyes. "You see."

The publisher, an intuitively generous man, could never resist an artist's need. He held out some greasy coins. "Don't spare me. Take full advantage of my kindness, my foolishness. Ruin me. I advance you this money on your next ten drawings for prints, but you must promise to deliver them soon."

"All right. But they're the last I'm doing."

"I tell you what I need, Sharaku. First that popinjay actor Stata Hangoro III, in 'The Iris Vendetta,' playing Fujikawa Mizuemon, and those two fools in 'A Medley of Tales of Revenge.' Nakajima Wadaemon as Bodara No Chozaen, you know the belly-laughing scene with the boatman."

"I know." The young Noh dancer seemed unexcited, and still moody.

The publisher was going to say something about the ingratitude of artists and their inability to give the public what it wanted, but three people had just entered his shop and Tsuta-ju was bowing before he realized that one of them was a giant white man in native costume, with a head of yellow hair and blue eyes. The artist Hokusai stood by the giant, grinning at the shock to the publisher's nerves. O-Kita Mitsu, the famous geisha, was the third, and Tsuta-ju stood in amazement at this good fortune to his shop. O-Kita's two maids, standing in the doorway and giggling in the background, only made him understand more deeply the honor the street was sharing. Many people crowded around staring at the giant.

"Ah, Hokusai," said the publisher, recovering. "You always amaze me. Always do something to make the neighborhood jump like a cat with pepper under its tail."

Hokusai wrinkled his eyes as he made a mocking smirk at the publisher. "Tsuta-ju, you peddler of spoiled paper, this is Heacock Sir, a great collector in the world of art, an honored guest of the Shogun. He comes from other shores and has seen much, even where they paint on cloth with pastes of oil."

"Of course, of course." The publisher was bobbing like a float on a fish line. "I know the Dutch from their prints. Their envoy who sometimes comes to our city to visit the Shogun.

The Dutch too buy prints. But I forget my duties." He clapped his hands and hissed at his two shop clerks. "To the Moon teahouse. Bring back two pots of tea, with cakes and tidbits."

Hokusai added, "And several bottles of good *sake*. Make it a Tokkuri, a choice gallon of it."

Daniel Heacock was looking around the shop, "It is hard to get good prints at Nagasaki."

"Barbarians there," said the publisher, looking up at the giant. "They blow their noses on their robes and eat crows. May I beg the reward of introducing you to my best print maker, Toshusai Sharaku."

Sharaku was staring at the beautiful geisha. He had to be jabbed in the ribs by the publisher's elbow before he bowed to the strange tall man.

"I own one of your prints," said Daniel. "I had never heard of you before I saw it. But Hokusai here says you have done over fifty in the last few months."

"I try," said the young dancer. "I am not really a professional print maker."

O-Kita was curious to see how much more blushing the skin of this sensitive young man could take. She said, "You look so young to be a master print maker." She raised her semicircle of eyebrows, called three-day moons, into a questioning position.

The flush on the skin of the young man darkened two shades. "Oh, to be sure. I have just begun this year, and I shall not do many more. They don't sell."

The publisher said, "Oh, they sell, but not as fast as some."

O-Kita put a hand on the young man's arm and smiled. He shyly hung his head and swallowed hard. What a booby, she thought, and what a fine slim body and sensitive face, and already on the road to ruin with Hokusai and Utamaro and all the other artists.

"You draw the geisha?"

Sharaku dared not look up. He felt pleasantly incoherent. "No. I work mostly from the theater and the *sumo* wrestlers."

O-Kita again gave him a professional smile. She clicked her fan open, and turned to join Daniel who was looking over a pile of prints. He held up a print and took her arm while he whispered. "Stop making the boy blush. Women certainly can be cruel."

"He is a shy one, isn't he?"

"And a great artist. So show some respect."

O-Kita banged her fan shut. "You are perhaps a little jealous?"

Daniel laughed and drew her closer to him. Women were all the same, he decided.

The publisher lifted his arms as servants came in with trays of food and drink from the nearby teahouse. "Let us all go into the back room. We are cutting one of Sharaku's best prints. It shows the director of the Miyako-za theater delivering a prologue. Come along, Sharaku; don't hang back, boy."

Daniel smiled at the young Noh dancer; he knew the full effect a beauty like O-Kita could have on a shy susceptible male.

Daniel had recovered from some of the gloom of the night before. His encounter with O-Kita, and his meeting with Hokusai, summoned by the geisha in the morning, and the sunlight of a fine day, all cheered him up. And now he was in the print shop of a publisher of these woodblock prints he had begun collecting four years ago to alleviate boredom while doctoring among the Dutch traders.

He had pushed aside his worries about the impending operation on the Shogun, about Foxy's fear of some suspected intrigue at the palace, even about the continuing warning signs of a seizure. He fought the attraction of the opium pipe which usually became stronger as an attack of his illness drew nearer. Just now Daniel was in love with this geisha. He had been harassed just before dawn by some remarkably vivid dreams of her, tangible remnants of which still amused his thoughts . . .

He looked with detailed pleasure across at O-Kita as they finished the tea, the *Naku miso* pickles and the *seimbe* cakes in the back room of the publisher's shop. From the street came the twanging discords of people in front of the theaters, vendors' cries, and the incoherent dirge of actors reciting behind thin walls. The fat publisher, trying to behave pleasantly blasé, waved a kimono-sleeved arm to the back of the room blocked off by bales of paper.

"Now if you will favor this too poor place, we will watch the cutting of Sharaku's print of the theater manager."

Hokusai set down his *sake* bowl and followed them. "They ruin our work, these choppers." But he said it softly, for a flaccid, innocuous-looking old man wearing large badly scratched Chinese glasses of soft crystal, was in one corner of the room. He was seated before a low table on which lay a cherry-wood plank onto which he was smoothing a drawing on rice paper, rubbing thin the paper which he had attached to the block.

Daniel stood between the publisher and the young Noh dancer. The cutter did not look up, but continued to smooth the wafer-thin paper. The drawing had been done with a slim brush and night-black ink.

Finally, satisfied that the drawing was ready, the cutter took up one of his little knives and made a swooping bold slash into the picture, cutting through the drawing into the block of wood. Then he made another slash, and another, and suddenly chips began to fly. With an amazing speed and an almost careless skill that seemed at every stroke about to destroy both drawing and wood, the engraver proceeded to cut away the white part of the drawing, leaving only the black lines.

Daniel said to O-Kita, "He's like a surgeon—no longer aware of the knife edge; he's too busy with the secrets of his subject."

O-Kita nodded. "You understand so much." Now she moved closer to him. She was proud to be with this tall stranger.

The publisher pointed. "Now watch. He is going to do the hair."

The cutter picked up a special little knife, really a very tiny triangular gouge, and began with a magical control of his fingers and the sharp knife edge to cut the fine, almost invisible, grooves that were representing hair on the head of the theater manager.

O-Kita gripped Daniel's arm. "It's unbelievable!"

Sharaku watched with a worried tilt of his head as the cutting of the block proceeded. "Be careful of the lines of the robe around the neck."

The cutter grunted sourly to himself and went on, at an even quicker pace.

The publisher indicated another boxed-in corner of the room. "Now here we have a print actually being printed. A full-length figure of the actor Ichikawa Komazo II, also by the young Sharaku."

The visitors moved past obstacles, and O-Kita again stood at Daniel's side, holding his hand. They looked down at another low table, six inches high in front, and sloping almost to the floor in back. The block of cherry wood on this table was being smeared with a heavy thick black paste with a wide brush.

"The paper is made of the finest mulberry tree pulp," said the publisher. "It has been sized with rice paste and alum. It has just the right amount of moisture in it. Oh, it costs like ten demons driving one to ruin."

The printer had placed a sheet of the paper over the inked block.

"Notice, please," said the publisher, "how he placed it with the little raised mark on the edge of the block toward his stomach. That is called the *kento* mark. Each block will add a different color to the print and each will have a *kento* mark in the same place. In this way the register of all the blocks of the finished print will be perfect. So."

O-Kita asked, "Every color is done on a separate block? The same design must be cut in each block?"

"Yes," said Hokusai. "They are just printing some proofs now in black, from the key block. Sharaku here will color the proofs so they can cut the color blocks."

The young artist, animated and nervous now, said, "Sometimes I wonder why they want the proofs colored. The printers have their own ideas about color."

The printer, a very thin man with a few snags of teeth left in a small tight mouth, looked up in disdain. "If the artist only realized how much a printer can add to a print."

The publisher frowned. "Good printers are hard to get. Don't annoy him."

The printer was rubbing the back of the paper with his

broad thumbs against the print. Then, taking up a small pad sheathed in some smooth material, he began to rub the paper at great speed.

Daniel asked, "What's that pad?"

The publisher said, "That's called a *baren*. It's covered with bamboo sprout skin, and is made of twisted bamboo twine. It gives a good grain to the print."

Daniel watched the great pressure applied to the print; it looked almost careless. The printer turned to smile at them, showing where all his teeth had once been. He flipped up the sheet of paper from the inked block and handed O-Kita a beautiful black print of a strutting actor.

"Oh, thank you," she said. "It's lovely! It's the actor to life, the vain goose, the strutting fool. Sharaku, you have a keen eye."

Daniel added, "And wit."

The young artist blushed.

O-Kita handed the print proudly to Daniel, although she was herself witnessing the printing process for the first time. "I want you to see how well we do this."

Daniel, the print on its soft silky paper in his hands, felt that electric excitement all collectors feel when they face a rare item. This still damp print was a masterpiece in a field of art not yet catalogued or collected; for that matter, not even known yet back in America. This pattern of a powerful wavering line, this perfect drawing, made into a perfect print of the prancing actor, Daniel knew to be unique.

"How many copies do you print?"

"After Sharaku gives us the colors," the publisher said, "we cut one block for each color and that may take another week or so. Then we will print two hundred first-class prints, at the most. After that the moisture in the colors swells and distorts the wood and the print is not clear. It takes often twenty-five days to print an edition of two hundred first-class prints. Of course, some poor publisher may then buy a used-up block, and go on printing up to a thousand copies of a good-selling picture. But these are bad prints, and the lines of the nose and hair will not be clear. So sometimes they chop out the damaged parts and slip in a new section of block and recut it. Also the cheaper printers use whatever color pots they have at hand, and not what the artist had designed. Believe me, honored sir, buy only in my shop and you will get first grade prints from the original blocks."

Daniel laughed and pressed O-Kita's hand at the sales talk. "At least let me buy this one, besides the ones I picked out in the shop."

"No, no," said the publisher coyly. "This one is a gift. Sharaku, sign it personally for the noble patron of our art."

The young artist looked pleased and picked up a thin brush. He fixed its point the way he liked it in some black ink on an ink stone, and putting the print down on a bale of paper, he quickly drew a set of beautiful letters in the left hand top corner of the print. He bowed and handed it to Daniel with a glow of pleasure.

Daniel took the print. "Thank you for this honor. What does it say? I read badly as yet."

The booming voice of Hokusai boomed out behind them. He was under the influence of *sake*, but not drunk, and feeling fine from all he had eaten. "Sharaku has written: 'I Toshusai Sharaku present this to the wonderful being from far off who collects my humble work.' Very good, Sharaku. You'll be a poet full of free rice yet."

"I thank you," said Daniel.

The young artist took up another print that had just cor
fresh and damp off the block. He lowered his head and fac
O-Kita standing by Daniel's side, dainty on her high clogs, h
large eyes looking at him, a polite smile on her face. Sharal
said, "If I might be so permitted, I would like to give yo
O-Kita, one of these unworthy things, for your great beau
which has fed me more than food this day."

O-Kita said, "How charming. I would be so pleased."

This effort seemed to leave Sharaku wordless. O-Kita nodd
to encourage him and he wrote on her print.

Hokusai snorted and banged a box full of paper scrap
"These damn print cutters. I always say to them don't add an
lower eyelids when I don't draw them in. And they alway
spoil my noses. They cut them to look just like the noses b
Toyokuni. And I hate his noses, which are against all the rul
of drawing. And now it's the fashion to draw eyes with a thi
line and a dot under it. These eyes are just as wrong as tl
noses. And as for printers—they print with mud. Is there an
sake left?"

O-Kita, leaning against Daniel, held up the print with Sh:
raku's new writing added, and read:

> "When I see the first new moon
> Faintly in the dusk
> I think of the moth eyebrows
> Of a girl I saw only once."

The young artist hung his head. "It wasn't meant—forgiv
me—to be read out loud."

O-Kita went to Sharaku's side, bowed and pressed his han
"I am honored. The poem is as fine as the print."

The publisher bowed in turn and Daniel took out from under his robe a heavy French watch in a gold case. They all watched him in amazement as he looked at the hands under the glass. He smiled and handed it to O-Kita. "It is a time machine."

O-Kita caressed the watch and looked directly at Daniel. He was aware suddenly that she was really in love with him. "It has been a delightful day," she said.

Hokusai said, "But I think we have time to show Heacock Sir our city. Come along, Sharaku. Your drawings were successful so you can join us."

The two artists left the shop, followed by O-Kita and Daniel, hand in hand.

11

Outside the shop Hokusai said, "Without a time machine I can tell it's early in the day. The Kabuki theaters are open now. We'll show Heacock Sir a real living art, not the pale stuff of the Noh theater."

Sharaku felt he had to defend Noh theater. "There is room for both."

"Of course there is," said O-Kita as they walked across the street toward the theater.

Hokusai inspected the theater posters set up on the busy street, pushing back hurrying people with his elbows. He held out his arms to make room for O-Kita in front of a huge red poster of flowing letters outside the Morita theater. "We're in luck. You can have *jidaimono*—historical dramas—or *sewa-nono*—dramas of contemporary life. Well, what do you want? Something meaty like 'Taikoki,' 'Sendaihagi,' or up the street the Miyako has a lovely thing—the leading part is being played by Kikunojo the second, the most beautiful actor of woman parts in all Kabuki."

Daniel puzzled over the poster while passers-by stared at him. "What are they playing here?"

O-Kita carefully spelled out the sign. " 'A dance interlude:

150

The Girl Without Make-up Who Is More Beautiful than Snow Wearing Lip Paint,' is in the play they're giving, called 'The Story of a Pair of Snow-covered Chrysanthemums That Blossomed in Izu.' "

Daniel asked ironically, "Is that the *whole* title?"

O-Kita said earnestly, "Yes. Shall we go in?"

Daniel nodded, and they followed Hokusai, who seemed to be known to everyone there, into the theater. The building itself was of plain wood. It was packed with people watching the stage, gossiping, eating and drinking from trays brought by waitresses. There was a pit, and there were galleries around three sides of the interior. Popular courtesans and geishas were looking down on the stage or chattering among themselves.

On the platform stage an actor dressed as a samurai knelt before a snowy background, carrying a lantern, and facing him was a beautiful woman in white carrying a baby. The top of her head was covered with a pale purple patch, and Daniel suddenly realized this must be Segawa Kikunojo II, the great actor of woman's parts. He nudged O-Kita. "Why is he wearing that purple patch on his head?"

"It is so ordered by the Shogun. All actors playing women's parts must shave their heads like that, and to cover it they wear the patch."

O-Kita, a famous beauty, was now recognized by the people in the theater and she bowed as she returned greetings.

"Why the Shogun's order?" asked Daniel.

"The court ladies fell so madly in love with beautiful actors playing women the head shaving was ordered to make them look ugly."

"Does it work?"

"No," said Sharaku. "The scandals are worse than ever."

Hokusai motioned a waitress nearer and ordered *sake*, a tea tray and some spiced tidbits. "I tell you this: actors lead the fat easy life. Applause, money, love or whatever else they like. Crowds following them, adoring women ready to leap from their *zubon-shita*, and we poor fools, Sharaku, Buncho and me making prints about them, we beg a few coins so we can eat."

Sharaku was watching keenly the action on the stage. A new play had begun with samurai, all hair, teeth, arms and varnished armor, hacking at each other. Actors in elaborate make-up were going through gestures and prances of great violence or sweeping gracefully into death or dramatic departure. The young artist by his side was powerfully excited by what he saw on stage. He seemed to be drawing with one finger in the air, as if copying some gesture, some tossing of head and arms, some swoop of robe or banging of bodies that seemed to be as much part of the play as the words. He couldn't sit still, and O-Kita had to tug on his robe to get him back in place by her side.

The young artist said to her, "I've just done a marvelous print of Segawa Tomisaburo the second. He's up there now. It's not a nice portrait. I tried to catch his manner of acting. I marked it 'Generally called Hateful Tomi!' He's really just an amateur."

Hokusai, wiping rice cake crumbs from his cheeks, smiled. "Listen, my boy, we were all amateurs once. And we still are. Wait till you've done a thousand, two thousand prints like the rest of us. Not thirty or fifty. You're still an amateur. We all are if we keep trying for something new."

Daniel was dizzy with the effect of the sword play, the love mockery, the swirling robes of all colors. He enjoyed the drive and power of the Kabuki, but its newness was overpowering.

"How long does this go on?" he asked.

"Six hours. There are three full plays," Hokusai said. He leaned closer to Daniel. "Tell me, do you know you are being followed?"

Daniel looked up. "Followed?"

"I can smell policemen anywhere. There are two fat fools along the wall, and they haven't taken their eyes off us."

Daniel looked, but was unable in the shifting crowd to be sure the rough-looking fellows pointed out to him were police, or that they were watching him. "Are you sure they're watching us?"

O-Kita gripped Daniel's arm in alarm. "Hokusai knows about these things. You have not offended the Shogun in some way?"

Daniel shook his head and reassured her, while a man dressed as a lion banged a drum on the stage. "They must be here to protect me. I am in Edo on a special mission. It would be too bad for Lord Ito if anything happened to me before my mission was accomplished. That's all it is."

O-Kita shivered and he took her arm. Silently she wondered if there were any connection between these watchers and her assignment from Prince Taira. Aloud she said, "Do you mind if we go back to the castle? I have never liked the police. Once they picked up a geisha I knew named O-Hisa and questioned her for two days about things she knew nothing of. They curried her face and nose with iron combs and when O-Hisa came back to us her beauty was destroyed and she drowned herself in despair."

Suddenly for Daniel the gaiety of the stage colors took on a sinister tone and the over-dramatic sword play on stage became too real. "Let's go," he said. "Back to the castle."

JOURNAL OF DOCTOR DANIEL HEACOCK

"A climax has come into my life. I accept life for the first time instead of fighting it. At night, not sleeping, I think it out—the relationship of a man to his world, a man's late adjustment to his life. Do I want this kind of love? I'm sure it's different from any that has gone before. Then why am I fighting off the overwhelming attraction O-Kita has for me? My illness is a poor excuse.

"Maybe it has something to do with moral values. But to approach life primarily from a moral angle is to retreat from the bigger truths.

"I thought I was partly dead, and that I would have to live with the epileptic seizures of the flesh and drag them along the way some carry their eccentricity. Odd how I once used to think of women—with my skin, a kind of pricking shiver, a sort of vibrating, erotic voice.

"Desire is not invented. Desire materializes, like vapor on a lover's window in a warm room. One couldn't wish it there. The weather in the place, if right, is enough. And I am in love, and all this writing about myself is nothing but whistling up courage to live again.

"I am no innocent traveler, and soon I shall be thirty. I know the agony of love—great loves, some say, are never worth the pain they cause. But does that make it any easier? I always assumed that when it came, this passion for one woman, one body, that I would be able to fight it off by logic, reason, and a healthy, cynical understanding that it was all one of nature's little traps. But somehow now I can't break free. I'm just a man and she is just a woman. There are in Edo thousands of other women I can get. And I don't want them, I want O-Kita. What happens to a man to betray himself like this?

"Is it only the trap of one body wanting another body? No, something else inside, the buried part, the secret part wants her too. What had I once wanted of this life? A woman who was alive and free. Free to love, free to be somebody a man could turn to. Now how did O-Kita tie up with all this? I remembered all those men in the social circles of Canton and Peking who had discarded their old wives and taken frisky young native fillies. And what good had it done them? The fillies, they soon found out, were just younger versions of their old wives. A man, it seemed, often made the same mistake twice, three times, four times. Maybe that is it. O-Kita is nothing more than a projection.

"I know, of course, I have not yet dug deep enough, I have not uncovered all the secrets inside myself. But whatever it is, O-Kita must be an answer of some kind. This is a brutal, blunt kind of male thinking; I don't feel this way about her at all. I adore her like any young fool with his first girl.

"I am concerned about those two men Hokusai saw. Were they following me? I spoke to reassure myself as well as O-Kita, but her story of torture is incredibly barbaric. Can she be involved in any of this? No, no—that's impossible. She's too lovely, too gentle to have anything to do with intrigue. But these boys can be rough, I suppose, I'd better watch——"

Daniel closed his journal abruptly, leaving off in the middle of the sentence, as Lord Ito came into the room. Foxy, who had been opening a bottle of *aomori*, a strong drink, bowed.

155

Daniel looked up in concern. "Anything wrong with the Shogun?"

"No," said Lord Ito. "His Highness sleeps. You will see him again at twilight."

Daniel decided this was a good time to discuss what had been bothering him since his examination of the Shogun the night before.

"Lord Ito, do you expect me to put up with the members of the court while I'm acting as the Shogun's doctor?"

Lord Ito smiled a very tired smile. "You feel we were too abrupt with you when you examined the Shogun?"

"I expect some respect for my profession, no matter what you think of me. After all, you are putting the Shogun's life in my hands, under my lancet as it were."

Lord Ito motioned Foxy to fill some cups. "It is a bad time for us here. Forgive us if we are not good mannered. *Go men kudasai*—please excuse me. That is the formal way of asking your forgiveness."

They drank and Daniel rotated the cup in his strong fingers. "I have been seeing something of your Edo. I like it."

"It was the company," said Lord Ito. "She is a famous beauty. With her chignon she is like a figure on a Satsuma vase."

Daniel sipped and said nothing. Lord Ito refolded the front of his Sensi silk robe. "I am a bad host. There was a time, not so long ago either, when my mind was all on the geishas. I never had enough of the *shirokubi*—the white-necked ones. Now there are other things on my mind. I would like you to join me. I am sponsoring some *sumo* matches. Come and be my guest of honor."

"*Sumo* wrestling at a time like this?"

Lord Ito handed Foxy his empty cup. "It is a good place to meet one's friends. One's true friends. I want you to know them. We can't meet here in the castle."

Daniel nodded. He wondered if Lord Ito referred to the men who had been following him. But he said only, "I hear your *sumo* men are very big."

"As big as you are, and much wider."

"Good. I was beginning to think my size made me a freak here."

Foxy put away the cups and went to get Daniel's robe for going out.

The *sumo* house was large and mats for the guests were placed around a padded circle. Daniel and Lord Ito sat down behind a barrier made of bales of rice. Seated near them were nobles who nodded and hissed greetings as they were introduced to Daniel. He knew now that he had been brought here to be inspected. To be met and observed. He tried to look around him without attracting undue attention. Perhaps he might again catch sight of the two men. But he saw only men of Lord Ito's own class. They were mostly young, but Daniel noticed some gray topknots among them.

Lord Ito explained, "The ring, as you see, is made of sixteen rice bales. One each for the points of the compass and each of the twelve months. A bale is removed from each side for an entrance." And then, in a lower voice, he added, "You are among true friends here."

"Do you ever do anything that hasn't a tradition?" Daniel asked, responding only to the first part of Lord Ito's speech. He decided to ignore the latter for the moment.

157

Lord Ito didn't answer as two huge men entered the ring and bowed in the direction of Lord Ito, the sponsor. An official with a wand-like fan of office followed them. The wrestlers were amazingly fat, with great flanks and arms, bulging buttocks, and cheeks like hanging melons. They wore ritual aprons of costly materials, and they rinsed their mouths from buckets of water.

Lord Ito said, "The biggest one is the champion. We call him the *Yokozuna*, leader of the *Maku-no-uchi*—ones-within-the-curtain."

Memory suddenly floated back an image to Daniel. "Didn't Shuncho make a print called 'The Strongest and the Fair' of this wrestler, Tanikaze, posing with O-Kita?"

"Yes, he did, but we don't call it by that title."

"It's my own title, I suppose. A fine print."

Lord Ito said, "The print makers did a whole series of great beauties and famous wrestlers. But it's vulgar stuff. Here is the *Dohyoiri*, the ring entry ceremony."

The ceremony of the entry of the wrestlers was impressive and rather like elephants dancing, Daniel thought. The wrestlers were stamping their feet, throwing some grains of what Daniel supposed was salt, clapping their hands and bowing to the sponsor, the official and the guests. The ceremony over, the two large men faced each other, their aprons off, wearing loin cloths, their large hands out, knees bent, their little eyes almost lost in fat. Then with a grunt they met, struggled for grips, locked limbs, grunted, heaved and panted.

"Doesn't look very scientific," Daniel said, observing the guests were watching him as much as the match.

"There are forty-eight different falls and throws. They must stay within those accepted forms. Ah! *Watch!*"

The great Tanikaze had suddenly side-stepped, twisting and gripping the man who faced him. They pushed, turned and then Tanikaze lifted, turned, and with a back throw tossed his opponent down. There was a sound of delight and the big wrestler bowed to Lord Ito.

The room was getting warm. The guests fanned themselves, the official made some remarks, and Tanikaze again faced the man in the ring. He won one more fall. He bowed and the ring held two more of the giants.

Daniel asked, "Are they Japanese? They don't look it."

"Oh, yes, they are, and they have the real *Yamato damashu*—Japanese spirit. They eat well and do nothing but wrestle."

The room grew warmer, but the sweat and smell of the huge men locked in fleshy combat was not unpleasant. Between matches Daniel inspected the guests again and again. He wondered how deeply he had become involved in some castle plot. He wanted no part of it. His life had taken an unexpected turn and he wanted to concentrate on his newly found emotional reactions. He glowed with pleasure, remembering that he was going to dine with O-Kita later in her rooms. Conspiracy was all nonsense anyway. One set of rascals is thrown out, and another set of rascals is put in.

The wrestlers had put on their ceremonial aprons again and were bowing to Lord Ito, who handed the three winners the traditional prizes: a bow, a bow string and a fan.

Daniel stretched and rose to get ready to leave. Then he saw the men Hokusai had pointed out to him in the theater. The men who were following him. So he was being followed, even here. He turned to protest to Lord Ito, but the young lord was busy with his prize giving. Daniel decided anger would get him nowhere; but he wanted this matter straightened out.

When Lord Ito was finished giving prizes, Daniel remarked almost casually, "I don't particularly like being put on public display this way."

"It is for your own safety," Lord Ito answered. "They will trust you now. They have seen you with me. Shall we go?"

Daniel nodded and followed him out, feeling even more uneasy than before.

12

It was already dusk—the sky was of muted gold and soot, with bats flitting like dried-out leather over the limbs of the cherry trees—when Daniel returned from the *sumo* matches. He was to examine the Shogun again.

This time the Shogun was lying in his great bed-chamber on sleeping pads behind magenta and green screens painted with flying cranes. The two old herb doctors, Pi and Mo, were there half asleep over a low tea table. Daniel examined the Shogun, felt his dry brow and took his pulse. The Shogun looked weaker, and he said nothing; but his eyes followed every one of Daniel's movements as if trying to understand what this odd stranger was doing to him.

Daniel stood up and bowed. He and Lord Ito left the bed-chamber and went to Daniel's rooms. Lord Ito was no longer the splendid companion of their trip to Edo. He seemed even leaner, and Daniel had noticed him at the *sumo* matches gnawing on his lower lip in some truculent expression of worry.

Lord Ito turned to face Daniel. "When do you operate?"

"The fever is still there. I'm going to give him some laudanum—a tincture of opium—to keep his pain down. In a

161

week the infection should subside and I will, if I think there
is any chance of success, remove the bladder stones."

"He can't live long if you don't operate." Lord Ito gave
Daniel a disturbing stare.

"That's true. And those brews Pi and Mo are drenching
him with are no help. Have it stopped. Now where do you
want the operation performed? I don't think it can remain
much of a secret here."

"That's true. I was talking to Prince Taira about that. I
don't trust the prince."

Daniel said, "I have no interest in palace intrigue, or who
runs the country."

Lord Ito touched Daniel's shoulder in a friendly gesture.
"Good. Don't get involved. I suggest we move the Shogun,
when you are ready, to my house. What will we need?"

Daniel got out a sheet of paper from his saddlebag and began to draw with a brush dipped in ink. He had torturously
learned in the last few years to write with a brush point; it was
still difficult but he had achieved a certain skill. His drawing
was not bad, and he now drew the plans for a large heavy table
of strong timbers pegged together for strength and braced
with cross bars.

"Lord Ito, I need a table about three feet off the ground
and built like this. With ring bolts in four corners. Can you
have it made?"

"Yes, what are the ring bolts for?"

"The operation is painful. I'll try to drug the Shogun with
sake and laudanum, but he may still scream and struggle. He
can't move—he mustn't—while I operate or I'll cripple him."

"You're going to tie the Shogun down?"

"It's the proper procedure, written down by the great surgeon, Ambroise Paré. If we treat the Shogun as a suffering human being, I'll need four strong men. They should be men who have never seen the Shogun, if that is possible, to keep this secret."

Lord Ito nodded. "I'll send for four farmhands from my fields in the west." Lord Ito wiped his face. "I'm a brave man in battle, Heacock Sir, but these butcheries on a table, you will pardon me, make my head whirl. However, we shall be ready when you are."

Daniel folded his arms and looked at the matting on the floor. "I may decide not to operate, Lord Ito, if I think the Shogun can not bear the shock of the operation."

Lord Ito said softly, "You will be in no danger at any turn of events if that is what you fear."

"You misunderstand me," Daniel said, and at the same time realized that Lord Ito understood his concern very well.

"Perhaps. But if you decide not to heal the Shogun, I will have you escorted back to the Dutch island. There will be no final payment, of course, just the fee you got when we started for Edo."

Daniel set his jaw. "You think it was the gold that got me here? That I'm as greedy as the fat Dutchmen?"

Lord Ito bowed with a stiff constraint of emotions and did not raise his head. "I have been wrong to say that. I know how much you like our country, how you collect its art. It was foolish and my mouth was sour with anger when I spoke."

Daniel took Lord Ito by his shoulders and smiled at the stern, expressionless face. "I'm a doctor and I'm your friend,

Lord Ito. As a doctor I'd say you were wound up too tightly; you'll go to pieces if you don't relax."

Lord Ito pressed Daniel's hand and left quickly.

Daniel stood still, rotating the paint brush in his fingers. Foxy came in, the angularity of his sly features dramatized in the lamplight. He moved with innate caution to Daniel's side, as if not wanting to break the mood.

"You are not eating here tonight, Heacock Sir?"

"No. I'm eating with O-Kita Mitsu." In English he added, "And wipe that smirk off your damn face."

Foxy made a scarcely perceptible grimace. "If you want exotic adventure I can get Hana-ogi, the most famous courtesan in Japan, to come here. She has been drawn by all the great artists—Koryusai, Choki, Utamaro. She is an expert from the *makurazoshi*—the pillow book of amorous ingenuity."

"No, no, Foxy, don't serve it up like a lobster hot and smoking on a plate. Aren't you ever lonely?"

"Oh, yes. I have very simple tastes. The street girls of the Honjo district, wisteria scent on white necks. No sad partings."

Daniel said, "I'll wear my *hakata*, the pale plum-colored one."

Foxy brought the robe and said in English, "If a guard stops you I will show you a gesture. Like this. See? It means you are on your way to a woman, and the guard will not bother you."

Daniel repeated the gesture with his fingers. "Really?"

"Of course if you are on your way to visit one of the Shogun's women I would not advise admitting that."

"You know damn well I'm having dinner with O-Kita Mitsu."

Foxy said nothing, just smoothed out the pale plum-colored robe on Daniel's wide shoulders.

The dinner in O-Kita's rooms at the castle was well planned. It began with *sashimi to kyuri*—cucumber and raw fish—and ended with *kinkan*—golden limes. The two little servants served the food, staring and making faces at each other in wonder at this giant whom their mistress was entertaining. Daniel sat in his splendid robe. O-Kita was in her best blue and brown kimono, the pins well set in her coiffure, and her graceful slim neck very white with powder.

Daniel lifted the cup of warm *sake* level with his eyebrows, held it to his mouth and said to O-Kita, sitting across the low table from him:

> "I may live on, exist
> Till I ache for this moment
> When I am so unhappy
> And remember it fondly."

O-Kita smiled and clapped her hands as Daniel swallowed the rice wine. She smiled earnestly, "I did not think you were sad."

"Oh, yes. I'm in love and I don't know what to do about it."

"What do they do in your country? It's the same feeling, I'm sure." O-Kita lifted her cup of *sake* and recited:

> "Even if I try to hide
> My love shows on my face
> So plain, he asks me
> What are you thinking of?"

Daniel looked intensely at O-Kita. It was late; the castle rested in silence all around them and the little maids had retired to their own quarters. Daniel rose from sitting cross-legged at the low table. His legs were prickly with stiffness. He went over to O-Kita and knelt by her side on the lime-yellow matting. Her eyes seemed glazed, her little mouth was budded into a nervously proud smile. He put his arms around her and was surprised to find her trembling. Under her robe his fingers told him she was limber and yielding, and as Daniel held her to him he felt the blood deep inside him stir and warm. For all the unreality of the situation he felt a tightening pain of pure pleasure.

He kissed her. O-Kita moaned and he kissed her again and he felt her kissing back fully and openly. The decorum, the control, the ironic politeness of a geisha dissolved under his fingers as he moved his hands up her kimono sleeves and touched her breasts.

She was saying something very rapidly in Japanese, but he could not make any sense of it. She seemed to protest the grip of his fingers on her. She broke free, leaned back and pulled the pins from her piled-up hair. It fell black and shiny like a torrent in flood, gleaming and strong.

Daniel suddenly felt the solid reality of the night. The room, the girl came alive to him, like a floor rising to meet his body. Gone was the dream quality, and now all his doubts were being fought by his desire. She rose to her feet like a sleepwalker and stepped out of her kimono and her intimate garments.

She faced him proud and naked, the perfection, the warmth, the nearness of her body choking Daniel as he moved closer to her. From somewhere in the castle came the sound of an opening or closing gate, the hammering of iron on iron, and Daniel mistook the sound for his heartbeat as he took O-Kita in his arms and all the universe seemed too small to hold their passion.

Later, much later, the sound of a flute reached them from far below the terrace. The sliding *shoji* screen of O-Kita's room was pushed back, and from their low sleeping pads the two of them could see the crooked knuckle of a pine tree bough, and beyond it the top of a red lacquered column. A row of dwarf trees in yellow glazed pots stood like sentinels outside on the terrace and Daniel tried to count them and gave it up.

O-Kita lay on her back with an arm thrown over her face, her long hair flowing and coiling over the pillow as if with a life of its own. They were both spent now, both aware of their love so lately dominant in them, and now released. There was a mellowing of experiences relived; their passion had melted down into a close companionship and tenderness. Their love had crystallized, with a lack of restraint and remorse, into an awareness of how much they meant to each other. Each wondered if the other knew; each hoped.

Daniel turned on his elbow and kissed O-Kita with a light fumbling pressure of his lips to hers. The active aggression of love that had filled the room was expended; now they were alone, and Daniel feared some sudden loss.

"I love you, O-Kita."

She smiled, eyes closed, as she put her arms around his shoulders. "Your skin is white, not as milk but as the inner bark of a willow tree. Your body smells like honey made of chrysanthemums."

"I don't know why, but at this moment everything seems *yoroshiu*—all right."

"You are so much unlike any man I know and I am amazed at myself. It is very odd but I am thankful."

"Happy?"

"Yes, but see me as I am. I am a woman. Not a creature in a painting on a screen, some beauty that lived four hundred years ago. I have a temper. I am greedy. I don't come to you innocent and shy, as a girl should."

He kissed her cheek, and ran his fingers over her damp skin. "You talk too much."

"It's a cold dawn."

Daniel stood up, tall, his naked muscles flexing and knotting his back, thighs, and calves as he went to the open screen wall and looked out. "It's all gray and the mist is creeping up from the sea. The tree tops ride like birds at sea."

"Come back to me. My skin protests the chill with bumps."

"Soon."

Daniel went to his robe folded on a chest and took out a cheroot and lit it. He stood sucking in cold air and cigar smoke, standing pale and mother-naked in the hint of dawn, filling the open space between room and terrace, pungent smoke rising to be torn to shreds by the first chill morning breeze.

"O-Kita," he said, not looking back at her or into the room, "I've come to the time of life when I want to decide on one woman, and only one woman. I can't change your way of life if you don't want me to. But if you did, I could become a doctor here, and we could have a house overlooking our own garden and a little stream and live out our lives with each other. In a calmness and a happiness neither of us has yet known, I think. I'm not perfect, or even near it. A man and woman begin by first creating themselves. There are certain things about me you should——"

"Who is talking too much now?"

He tossed the smoldering length of tobacco away, past the terrace. He closed the sliding shoji wall and came back to lie by her side on the sleeping pads. His skin was cold to her touch, rough with gooseflesh, and he was trembling. It was a long time before she calmed and warmed him to go back to sleep in her arms.

So love came to O-Kita Mitsu, a geisha, raised in hardship and much abused, aware of auguries and gods, and to Doctor Daniel Heacock, surgeon and traveler, marked by seizures and opium, exiled by himself, hunting refuge and peace.

No one at the castle was much interested in the affair of O-Kita and Heacock Sir. Daniel, when he had time to think of it, was surprised to find that he had had no symptoms of the impending seizure since reaching Edo and falling in love with the beautiful geisha. He decided he had been so busy for these few days—with O-Kita, examining the Shogun, avoiding all the plotters, and seeing the city—that his illness was diverted by activity. Every day he saw and examined the Shogun. The fever was abating slowly, and Lord Ito was having the operating table built.

Daniel and O-Kita did not keep their love in a closed room. They moved around Edo, enjoying equally fine weather and rains when they came. O-Kita would put on her elaborate twelve-layer kimono of the Heian period, and Daniel donned a fancy long-sleeved robe worn by the sporting young bloods, and pulled a cap over his head to hide his yellow hair. But his height and pale skin and blue eyes attracted a great deal of attention.

The lovers went to view the cherry blossoms at Asukayama and touched the famous memorial stone for luck. They paraded by the sea at Shinagawa, embarking dangerously in the narrow gondola, their hands trailing in the water, past the wooden bellies of brown ships tugging at the swift salt tides. They stopped at the Takashimaya, the famous rice-cracker shop in the Ryogoku district, a place known for its beautiful women. O-Kita chewed on a cracker and said with a smile, "You will leave me someday for one of these beautiful women."

"You may be right," Daniel answered in mocking tones.

"Everyone is beautiful here—the waitresses, the courtesans, the geishas, even the little maids."

"Not as beautiful as you are," he answered, as is proper among lovers.

He bought her a bunch of *ominaeshi*—little yellow buds, called the-woman-flower; when he found out it was also called the-harlot-flower he laughed and bought her two potted adonis plants which were guaranteed, he said, "to be perfect symbols of happiness and long life."

"Oh, yes, everyone knows that, Danhil. That is true," said O-Kita. She looked at him as if every glimpse was a pleasure and she could not get enough of seeing this giant who was becoming a well-known figure in the streets of Edo. The street girls in the downtown Honjo district threw gay remarks at him; "Chotto poi," the seller of black hemp kimonos, was proud to make the longest robe on record for him; and when

Daniel passed the Akatsuta-ya—the famous riverside wharf house of assignation—the girls would lean on their wooden window sills and shout down to him: "*Shibaraku*—stop a minute!"

O-Kita, when they were alone in the night, liked to lie against him and run her hand through his long blond hair. Their sleeping pads were under a large pillar print of a slightly erotic content that Hokusai had given them, saying, "You don't need friends right now." And they had to agree.

"I love you, Danhil," she would say (it was the closest she could come to pronouncing his name).

He would stroke her arms and think how perfect their life could be if he were assured of an income, had no illness of seizures, and were not now in danger from the intrigue at the castle. But, he decided, it was partly the danger that made the nights with O-Kita so full of sweet tensions, of vibrating pleasure, a whole lifetime of close companionship distilled into a few days.

One day when Daniel came to her room and took off his cap, O-Kita screamed and shouted, "Oh, oh, you haven't done it, you haven't done it!"

Daniel felt like a little boy caught in a childish thing. "But it's the way all men look."

He had had his head shaved into the popular male hairdo, leaving only a fringe and a fine topknot which had been dyed black.

O-Kita rolled her head.

Daniel felt dejected. "But darling, I even have a topknot. I'm Japanese now. *Umai'zo*—bravo!"

She fell weeping into his arms. "But you're not. You're my special man from the fairy tale, who came to me on a leaf when I was a child."

"You're too old for fairy tales, O-Kita."

"I never minded you not being Japanese—I gloried in it. I didn't want you to try and become like all the others."

"Who can know a woman's mind? I thought you'd be pleased to see me like this." He ran his hand over his handsome bare skull. "It's comfortable, too."

She laughed suddenly and wiped her eyes on a paper napkin and smiled.

"I love you so much, Danhil."

"I know, darling," he said in English. "Damn it, don't I know it, sweetheart? Don't I know it?"

"What are you saying?"

They made love in joy, fulfilling their overpowering desires, their need for each other.

His blue eyes and his great height Daniel could not disguise, and he didn't try.

O-Kita carried a large apple-green grasshopper in a cage as they continued to explore Edo—the red maple trees at Karsan temple, buying a turtle on a string for O-Kita's growing zoo, having tea with some famous actor of female roles. Later on O-Kita, a great and cruel mimic, would act out for Daniel, with all the smirks and limp-wristed skill, the mannerisms of the actor. They would laugh and play and kiss and struggle in each other's arms and drink a great deal of the warm rice wine. In the morning Cat, the little maid, would come giggling

172

to them with a tray holding two cups of *mukar-zala*—the morning pick-me-up drink.

Daniel's head would sometimes ache, but O-Kita would politely mock him, sitting on the sleeping pad. "You are not a great drinking man, like Utamaro or Hokusai."

"I am, but on my own grounds. Gin, bourbon-and-water, good rye whiskey from Kentucky. But this slop poisons me."

"*Kenhuckee*," O-Kita repeated. "What a funny word!"

"It sounds odd to me, too, O-Kita. With you I've forgotten who I am, and where I come from. I'm nobody, I'm nothing. It's so sad. Have Cat bring us two more pick-me-ups."

"It's your headache makes you sad, not O-Kita? Not my love, is it? Not the fine times we have and the happiness, so much happiness?"

She looked so questioning, so worried, Daniel had to laugh, take her in his arms. He dressed in his formal *hakama* robe, a gift from Lord Ito. He pulled his topknot into place and asked, "What shall we do today?"

JOURNAL OF DOCTOR DANIEL HEACOCK

"A man descends within himself at a time like this, and alone makes terms with his life. I am very near a big seizure of my illness; yet I push it aside and let the symptoms pass as just a result of my love for O-Kita.

"In a way I am surprised to admit that I am happy, actually contented. Despite all the pressures, all the peculiarities of our situation, there is an almost everyday normality about our relationship. We share the privileges of love in rooms warm and intimate. I am seeking instinctively for reassurance . . .

"In love I find that every moment seems an eternity, and

in passion all of eternity is only a moment. O-Kita accepts physical love fully, with pleasure and no sense of sin.

"Many writers have tried to express the agonies and exaltations of physical love, and most have failed. It either descends to the mere pornography of verbal pictures, or becomes a symbolic evocation, drawn in words worn too smooth and stale by older poets. The physical passion cannot easily be analyzed, because this intense sensation is an overpowering of reason.

"O-Kita is a new art to me—not Greek or Gothic. Her hands are long, her body is milk pearl and smooth like a child's, the muscles round out the forms into lines of artful purpose. The legs are long and the feet and toes beautiful.

"O-Kita says the women out here can remain austere, that the events of the natural world do not baffle them. They remain charming and somewhat theatrical; I doubt if there is any other world that gives its citizens such a quality. Their emotions appear to be transfixed, released by love, and projected by busy minds into what are, at times, overflowing, spontaneous qualities that make them good company and interesting lovers. The borderline between the full, wonderful moment and certain awkwardness and naiveté is always narrow.

"I wish I could settle down here, with her. I wish I were sure the Shogun will make a good recovery. I gather indirectly from Lord Ito that there are many political forces at work, pulling in different directions. Will they ruin my hopes?"

13

It was two full weeks after Daniel had first examined him when the Shogun, his fever somewhat lower, was secretly moved to the house of Lord Ito.

It was a dark night with a hint of blue rain clouds and a moon that seemed reluctant to come out. Great fires burned in clay pots in the lanes around the house, and the swords of troops in the neighborhood fields were highlighted by the leaping orange flames. There were also samurai in Lord Ito's gardens, wearing their helmets of riveted bronze, horned and winged, corselets of black sheet iron high in back, and always the two swords protruding from their belts. It looked to Daniel, arriving with Foxy in a palanquin, like a scene from an ancient war drama.

A retainer let them into the house. Lord Ito himself met them with a bow, his lean handsome face serious. Daniel asked, "Isn't all this protection destroying the secrecy of what's going on here tonight?"

"The Shogun came at dusk with some of my retainers. The soldiers and samurai are my own; they are faithful to me. They have been told this is a conference on grave military matters. There is a rebellion in the north."

"How is the Shogun?"

"He says nothing. He waits. The pain never leaves him."

"I wish we didn't have all this army around us. I need quiet."

"They will be quiet. Heacock Sir, if the Shogun dies there will be civil war. We have announced that the Shogun has gone to view the rebel situation. I want no news of tonight to get out of here . . . whatever happens."

Daniel took the medical case from Foxy. "They, whoever they are, want him to die here?"

Lord Ito bowed and said softly, "You understand."

"Where is the table?"

"In the next room. The lamps are hung overhead. The four strong men who will aid you are also in there. The Shogun has drunk the medicine you ordered. He will be brought in when you are ready. In any event, I guarantee your safety with my honor. One thing more . . ."

Daniel had opened the medical case and was admiring the shiny unused instruments. "What is that?"

"There must be an official witness to the operation. For a report to be made to the Imperial Council at some later time if need be."

Daniel grinned, feeling taut and warm. "It's a sight not very pleasant to watch. Whom do you suggest?"

"I will watch you perform with your great skill."

"All right. Go and have the Shogun brought in. He should be drowsy from the laudanum. Under no conditions is anyone to come into the room while I'm operating. Warn the guards to keep everyone out, no matter what they hear. Oh, and have a stiff drink of *sake* yourself before I begin the operation. I fainted at my first one."

"I shall not faint." Lord Ito left them.

Foxy shivered as he looked at the instruments with the beaks, hooks, cutting edges, all set deep in their nest of velvet.

"These can heal? Criminals are sliced in torture by things like this."

"They have healed. I have been more successful than most. I believe there is something in the unused steel, a chemical only in a freshly-made set that sets up a reaction of some sort with the cut flesh that helps it to heal."

"What is it?"

"I have no idea. Once I heard a doctor in Edinburgh tell about some Dutchman who built a powerful magnifying glass and saw tiny beasts in a drop of water. He suggested they might feed on wounds and kill patients. But that's nonsense. These things, if they exist at all, come from the body, and so they can't harm it. No, it's a reaction of fresh steel on the body fluids."

"I am sure you are right."

Daniel tried to retain his professional calmness. He would need it here tonight. This was no matter of dosing a patient with a milk posset, or treating a tumor with bloodroot and caustic paste; this was major surgery, and he would perform it in a place where things like this were never done.

He stripped off his robe and stood in a gray *happi*, a short jacket-like garment usually worn by workmen; it gave him freedom of movement and left his arms bare. He flexed his big shoulders as he waited for the Shogun to be brought in. He was a fool, he decided, to have become a surgeon. If he were not a surgeon, his illness would not have interfered so totally with his career. He had never before realized so clearly what a handicap it could be to him—now, on the brink of a seizure, and scheduled to perform a major operation in a matter of minutes.

He was still troubled by the symptoms of his illness—had, in fact, been kept awake much of the night before. He prayed that he wouldn't be bothered during the next few crucial hours. Could he ever hope to have a normal life, as other men had?

How much better off were the large paunchy London doctors in their wigs, tapping the gold heads of their canes and treating with some vague powder scrofula of the vital organs, palsy, pleurisy, and the pleasant vapors of foolish and pretty women. Old Doctor Barrett, who used to lecture on anatomy, would say to them in the light of a bayberry wax candle held over some half-dissected cadaver, "So, gentlemen, the whole and total picture of our ignorance ends in wonder and pity. As doctors and surgeons, you must have some aggressive pride; if necessary, cultivate a deceiving appearance of knowledge. I fear that only a few of you should be trusted with the cutting knife. However, I am here only to instruct. . . ."

Daniel brushed aside the memories of his apprentice years and realized his hands were damp. He washed them in a basin and took a towel from Foxy.

"See what's keeping the Shogun," Daniel said.

"It's better not to show one is impatient; it destroys the confidence."

"Spoken like a London sawbones."

Foxy timidly pulled on Daniel's arm. His usually happy face had a pale green tinge in the lantern light. "You will not need me?"

"Oh, yes. I do need you to assist me, Doctor Foxy. You will hand me the needle and thread when I need them. And I may be involved with complications in the bladder, so you will hand me any instrument in the case I call for. You know right from left?"

"To be sure. Right, left. See?"

"I'll call for first, or second from right, or first, or second from left. Let's go in."

The room they entered was not large, and it seemed smaller because of a dozen lamps hung from cedar beams in the ceiling directly over the stout clumsy table that Daniel had ordered built.

Four solid, silent men were just placing the Shogun on the table. He looked dazed but calm, and his breathing was just a little labored.

Daniel, with no sign of greeting, began to tie the arms and legs of the Shogun to the ringbolts set in each corner of the table. He was cold, almost brutal, and swift. The Shogun was to him no longer a powerful ruler; he was only a sick person, a problem in flesh and tissues, whom he, a doctor, would try to help. He noticed Lord Ito standing at the head of the table, sweat gleaming on his shaved poll. Daniel smelled *sake* and nodded at Lord Ito, wishing he had taken some himself.

He flexed his fingers and opened the robe of the Shogun. The naked thin body, heels pressed to buttocks, was rigidly held to the table by bands and four strong men. Quickly Daniel ordered the four men to remain at the corners of the table and hold the body firmly. "He can't move; he mustn't move or all will be ruined. What you are about to see is not magic; but it is the rebuilding of a part of the body in need of repair."

The four peasants blinked and their huge muscled arms held firm to the patient.

Lord Ito said, "They will obey. They are farmers who kill cattle. They will not become ill at the sight of anything."

The Shogun swallowed and his eyelids fluttered.

"Good." Daniel felt the Shogun's brow, ignoring the dark eyes. He felt the pulse and picked up a lancet and a grooved guide. He wished he believed in the power of even a hasty prayer. What he was about to do had to be done quickly by feel, through cut tissue, through flowing blood, and with great and swift skill. He pushed the oiled guide tube into the urinary passage with a powerful thrust. The Shogun began to moan and stiffen. "Don't let him move!"

Daniel cut sharply into living flesh that flowed red at the severed edges. The Shogun began to scream.

Three minutes passed. Daniel's gown was smeared with gore. Several times he had dried his hands on towels now tossed onto the matting. The Shogun had stopped his hopeless struggling; only a whistling scream came from him at short intervals.

Daniel wiped the sweat from his face with his arm and said to Foxy, "The dilator!" In English he almost shouted, "Second from the left, goddamn it!"

It was hard getting the dilator in place in the bladder. The tiny, crooked forceps went deep again. He had so far been unable to grasp the stones with it. He began to try to grip the wet slippery objects again. This time Daniel had the larger stone. He twisted. The Shogun found strength to protest in an animal bleat. Daniel held up the ragged cruel-looking stone to the light and threw it with a clatter into a basin of water. He probed again quickly for the smaller stone, feeling he would fall unconscious if he could not soon escape from the heat, the slaughter-house smell, the glare of the lamps.

His head was filled with the giddy lightness that sometimes preceded a seizure. A hell of a time for an attack!

The Shogun's lips were losing color. He leaned over trying to listen to the heartbeat. It was faint.

Daniel said to Lord Ito, whose face was white and tightened, "I wish you had a doctor who could sew up a wound in case I fail to finish."

"You know we have not. Is anything the matter? He is breathing weakly."

Daniel lied. "No." His vision was dimming now. He shook sweat out of his eyes and probed. The smaller stone was caught by his forceps. He felt the jaws of the tool close on it, and drew it out swiftly, not caring now what pain it caused. He felt close to collapse from the heat and smells and tension, and he was in panic that he might faint or have an attack before he could complete the operation.

With the second stone out, Daniel recaptured himself, holding firmly to the edge of the table for a moment. Then he inserted a grooved scraper to get out any grains of sand or clotted matter that might keep the wound from healing properly. He motioned toward the silk threaded needle and Foxy handed it to him.

Daniel worked quickly now, automatically, almost without knowing what he was doing. He had been well taught in

England, by Doctor Smollet himself, an old naval surgeon with a brandy-red nose. He knew the best way to sew up wounds, and he was careful to properly tie the knots.

When he had finished the Shogun was unconscious and did not protest as Daniel put on the thick cotton bandages over the cut, gashed, and sewed tissues.

Daniel's fingers were numb and he was shaking. He managed to control his voice, speaking in a low, hoarse croak. "Foxy, untie the patient. Then have him carried to bed. Lord Ito, have him watched so he doesn't turn or tear at his bandages." He turned to Lord Ito. "It's important to have him watched."

Lord Ito stared expressionless at Daniel; then like a ballet dancer, he gracefully folded into a jointed doll and sank to the floor in a flutter of silk.

Daniel turned and plunged his head into a bucket of water, splashing it over his hair and dipping his arms in it to the elbows. He took up a towel and dried his hands and face, watching the Shogun, under Foxy's orders, being carried out of the room. "Careful, you sods—don't tear open those stitches!"

Then he turned his attention to Lord Ito, prone on the floor in a heap. Daniel took up a dipper of water from a fresh bucket and tossed it down onto the man's face.

Daniel cracked his knuckles, rubbed his aching back and kicked and flexed a cramp out of his left leg. He poured himself a large measure of *sake*, drank it down in a gulp, coughed and hunted a cheroot among his medical litter.

He had the roll of tobacco burning well and was inhaling huge lungs full of the savory Java leaf, when Foxy came back.

By then Lord Ito, looking drained of strength, was gulping a cup of *sake*. Daniel knew better than to mention Lord Ito's fainting; a great lord could not lose face in such a manner.

JOURNAL OF DOCTOR DANIEL HEACOCK

"I have just come from performing the operation on the Shogun (two stones—successfully withdrawn). I am back in my room at the castle, and Lord Ito's house is a good three minutes away from here for a good runner. I wanted to stay there but it was thought wiser that I not be found at the scene if something should go wrong (that could only mean if the Shogun dies). I am exhausted. I can't sleep. O-Kita must be asleep already and I don't want to awaken her. Besides, in my present state I would blurt out everything, and if the Shogun should die I don't want her to be among those who know why I was brought here.

"I will smoke a pipe to calm myself. I have come to believe the oriental philosophy that opium is more of a benefit than a curse to certain people. I think I am one of those people. Opium, or O-Kita; both are the drugs I need. They are my religions, I suppose. (This might well be my last will and testament if anything goes wrong with the Shogun.)

"Suppose he starts to bleed? Or worse? What will happen then? Will O-Kita be involved in it with me? I mustn't let any danger to myself harm her too.

"O-Kita . . . O-Kita will not come, and I dare not go to her . . . I will smoke two pills now and sleep."

The next morning Daniel awoke late, calm and unshaken. After he dressed he went to see O-Kita.

"I can't stay. I must be at Lord Ito's house. But I don't expect to be away too long."

"Sharaku is taking us to the Noh theater today."

Daniel kissed her. "Aren't you going to ask me where I was last night?"

O-Kita shook her head. "That would be very foolish. If you were with the courtesans you'd lie, and if busy with your mission, I hope it was successful."

"You've been listening to court gossip," Daniel frowned, wondering exactly what that gossip was, and whether it would affect him or her. "I'll know about my mission in a few days. I'm sure I can go to the Noh theater with you." And in English he added, "Damn it, darling, you're a beautiful, beautiful thing."

O-Kita bowed, and smiled behind her fan. Whatever his mission was, she knew he had powerful friends at court, which meant he must also have enemies. She wished she had her amulets, the sacred bones and inscribed tablets hidden away at Madame Hairy Lip's teahouse. Would she ever see the teahouse again and pick up her old life? How could she stand it alone, without Danhil, without this man she loved?

Every second or third day, for two weeks now, Prince Taira or one of his agents would, almost accidentally, meet her in the gardens. She would be questioned—and she would answer so little. In truth, she knew nothing of what she was asked. They had wasted their time, their money to employ her for this. She did not like these encounters; they frightened her.

She frowned, and thought again of Danhil. The big man was no longer frightening, but he remained fascinating. Her sadness dispersed like leaves in a wind. She knew nothing remained constant, especially illusions.

Lord Ito had recovered his color but seemed shocked by the memory of the operation. There were still samurai in the garden, but the soldiers were withdrawn or out of sight. Lord Ito said to Daniel, "We have had to watch the Shogun all night to keep him from rolling over. He did not tear at his bandages."

"Has he eaten anything?"

"Some gruel, some warm wine and tea, but he's weak and dazed."

"Any pain?"

"He complains of belly pressure."

"A little gas. I'll tell you what to do for that. I'll see him now."

The Shogun rested on sleeping pads, flanked by Pi and Mo who were brewing some mixtures on small charcoal fires. There was some color in the Shogun's face and his eyes were not glazed, only unfocused.

Daniel decided not to keep up the game that he could not speak Japanese. "Your Highness has come through a great ordeal."

"By O'Tsuki-sama we shall look at the moon and give parties."

The Shogun, Daniel saw, was still only semi-conscious, and very weak. He examined the bandages and sniffed them. No sickening sweet smell of rot. He probed with his fingers gently around the groin. No sign of rigidity, no discoloration of exposed areas flaming with infection. Lucky so far. He felt the damp brow and took the pulse of the Shogun. A slight fever and a fast pulse. The Shogun was in great discomfort.

"Your Highness must rest, and take broth of chicken."

Pi, with a characteristic shrug, handed Daniel a cup of green herbal mixture. Daniel sniffed at it. "What is in here?"

He recognized none of the things Pi told him were in the brew. Daniel looked at Lord Ito. "If you say this is harmless, he can have it. But I'd rather he took only what I give him."

They walked out of ear range of the figure on the sleeping pads.

"It's made of medicinal herbs that can do no harm. How is the Shogun?"

"In shock, naturally; it's a brutal operation. And pain is coming now as the angry flesh, torn and cut, heals and the stitches grab hold. I'll give you some more laudanum for him when he gets in a bad state. But he's to stay on his back and not touch the bandages. I'll change them in two days. If they begin to smell bad call me at once."

"You fear something?"

"Blood poisoning is often the result of all a surgeon's hard work. An infection that spreads like fire in dry grass. Most surgeons lose a great many of their cases that way. I have been lucky in this operation, so far."

"We shall obey you in all you say. But be careful of what you do and where you go. The Shogun needs your services."

"Aren't your police protection enough? You have two men following me everywhere I go in Edo."

Lord Ito sighed as if such levity were out of place. "How long will it take the Shogun to recover?"

"If everything goes well, he'll be on the road to safety in a week. In two weeks the scar tissue should be strong enough for him to walk. He'll be weak and he'll find some of his natural functions painful but he seems to be a man of strong character."

"He is the Shogun."

Pi shouted, "His Highness is passing blood in his urine!"

Daniel smiled. "Good. If he didn't or couldn't, we'd all be in trouble. I'll be back at dusk to check his condition again."

Lord Ito followed Daniel to the door. "Heacock Sir, the next two weeks, while the Shogun is recovering, will tell us if there is to be civil war. So take no risks."

Daniel nodded. "I have always felt that all our lives we are living under sealed orders."

"That seems true," said Lord Ito, bowing.

BOOK FOUR

The King of the Infernal Regions being very old is retiring from business; he has built a pretty country house and asks me to go and paint a picture for him. So I have to leave, and when I do go I shall take my drawings with me. I am going to take a studio at the corner of Hell Street and shall be happy to see you whenever you pass that way.

Last letter of the artist Hokusai

14

It was a gray-pearl day with a mist hanging like an opaque skin over Edo. A citron-colored rain had just stopped falling, and people out walking printed their inky reflections in the wet spots.

"The word Noh," said Sharaku, "is written with the Chinese character meaning 'to be able.' It also signifies 'talent.' So one could say the Noh theater means 'an exhibition of talent.' "

Daniel said, "It has tradition."

Hokusai scoffed. "It's seen its best days. The people like the Kabuki theater better. Anyway, four hundred years ago Noh came out of something called *Dengaku no Noh*, field music shows, with lots of jugglers and acrobats. So it wasn't always for the great lords."

"Stop teasing the boy," O-Kita said, taking Sharaku's and Daniel's arms to walk between them. "Tell us more, Sharaku."

"Well, early Noh combined with Sarugaku or monkey music, as they called it, and with the Shinto song-dance which . . . which was . . . well . . ."

Hokusai laughed. "He's ashamed to say it. It had its origin when the Goddess Uzume tried to lure the Sun-god from his

191

cave. She bared her breasts, let down her skirt, and danced."
Sharaku blushed, the blood in his face turning him scarlet.
Hokusai went on, "The song goes:

> 'I will lift up my petticoats
> And warm my *fuguri* at the fire.' "

O-Kita laughed, hitting Hokusai playfully with her closed
fan. "You are a low kind of man, but amusing."

They went into the theater Sharaku brought them to and
sat down. In front was a smooth platform made of polished
hinoki wood; on the back wall only a pine tree was painted.
There was a curtain to admit actors from the side. The audience, a small one of mostly elderly people, sat around three
sides of the stage. Four musicians were in a recess at the back
of the stage; a stick drummer picking his nose, two hand
drummers, and a lean man now playing on a piercing flute.

Hokusai said, "He's the bridge man, the flute. They give
about four plays a day here and when two actors aren't playing well together in harmony, the flute bridges their differ-
ences. The drums heat up the audience to excitement. You'll
see."

O-Kita said to Sharaku, "Was it exciting, being in Noh?"

"I was raised in it. I never knew any other life."

Sharaku was studying his hands. O-Kita pressed his arm
to show he mustn't be embarrassed by Hokusai's continual
heckling.

Daniel had somewhat accustomed himself to sitting cross-
legged. A row of actors came out, looking like colored silhou-
ettes, and began to sing in shrill voices, reciting something
Daniel couldn't follow.

"The unison singers," said Sharaku.

Two actors appeared, one masked as a woman. The costumes were very elaborate, and in bright colors. There was almost no scenery or props, and one of the actors used his fan as a knife, then as a brush, and also as a sword. The actors began an odd movement of slow steps and solemn gestures.

Hokusai said loudly, "They call it *mai*, a dance, but I ask you, is that dancing? Dogs crawl better."

Sharaku said firmly, "I was a dancer like that. I still am."

Hokusai closed his eyes and fell asleep. Daniel tried for a more comfortable position. He watched and listened; by the time the second play was on he was able to follow the stage action and get some meaning into the words.

"And this hate is payment for past hate," said an actor.

"The flame of hate . . ." another stated.

"Consumes only itself," the first actor completed.

"Didn't you know that?"

"We know it now."

The chorus, silent for a few moments, suddenly began to wail:

> "O Hate, Hate
> Her hate so deep that on her bed
> Our lady moans.
> Yet she shall live
> In the world again!"

The chorus woke up Hokusai. "This damn thing still on? I've had enough. Let's go get a drink."

Daniel agreed and they all followed Hokusai out of the theater as the flute music grew louder.

Madame Hairy Lip's teahouse was in a state of scatter-brained excitement that even Madame herself could not control. For once her stern look, her "harump-harump" of disapproval coming from deep in her throat, did not quiet the geishas, waitresses, maids and other women who made up her establishment. O-Kita and her two little maids had come back from the Shogun's castle for a visit. There were wild rumors that O-Kita had been made a concubine in the Shogun's seraglio, had been married off to a prince, was entering a Buddhist nunnery, was setting up a teahouse of her own, and even that she had become bewitched by a giant with blue eyes and was going off to live with him on some far distant mountain top. But the real reason for O-Kita's visit was not even suspected.

In the teahouse garden, on the pebbled paths by the sword-leaved irises, the little maids gossiped as they played *jonken-pan*, the finger game. "Oh, yes, you can see the giant with the blue eyes walking with her in the streets of Edo."

Cat, shaking out O-Kita's cushions, just smiled and said, "Well . . . a lady doesn't gossip about these things."

First O-Kita had a long talk with Madame Hairy Lip. Then she went to her old room. She bowed and then kneeled to the Buddhist shrine there. It was finely carved and gilded, and there were images of Buddha, Kwannon and Amida, good ancient bronzes that Hokusai had found for her in the proper shops.

She was upset. Just that morning she had again met an agent of Prince Taira. They wanted more and more information from her, and she had so little to give. At first it had seemed that they just wanted her to watch the blue-eyed man and Lord Ito, and as was usual among the geishas in such situations, she had obeyed without question. But now that they knew of her relationship to the man from far away their questions had become more insistent, almost sinister. She wondered if they were not planning to destroy him, and herself at the same time. Yet how could she suspect this and not warn her lover?

Was she trapped in the center of some plot in which both sides already knew all that was going on? She was confused after the events of the last few days. It was such a sudden change from the sheltered existence she had led even as the most popular geisha at the Kataya teahouse. To be a spy for such an honored man as Prince Taira! And to be in love with a blond giant! But what was she to do? Should she tell Danhil about her assignment from the Prince? She could not definitely say that harm was intended. Better to say nothing, at least until she could tell more. Long training had emphasized discretion, silence.

She shook her head clear and continued praying. She bowed her head low and whispered a special prayer. She realized that in questioning the motives of those above her she was not being a proper geisha, not being a respectful woman. No woman she had ever heard of, and certainly no geisha, dared ever to think that her opinions could matter to any man.

It was better to submit, to pray as she now did. *"Namu myoko renge kyo,"* that Buddhist text which expressed her faith and brought her peace. "Adoration of the wonderful law of the Lotus Scriptures." And then she added, "Protect my love of this man Danhil; save me from Prince Taira, oh gentle

Gautama, and in all my steps be you with me to watch and guide me."

The sliding partition behind the shrine was pushed open and Madame Hairy Lip stood there.

"*Irasshai*—please come in," said O-Kita, bowing.

"Never mind that. I am in," said Madame Hairy Lip. "I suppose you think you know what you are doing in letting this barbarian buy you out of my teahouse. But I think you are making a mistake. You could have made something of yourself here, and saved your money. In time—after all, I am old— you might become an adopted member of my family and take over this teahouse as I did once."

"I am honored, very honored that you should even think this way of me."

"You always were too clever, O-Kita. But I saw something in you, even when you were young. I don't suppose you will change now. The hairy rascal says he's in love with you?"

"I will not change my mind."

"Anyone else I could understand. A lord, a prince, even a fat merchant—but this outsider!" Madame Hairy Lip leaned closer to O-Kita. "I hear in love he is like . . ." she went into some obscene gossip she had heard.

O-Kita laughed politely. "It is nothing but what is usual between a man and a woman."

"What will you get from it, O-Kita? I remember my father telling me about when the Chinese and the Hindus used to come to Edo, and before that in the olden times the Portuguese and others, and the girls became foreigners' mistresses.

It didn't end well in almost all cases. Ah me, why talk to you of serious things? Life is a vapor."

O-Kita stood up, head down respectfully. "I must return to the castle. Everything has been arranged to your satisfaction, Madame?"

"Yes, I have received the money for your freedom." She handed O-Kita a folded paper. "Here is your release. And when he marries you let me present you with the ritual red mullet in the basket, the rolls of silk and the dried fish—everything that is tradition for a fine wedding."

"No one has said anything of marriage."

"The man never does, most of the time. A woman has to remind him."

"I am thankful for your advice and for raising me properly so I am not ashamed of my manners or my talents wherever I go."

Madame Hairy Lip smiled a thin smile and said, "I turn out a fine girl, polite, limber as a hemp-palm tree. It's a tradition here."

She turned and went out without saying any more.

O-Kita was aware she was taking a bold, perhaps too bold, step. In leaving the security of this teahouse she was cutting herself off from a destiny that could have carried her into placid middle age and a comfortable old one. Yes, she could even have married a good fat rice merchant some day, or perhaps become in time mistress of this grand teahouse and raise up others properly with the right manners and ways.

She began to gather her possessions, everything she was taking with her. The screen and the paintings would be sent

197

for. Now she piled up some sword guards that she collected, boxes of hairpins for her coiffure, white bronze mirrors, her little lacquered cosmetic cases, her robes, clogs, and colored sashes—really so little to show for all her years in the place.

She wanted to escape quickly. A panic suddenly gripped her. She shouted: "Cat! Cat!"

It was all too much for O-Kita now; the walls were leaning in on her and it was just like the hot rainy season ten years ago when the earth had been shaken and cracked by the big earthquake, and they had all run out as they were, naked, from the bathhouse into the garden, and the world seemed about to stand on end, like a rice dish.

Cat came in and saw O-Kita's face. "You called? What's the matter?"

O-Kita came away from her memories of the earthquake and the walls fell back into place. "Have this and the shrine figures taken to the castle. The rest isn't worth taking."

"May I have the umbrella and the broken hairpins you don't take?"

O-Kita nodded and bowed in the direction of the shrine once more and said the prayer: "*Namu amida butsu*," and went out.

In the house of Lord Ito Daniel scientifically, professionally examined the Shogun. It was now ten days since the operation. The fever was gone. The wounds seemed to be healing neatly in their tight stitching. But there was still an inflamed section on the groin that worried Daniel. He pressed firmly on the Shogun's flesh. "Does Your Highness feel pain there?"

"Just a little, but not anything like it was before."

Lord Ito, kneeling by the sleeping pads, looked up. "It is of vital importance that the Shogun show himself at the castle. A certain group has been questioning."

Daniel closed the Shogun's robe, and bowed. "The cure is not yet complete. As I told you there is an inflamed area, which I think will subside. But there could be a flare-up of infection. The flesh could tear and the stitches break if there is too much movement. Wait another five or six days."

The Shogun in a low polite voice said seriously, "As a doctor you speak well. But I have a nation to govern. I must show myself at court. If I am carried out of here with care and remain seated during a short period of ceremony, do you see any danger?"

Daniel bowed again. "I would prefer you to remain here a few days longer. However, I know you have your duties of office to perform. We can risk it, Your Highness."

The Shogun looked up at this tall man in magnificent Japanese ceremonial robes. His head was shaved and the fringe and topknot dyed black, making his odd unslanted blue eyes even more startling and unexpected in the serious face. He owed this man his life, but he was the Shogun and every man owed everything to him, even this outsider.

"You will be rewarded," the Shogun said.

Daniel stood, head bowed, and said, "I would like to settle in Edo and become a doctor here. I would like to offer my skill to healing the sicknesses of your people."

The Shogun, expressionless, looked at Lord Ito. These were strange creatures, so lacking in manners.

Lord Ito pulled on Daniel's sleeve. "The Shogun is tired. Tomorrow he will go by palanquin to the castle for an appearance. We shall talk again of your plans another time."

The Shogun sank back on his pillows. He was too thin, his hand was unsteady, but his color was better and there was little pain. Daniel and Lord Ito bowed their way out of the room.

Daniel turned to Lord Ito. "I don't mind protocol and all that nonsense, but my request was serious and you prevented the Shogun from considering it."

Lord Ito smiled and patted Daniel's arm. "I am your friend. What can be done will be done. But not just yet."

"And why not? You heard him say I was to be rewarded. I don't want boxes of coins, or a castle, or sixteen dancing girls. I want to settle down here and practice my trade. Is that asking too much?"

"Yes, it is. The Shogun doesn't permit foreigners here. But in good time he will say yes. You see, you are not here as a doctor and surgeon. It would be too soon for you to openly practice your profession. Wait a little while, till the Shogun is stronger, till he again takes control of his affairs. Wait until the questioners at court are answered. A little time, a little time, Heacock Sir."

"How do I know how much time I have? I never wanted to be settled before. Now I want a home, to practice my trade normally. Is there anything wrong in that?"

"No, no, of course not. I know that here things move too slowly for you. We shall try and move them more quickly. But not quickly enough to do harm—to anyone."

"I'm sorry, Lord Ito. It's been a harrowing time for me. The Shogun still worries me, but he has come through the worst of it. He's a brave man."

"Come to the castle courtyard tomorrow for his appearance, and see how brave a man he is."

Daniel laughed. "You're a country of such perfect little landscapes and such cruel melodramas. Just when I think I know you all, I don't."

Lord Ito bowed.

Daniel went on earnestly, "Lord Ito, the Shogun's condition is good, but his operation was a hard one. I am really fearful about moving him too much."

"It must be done for the good of the country. He must show himself."

"All right. But continue him on liquorice, cinnamon milk, rose water and white of eggs."

"Will they make him strong?"

"They will heal him. There was a lot of damage done by those stones. They're solidified," he added in English, "uric acid of renal origin."

"What does that mean?"

"I don't know the Japanese words. But it's the kind of stones they are. They weigh a good ounce between them and the Shogun is a lucky man to have survived them. I've seen these operations go well half a dozen times, then septic matter sets in on the next half dozen—and yet the same surgeon and the same tools were used. Of course I suspect the difference is in using a new set of instruments. I'm not sure why."

"You worry too much, Heacock Sir, and that is good for the Shogun. I was going to tell you later, but the Shogun has a fine honor for you."

"A man can't eat honor. I want to settle here."

"You are to be made a noble, and a samurai of the court. You will be entitled to a crest, and to wear the two swords, and you will have your own iron sword guards forged by our best steel makers."

Daniel nodded, not at all elated. "I thank you, Lord Ito, and the Shogun too, for this honor. And I have something for him too. I'm adding a cooling, demulcent drink to his list —lemon juice and syrup of radishes, as used in the best English hospitals."

Lord Ito said softly with affection, "You are a strange fellow, and my friend."

O-Kita was still troubled; to calm herself she sat on the mat in her room at the castle arranging flowers. She arranged in a large red bowl the chrysanthemums, bits of bark, stones, leaves and sections of branches, conscious of the principles of flower art: Heaven is the main principle symbolized by the upright stems; subordinate to it was a horizontal principle, Earth; and the binding motive was Man. She bent twigs into V-shaped forms on the right side to denote Man. It was an impressive arrangement of the white and yellow flowers; the interlacing twigs and branches were all planned in O-Kita's mind for a place under a hanging scroll. The arrangement was to become part of the scroll and yet not cover any of the picture or its writing. She dusted her fingers, remembering a favorite poem:

> *Kigiku siragiku*
> *Sonno koka no*
> *Nawa nokumo kana*

> Yellow chrysanthemum
> And white
> Any other colors do not matter.

Cat came in and bowed. "Prince Kwammu Taira," she announced, pronouncing the name too distinctly.

There was tightness of breath as O-Kita nodded for Cat to show her visitor in. She felt no confidence in herself, and her will turned to tumbling water. The old prince came in, looking more like an old turtle than ever. He brought no gifts with him this time. He walked to the *shoji* screen and shut it, blocking out the view of the gardens beyond the terrace.

He faced O-Kita, bowing low on her knees before him. "Your reports have been short and not very informative," the refined voice said.

"I am unworthy of the task, Prince Taira. I am untrained in such work, and I know very little."

"But you can tell me more than you tell my agents," said the prince. "Whom has Lord Ito been entertaining?"

O-Kita looked up fearfully from her kneeling, bowing position. "His usual friends. Lord Hirata, Kitagawa, Komuro. Prince Mimura, Otsuka, the merchant Okubo."

Prince Taira waved off the names as if they were nothing. "These names we know. No, I mean in private, when you and the big hairy one go there. Who is there?"

"No one worthy to mention; the servants, sometimes an artist, or a dealer in bronzes."

Prince Taira inspected his old hands, hands slim and very well cared for, with long thin fingers. "O-Kita Mitsu, listen to me. You are in great danger if my anger should strike you. Now with care tell me, was there ever present a Lord Nishimaka, any of the *daimyo*—Hatano, Dairoku?"

"I never met any of them."

"A Prince Ganko, Otojiro?"

"Not to my knowledge."

"Any outside lords or members of the Shogun's council? Think hard, speak true."

"Only those I told you of first. No one else."

Prince Taira seemed unsatisfied. Yet he smiled at her. "Was there any talk of the Shogun's health, and worry over who would replace him in case of his death, his sons being too young to rule? Come, speak up—let us not think over our answers. Well?"

"I never heard such talk. They talk mostly of the woodcut prints, scrolls, screens, and personal matters."

"Was there talk of the rebellion in the north, and the Shogun sending an army against it? And of who the general might be?"

"No, no, no such talk." O-Kita had sunk her face to the floor and with her head down, was sobbing, trying to keep the sound of it from reaching the old prince, who was staring indifferently at the top of her shiny black hair.

"You have not served me well. The police that protect the castle will come and question you again. You had better answer in more detail. I never threaten without purpose."

She was aware the old prince had gone but of little more as she lay in a faint on the yellow matting.

15

Daniel was present when the Shogun appeared for a brief ceremony before a large crowd at the castle courtyard. Daniel examined him afterward in his bedroom and there seemed to be
no ill effects. Two days later he was able to remove all the visi-
ble stitches from the healing scars. "Your Highness is making a
fine recovery. There isn't much more I can do for you. If all
goes well, in a month or so you will be fully recovered."

"We trust your skill," the Shogun said.

"In a month I would like to give you a full physical examination. Do not strain at anything. Moderation in all things, Your
Highness."

The Shogun, dressed in Sendai silks, permitted himself a
small grin. He was tired but pleased at his recovery. "Lord Ito
tells men you would settle among us and be a doctor?"

"Yes, I have made such a request." It was evidently court
etiquette to ignore a direct request to the Shogun.

"I have intended honors for you. You saved me from becoming a dead man, from having the priest put the sacred razor to
my forehead to avoid the punishment of Hell. I can wait another fifty years for that now. Yes, I shall certainly reward you."

"I am pleased you think me worthy. But being permitted to

live and work in Edo is what I want most. Not just honors."

The Shogun frowned and motioned Lord Ito nearer. On his knees Lord Ito listened as the Shogun spoke very low into his ear. Lord Ito rose, bowed and motioned Daniel to follow him out of the Shogun's bedroom. On the upper terrace the two men stood looking at the moat and gardens below them, and the smoke from the city and the even green of the parks. They could hear the cries of the fish peddlers, the drums of blind masseurs announcing their services.

Lord Ito said, "You are a strange man, Heacock Sir. But I think you are a fine one."

"This flattery means there is some sort of barrier to my wish?"

"The Shogun has problems of rebellion. There are certain people at court who must be dealt with. He cannot just yet permit you to become a doctor in Edo. People would guess you have been treating him for something serious. It would cause talk; talk could aid the plotters."

"I'm not going to hunt bugs and insects, if that's what you suggest."

"No. Go away for a month or so. You may take some of your friends. I have a fine house in the north, among the rice fields, and on the shore. It's a very primitive country and yet beautiful. The house is very fine and has much ancient art in it."

Daniel looked off toward the busy bridges, at the traffic of boats in front of the rice warehouses, at the crowded streets and the people moving with familiar ease through their city. "You expect trouble and want me out of the way?"

"It's more than that. When you come back it will be easier to grant you your wishes."

Daniel faced Lord Ito and looked him directly in the eyes.

"I'd want to take some people with me. Some friends, as you suggest."

Lord Ito made a gesture of indifference, showing the palms of his hands held up. "All right. I know your friends here. Take the geisha, invite the artists to join you later. But be careful. I am not as sure as you are you will find all you want in this country."

Daniel nodded in agreement. "I am not sure about anything. I am just following my instincts. I'm tired of following my intellect."

"Don't follow your instincts too far, my friend. Our ways are not yours. Our relationships toward people, certain people, are not the same."

"Are you trying to tell me something?"

Lord Ito laughed politely and leaned his head to one side. "*Go men kudasai*—excuse me. I know you well by now. One can tell you nothing. You hear only what you want to hear. You have saved the Shogun's health and life. Trust me. If there should be anything that needs your attention here, I shall send for you. Meanwhile, enjoy yourself. I can not. I must be here and on guard for the Shogun's safety. I will give you a procession for the journey. Remember, you are under the Shogun's protection."

Daniel wanted to shake hands but he restrained himself. He no longer felt like an outsider; he need not keep up old social habits from a different world.

That night Lord Ito, wearing the ceremonial robe of a samurai, sat drinking heavily in the house of Hana-ogi, the most famous and beautiful courtesan in Japan. She had been drawn by the famous Yoshiwara artists Koryusai, Choki, Utamaro, and the prints of her face and body sold in great number. Lord Ito, fingering a folding album of erotic prints, let the little maid refill his *sake* cup. It was taking him a long time tonight to feel the bite of the alcohol.

He wondered if Heacock's procession was already outside of Edo, resting for the night in one of the inns on the road to the north. What a fool about women the big man was! Lord Ito wondered what it was like to feel that foolish and happy over one particular woman, and her alone. What would it be like, he wondered, to know for sure you did not have to buy her favors, even if you were Lord Ito, and somewhere soft music was playing, and Hana-ogi herself was preparing to come to you. Lord Ito had an instinctive antipathy to whores; his sensibilities were drawn fine like wire. The day of peace would come soon; he could die in the coming struggle for power, or he would emerge as the chief lord on the sword-side of the Shogun. And he would marry some *daimyo's* or prince's daughter. But it could never be with the personal pleasure that he had seen in Heacock Sir's face that afternoon.

Lord Ito had once had a wife, but she died three years ago. Heacock Sir had fought for two weeks to keep her alive on the Dutch trading island where they were living, but the bleeding lung sickness had won and her ashes now rested in the family tomb under the willow trees. That was how he had first met Heacock Sir. Lord Ito had been young and he had never loved his wife; his world had been the court, the soldiers' march, the sharkskin sword handle, the ambition to carry proudly the family crest to honor with dignity and spirit.

Two little maids were bowing, but he sipped his *sake* without looking up. He could smell the scent that Hana-ogi imported from India, the hair oil from Java. She came in and bowed before him.

The most desirable woman in Japan, Lord Ito thought—which meant, of course, in the world. She sat down beside him laughing that deep rich laugh of hers; she was shameless and too bold, yet she remained well mannered and polite. "Lord Ito broods tonight."

"Do I?"

He looked at her. Large and tall for a beauty, if the modern standards were to be believed, but with a great grace and soft to the touch, with a slender waist, and exquisite skin under the white powder. Her neck was sensual in its grace and perfection. Her features were marvelously matched; the curve to her nose and nostrils had a passionate pulse of their own. She was neither too brazen nor too obvious. But she was bold, aware of her price and her skill. This was no nun from Hokkeji temple.

"Soon it will be time to transplant the rice up north," said Lord Ito, thinking of other things.

"You want to talk of other subjects than Edo?"

Lord Ito looked into the mirror on its red lacquer stand, so that he saw two images of Hana-ogi.

"You are very beautiful, Hana-ogi, you always are."

The courtesan waved her little folding fan. "Perhaps I shall send for the geisha. You seem too bemused to care for me."

"Tell me something amusing," Lord Ito said. "Tell me how some men enjoy themselves greatly."

"When I was young and just beginning as a courtesan, when there was a shy guest we would play a game called 'naked islanders,' such as are seen on the old maps. All of the courtesans would disrobe. The first time I played I blushed and turned pink all over. And the guest saw my skin and was no longer shy. With a sated old man, of course, it is harder. We would imitate bats crying, or the wooden clappers of watchmen. The procuress would chant obscene prayers, saying a service for the death ceremony of the guest who was sitting there alive. We'd burn toothpicks instead of incense. Then we'd feed the jaded old man *nerigi*, made of hollyhock, that fires the desire. One old man asked me to marry him, but respectability is dull and a wife has to blacken her teeth and get beaten with bamboo rods, and there is childbearing to distort the figure. I like being visited by handsome young lords. A short life and leaving a body beautiful is the best."

She was undoing his sash and they would soon, she whispered, be *najim*, intimate. The great sadness and loneliness began to move out of Lord Ito, and he was proud, being a great lord and a handsome man, to be able to afford the attentions of Hana-ogi.

She was reciting:

> "In the dawn while I know
> It grows dark again
> I dislike the coming day."

Lord Ito leaned over to blow out a lamp and Hana-ogi said, "No, no. It is bad luck to blow out a lamp. One must shake it out for good fortune and success in love-making."

She shook out the lamp and the room was now very dimly lit. She caressed him with the touch of a cat cleaning itself, and he put his hands up the sleeves of her kimono where they were slit, and he held her breasts in his cupped hands. Being young and now fully aroused he thought of poets who made of this distortion and grotesqueness, of extravagant grimaces and squints, emotional ecstasies hard to reach and hold on to or believe.

"When were you born, my lord?" asked Hana-ogi, her mouth open and her eyes on his and her lips touching his.

"The year of the Flaming Horse." He pulled her to him and the reality of her reassured him to the experience.

"The year marked by the coincidence of fire with fire. It is a dangerous year to be born, the old astrological fools say."

She too was now alerted to panting desire by his touches and his caresses. Or so she seemed, for she had greatness in her art. He opened her robe and she opened his and he had only time to remember that everything is a passing world of dust and defilement as he took Hana-ogi to the pillows. He forgot in his warm blood the pride and nobility of his name and the duty of a warrior; even the rice fields of his estate were far away. Only the courtesan Hana-ogi was very close and beautifully touching him as he fondled her, and soon, in the poet's words, they "cried out beyond the edge of dreams."

Lord Ito's country house was in the rice country to the north, a world still half water and half mud, on which the land was terraced among long fingers of dark brown water that cut into the land.

Daniel and O-Kita found it a lovely happy place. The muddy terraces were fertile and the plant life grew with a shout—rice grass and sedge, and flowers, rare and of beautiful colors. Threading their way through the overgrown water lanes went the farmers in their skin-thin flat boats which were reported to ride in a heavy dew and race over a wet road. The rice waters were dark and thick, changing from pure purples to jet blacks and on a clear day to a nice clay color. Certainly, Daniel saw, there was no such thing as a crystal clear rice terrace.

O-Kita and Daniel and Cat and Foxy lived cut off from the world of Edo, in this newer world of seatide and terrace mud, a world of farmers and fishermen. The villagers took pride in their past and knew more of nature than the thin-lipped sharp natives of Edo, who felt some folk hero forefathers in their blood and who yowled old songs that remember wars and loves beyond the understanding of village minds.

The sea and rice world needed muscles for raising levees and digging canals. There was a time to fish the tide runners, both salt and fresh; a time to hunt the small fur-bearing animals; and a time to gather roots, seeds, fungus, moss and a time to dry them, eat them, and store them. Rice was the survival crop planted in May in six inches of reeking water; men and women and children bent, bent, bent, and pushed shoots into the mud. They also grew soy-beans.

One thing O-Kita and Daniel never understood too well was the local speech, which was a strange dialect.

"We're alone," said O-Kita that first night, as she prepared her hair in the bed-chamber and Daniel made notes in his journal by a country lamp burning rapeseed oil.

"It's a new world," Daniel said, closing his journal with little written in it. "All sky, sun, rice and frogs."

They did not feel lonely. They went out in boats, out past the cypresses dying in salt water and past the orange flower and the indigo iris. The inlet shore was thick with growth. Daniel identified water hickory, tupelo, bald cypress, and locust. Over everything were ferns and creepers, palmettos and the green gold of choking vines.

The old fisherman who took them out in his boat said to them, "The greatest trouble in boating is the water hyacinths. They are beautiful, but they are thick and they choke up the waterways. You can almost walk on them."

O-Kita pulled on a trailing vine of them. "They are pretty."

The old fisherman said, "It's harder to get the boats to sea."

"The bulb is good to eat," Daniel said.

"But who can ever eat it all? They make a mat of flower and leaf that hides lakes and streams."

Better than boating, Daniel liked to walk while O-Kita trudged along, followed by little Cat carrying an oiled paper umbrella and wailing, "It's dangerous. People sink into the mud and never come up, Foxy says."

It was a jelly-like land, a quavery land in spots that could suck down a man or an animal, Foxy said, and lick its muddy lips for more. Even the natives respected it and walked with care.

But it was fertile, Daniel saw. Grass covered it, salt cane, patches of oyster grass, the waving cattails. A native could read the condition of the bogs by what grew on it. Humus, ooze, and roots made a wet shaking world of their own. Daniel liked to explore it. O-Kita shivered all the time and held his hand tightly.

After a day of crossing from land to island, from swamp to peaty shore, O-Kita and Daniel would soak in hot baths in oak tubs. Then they dressed and found it good to sit and spoon up shrimp soup and red bean stew, which was the native fare.

At night they made love and afterward lay listening to

hawks and owls hunting, to insects singing, frogs courting, and their own hearts pounding.

JOURNAL OF DOCTOR DANIEL HEACOCK

"This is the year of the Tiger—1793 was the Ox and next year, 1795, is the Hare.

"This morning the weather was warmer than it has been yet. I walked naked to the hanging bucket to get a dipper of water. Foxy was pushing straw into the bathhouse furnace and Cat, plumper than ever, was laughing and choking over one of Foxy's jokes. We all bathed together in the almost scalding water. Cat scrubbed my back and Foxy swam under water imitating an old frog. At noon the woman who cooks brought her sister; both blacken their teeth with lacquer, as do most of the married women of the village. They sold us chickens, and I played *shogi*, which is a native chess, while a meal was prepared. I lost as usual. Foxy is a very fine player.

"I have bought O-Kita a Chin puppy dog, a Japanese kind of spaniel. It is small and bright, with a short nose and a prominent brow. O-Kita has named it Flysnapper and he is becoming a problem. O-Kita likes to carry the puppy in her sleeve and take him to bed with her. He barks when the lanterns are lit in the garden, and he digs into the mats and sniffs in corners when Cat is trying out hairdos on O-Kita. O-Kita has discarded the *tsub-ushi-shimada* hair style worn by the geishas, and now favors the *chocho-mage*, a butterfly effect, or the *shima momo-ware* worn by unmarried girls.

"This morning as I was cataloging my woodcut prints (I have gotten Toyokuni's five sheet set of the main street of the Yoshiwara), there was screaming and the sound of a slap and I went in and found poor Cat in a corner, howling and holding a very red and puffy cheek.

"O-Kita was pacing the floor kicking at the train of her kimono. 'The beggar girl! I'll send her to the blind masseurs!'

" 'What did she do?' I asked.

"Cat wailed. 'I was only trying it out; the *maru-mage* style.'

" 'You women,' I said, and tossed Cat some rice sweets and went out to the garden where Foxy was sitting smoking his long bamboo pipe and scratching one naked leg with the other. I said, 'They had some womanly argument. Why would O-Kita resent having Cat put up her hair *maru-mage?*'

"Foxy knocked out his brass bowl and grinned. 'It is the style worn by married women.'

" 'I see. Just what are the marriage customs here?'

" 'You have skipped the first meeting, the *Miai*. But you can still have the *Yuino*, the exchange of presents. Rolls of cloth, kegs of *sake*, fans, such stuff.'

" 'All this is still not a wedding.'

" 'No. The ceremony is held in the house the bridegroom lives in. The bride's things are sent there. Then the bride appears in the headband, the *tsunokakushi* or horn cover. To get married is easy. It's called *San san Kudo*, meaning you take three drinks of *sake*, then change cups, take three more drinks, change again and take three more drinks. You feel pretty fine by then, I am sure.'

" 'I should think so. What else?'

" 'That is really all, and everyone is really getting drunk now unless you want a Shinto shrine ceremony, which has nine more drinks of *sake*. You are thinking of getting married, Heacock Sir?'

" 'O-Kita says November and December are the favorite months to get married, for the best results.'

" 'That would be mostly the months of Ju-ni and Uri. Our calendar is not like yours. May I ask how long shall we stay here?'

" 'Till Lord Ito recalls me to Edo. It's a fine big house he has here.'

" 'I heard the family ghost again last night.'

"Foxy swears the house is haunted by a beautiful woman who walks with her throat cut, her face drained white and bloodless. Foxy says she lives during the day in the space under the hung ceiling, but I have never bothered to look. In the big room where we spend most of our time, he points to certain stains as the dried blood of a samurai who raped the daughter of a great lord and was cut down by the guard as he tried to flee naked into the snow outside. Japanese stories have few pleasant endings. But all are heroic.

"The room is paneled in paintings said to be by Kano Tan-nyu; pine trees and eagles, with a background of gold leaf rubbed with white. The hipped roof has tiles turning green with age and when it rains we have the *shoji* screens open and sit on mats drinking tea while O-Kita sings and plays and Foxy studies some move on the chessboard. Cat tends the pan of glowing charcoal on which the tea is being made. The little dog Flysnapper sits watching us, head to one side, and the green rain falls and the stones in the garden turn black and shine with wet and then it is time to light floor lamps. I feel we are suspended in time, locked into a moment that is as eternal as anything men shall ever feel, and it is as satisfactory as anything I have yet known. Then the dog barks, Cat burns her hand and the wind drives the rain in on us and we must close the screens, and the moment is shattered.

"I am really enjoying this life. I wonder how long we'll be able to go on like this; how long until I receive a summons from Edo. I wonder if all is well with the Shogun's health— political as well as physical. More than before I realize how much my future depends on him."

16

The days passed quickly, for Daniel cataloging his woodblock prints, for O-Kita playing music and singing. They ate breakfast and then spent the morning, with the little dog Flysnapper, along the shore, both sketching, blocking in ideas and coloring square bits of paper with little color notes that they hoped to design into scrolls. It was a new interest and both knew they had little talent for it.

Daniel invited his spirits to loaf and with the sketchbooks filling up he enjoyed the hot stab of sun—a lacquer-like Chinese red—growing stronger and stronger until it boiled over and he and O-Kita took shelter in some garden. They would go walking into the foothills—listen to runner birds in the newly cut fields and measure with cheerful eye the distant mountains and the leaning pines and the line of low farm buildings and trees and the full rustling flow of the streams.

It was strange to walk across a field of stubble and feel stirring under them an echo of an earthquake and hear muffled the distant thud of the earth groaning.

O-Kita, Cat, and the dog would run quickly, following the leaping grasshoppers until with one spring the insects would go over the edge of the world and Cat and the dog would drop after them, clinging to terraces and bush, dropping at last into a lower field. Then Daniel and O-Kita would come down and join the laughter.

Coming home at dusk they would pass the little bent-over farmers who, in rice straw hats, would politely stand aside to let them pass. After Cat was asleep and Foxy had gone to the village inn, Daniel and O-Kita would sit looking at the sea and the white ghosts of ships.

"Did you have a good day, O-Kita?"

"Yes. Any word from Lord Ito?"

"Nothing."

"Do you mind very much?"

"Not really, O-Kita. I like it here with you. I wish we could stay here forever." And he would hold her close to him in the dusk.

In the hour of the Rat, as the Japanese call it, which was between eleven and one o'clock in the night on Daniel's silver watch, he came awake with a start. O-Kita was breathing softly at his side. From the distance came a drumming sound that lacerated his nerves. He listened anxiously for a long time and when the hour of the Ox came, from one o'clock to three in the morning, he was sure he heard the sounds of an army on the march.

He got up quietly and put on a heavy night robe. He went out on the porch and looked off to the south still in darkness. He could just make out the points of spears and the curves of horses' necks and wide wing spread of a horde advancing across the fields, bands of men swallowing up the landscape like a slow flood. He stood a long time and was joined by a shaky Foxy, who had also heard the sound of troops.

"There must be war against the rebels in the north, Foxy."

Foxy shivered. "It may be the rebels themselves coming down."

"Not from that direction."

Foxy, with no capacity for violence, said, "We better hide the women, and the wine, and if they want to cut our throats, show them the paper from the Shogun. But it would be best and smartest to run away to the hills and live in caves."

Daniel frowned and told Foxy to wake O-Kita and Cat and the women with the black teeth in the kitchen. The pictures of war he had seen in the old prints were not too reassuring.

Shortly afterward some gray ghost-shaped scouts came riding into the nearby fields and then three mounted men in armor rode into the garden. Their horses were black stallions with red saddle cloths. The men wore horned helmets and the heavy red and black iron armor of war, not the ceremonial patterns of the court which Daniel had seen before.

The riders looked like great crabs or lobsters in a new kind of fearfully shaped shell. Daniel was wondering if he and his household were all to die here when he heard Lord Ito's voice under the biggest of the helmets, shouting with an amused tone.

"The gardens look fine, Heacock Sir."

O-Kita and Cat, sleepy and frightened, came out on the porch. Daniel bowed, suddenly relieved after hours of anxiety. "We have enjoyed the place. You bring a large escort for a visit."

Foot soldiers came running up to hold the horses, and Lord Ito dismounted stiffly, walking with difficulty in his battle armor. Two men removed his helmet and another unloosened some of his armor.

"They go to war against the north where the rebels are active. It's sad to know one must create chaos to make a world. I came along this far with the army to be with you for a few days."

Daniel bowed again in relief. "This is an honor. It's a fearful looking army. More like demons than soldiers."

Lord Ito smiled as he came up the porch steps. "Even our armies seem like works of imagination rather than reality to you, don't they? But I think this will be a short campaign. I hope so. I don't like to keep such a loyal force away from the court for too long, especially at this time."

The two other riders, large, brutal-looking men, joined them. The advance guards were moving swiftly past the gardens, filling the lanes and the green shoulders of the roads. Cruel and hairy, walking or on small swift horses, their lances and spears ready, they soon melted into the deep blue landscape ahead. Then came the samurai, heavy and large, on big horses, with the clanging of rein chains and loose armor, the terrible designs of their helmets seeming fit only for the night they were riding in. Lord Ito raised his hand in a benediction to them.

The black-toothed old women brought out tea and *sake* and little soy-bean cakes. Daniel and Lord Ito sat cross-legged on the porch mats of the house. Daniel watched as the baggage carts passed, the porters stooping under bent bamboo poles, the solid wooden wheels on the carts booming like drums. This was the sound that had awakened him hours earlier.

The dawn hinted its approach after hesitant glowing, and the army in black and red and gold, shading off to brown and gray and a dusty yellow, continued to pass. Everything was dusty now, the air thick with the earth. And the leaves were coated white in the gardens. Even the brook had a film of floating dust and the goldfish were nervous and unquiet. Then suddenly the army was gone like a ghost at cock-crow. The sun was up. The dust still hung golden in the air, but there was no more army.

Daniel was stirred and awed by the sight of the army. Lord Ito seemed elated. He swallowed his *sake* and said, quietly but with great pride, "We are a remarkable race, and death is not the end for us, as it is for other people!"

Daniel asked, "How is the Shogun?"

"He works too hard. He makes too many appearances. I know you will not approve. But his health is a great deal better."

"The wounds have healed?"

"All but in one spot where some of the stitches inside have broken through to the surface. It is not bad, but he wants you to examine him."

"How is the situation in Edo?"

"Everything is under control." Lord Ito appeared reluctant to discuss this subject, but Daniel was not satisfied.

"Isn't it dangerous to send the army away to war if there is danger in the city?"

Lord Ito said after significant silence, "You have been happy here?"

"Yes, very much so. Do you think the Shogun will let me practice as a doctor now?"

"You are invited to attend his great meeting in the courtyard of the castle on the festival of O-Bon. First for two days the people will visit the tombs of their ancestors, and invite the spirit to their homes. After that the ancestors are escorted back to their resting places and the Bon Odori is danced."

"That sounds very interesting."

"Now I must go to the family altar in this house and grace the presence of my family's memorial stones with some prayers."

O-Kita was upset by the presence of Lord Ito. She said to Daniel, "He does not like me, and I am tired of his house. The country is not for me. I am a city girl."

"Lord Ito isn't much interested in women, but he doesn't dislike you."

"He is the lover of the great courtesan, Hana-ogi, and he has enjoyed many geishas in his time. These lords take love by holding back everything."

"You imagine things. He has a war and a rebellion on his hands. Cheer up. I've never known this bitter side of you."

O-Kita did not cheer up; not until the next afternoon when two dusty tramps, walking with packs and sticks, came to the house and turned out to be Hokusai and the young Noh dancer turned print-maker, Sharaku.

Hokusai spit in the road dust, slapped his travel-soiled robe, and said, "I tell you it's dog water, not *sake*, you get on the road. Well, Heacock Sir, you look more rooted in the country than a farmer's valuable dung pile. And you, O-Kita, are the

223

true country wife. I expected to find you with your teeth painted black plucking a goose."

"No, no. I've had enough country."

O-Kita was happy to see her city friends.

Hokusai said, "When I told this puppy I was coming to visit you he couldn't stand still until I said he could come too." He whispered to O-Kita, "I think it is you, and not the fine shore country, that attracted him."

Sharaku took her hand and smiled. He blushed as much as ever, but he seemed not so shy. "I was doing nothing."

Hokusai took the cup of *sake* Cat handed him, sipped, sighed, and groaned. "You wouldn't believe it but this young fool has given up print making. He turned over his last designs to be cut in some future time, and he is rejoining his dancing troupe."

Daniel shook his head. "You are among the very top artists, the best of them all, Sharaku."

"No, no. No one buys, and the publisher is discouraged. He has asked me to do popular subjects; what sells."

"What up the devil's nose does it matter?" asked Hokusai. "They will forget your bad work, and remember only your best. Ah, Lord Ito, I touch my chin to the ground in front of you and gnaw earth."

Lord Ito had come out and was amused at the mock bow Hokusai gave him. "If you didn't have to perform in the Shogun's courtyard soon at the O-Bon festival, I'd show you how to make a proper bow to a lord."

"I have the most marvelous new stories of what is happening in Edo, and if we can all get drunk I will tell them. Utamaro is again in trouble. Poor chap—some woman he loved is dead so he drinks. And they say we do too many prints of gay subjects, that our art encourages frivolity and immorality. Our Shogun presses us artists hard."

Lord Ito nodded. "He is right. It's a vulgar art, not justified by tradition. I am surprised Heacock Sir collects it."

Hokusai wiped his nose on his sleeve, winked, and drank again deeply. "Utamaro has greatly offended the court in his series about the great military hero Hideyoshi amusing himself with his five concubines. The court is furious. He has been sentenced to fifty days in prison, with his hands held in chains. Imagine an artist's hands chained up. It is too much. More *sake*, I weep."

Sharaku had wandered off to join O-Kita and Cat in the garden. The three older men sat and drank and talked. Hokusai gave them the gossip of the theaters, brothels, teahouses and artists' studios.

By dusk all were very drunk, and Lord Ito was making lists of his enemies to put to the sword. Hokusai was performing a dance, with vegetables from the kitchen stuck into his clothes and piled on his head. Daniel was singing a sea chanty, "Blow The Man Down." Sharaku, Foxy, and O-Kita somehow got them all to their sleeping pads.

The next morning they rose late and soaked in the hottest bath water, groaning and holding their heads. It was afternoon before Lord Ito's procession and the household started back to Edo. Lord Ito and Daniel rode ahead on horseback, Hokusai and Cat were in a cart, and Sharaku walked by the side of O-Kita's litter, retelling the famous old story of Gengobei, the

Mountain of Love. In the cart Hokusai fell fast asleep and Cat tickled him with a straw.

JOURNAL OF DOCTOR DANIEL HEACOCK

"We are back at the castle, and O-Kita is unhappy. She says over and over she thinks Lord Ito dislikes her. But I think she did not want our idyl to end. I know I didn't. Will I ever have such peace again?

"O-Kita is part of me, and her body, the caprices I share with her, are my life now. With her I have again reached a plateau of excellence. There are no signs now of a seizure. Whatever remains of my life will be a series of mornings and evenings with her.

"I saw the Shogun immediately after my arrival here, and removed the last of the stitches. He is really doing quite well.

"I went walking after I saw the Shogun. I like walking these streets, inhaling festival dust, the smell of old paper, the odors of beans, rice, pickles and fish that come from the small eating places. I am aware of the orange color over the city, its patched historic appearance, the glimpses of green from the park with the servants leading and pushing the overdressed children, already tacky from rice candy, through the streets. Even the life of the poor I get used to. The soot and dust, the chicken droppings, and the general sense of pulsating life in the gutters. Perhaps it is my mood. And I thought of escape. I wonder why escape should come to my mind now? Perhaps I sense the future. But I am too much at ease to think it out today."

17

It was a warm day and sunny and the court nobles and officials, and many guests, were packed on the roofs and balconies of the castle. The Shogun in yellow silk sat high up on a balcony, surrounded by his officials and the soldiers of the palace guard. The lords and princes from the entire island were happy to be so close to the Shogun.

Lord Ito stood in the back of the Shogun's balcony and he looked across to a balcony were Daniel and a pale O-Kita were talking to the artists Hokusai and Sharaku. Lord Ito was not happy. He wished this public ceremony were over; the world seemed too full of deceptive consolations.

The artist Hokusai descended from the balcony. The artist stood in the vast empty courtyard with his arms folded while a boy held a huge ten-foot broom toward him.

Hokusai, well known for his surprising tricks in public painting, bowed and took the broom. Twirling it in front of him, he addressed himself directly to the Shogun on his balcony overhead and bowed very low.

"Your Highness, I am honored, much as I do not deserve it, in being permitted to entertain you again with my art. I have painted with my fingers, with toothpicks, with a *sake* bottle, with an eggshell. I have painted with my left hand from the bottom up, from left to right, and I must add in all modesty, the paintings turned out better than I had expected. Once I even painted two flying sparrows on a grain of rice."

Two boys were carefully carrying out a pickle vat on a litter, a vat full of black ink, several gallons of black ink. Daniel turned to O-Kita. "What is he going to do?"

"I suppose paint the courtyard," she said listlessly.

"But it's about two hundred yards square."

Sharaku nodded. "That's why he's asked everyone to be on the balconies and the roofs."

"He's a wonderful devil," Daniel said. "What's he up to this time?"

Sharaku handed O-Kita back her fan; she had dropped it as Prince Taira stepped out on a nearby balcony. Sharaku said, "In the courtyard of Gokokuji temple, Hokusai once did a painting as big as this. He's beginning."

Hokusai had dipped his huge broom, its head as big as a water buffalo's, into the ink vat. "And now, Your Highness, so big is this thing that only from above will you be able to see what I am about to draw."

He lifted out the dripping broom and began to run around the courtyard dragging the ink-loaded broom across the yellow courtyard tiles. The two boys with the barrel of ink on the litter followed him. Hokusai danced here, danced there, always dragging his broom, stopping now and then to dip it freshly into the ink vat, then stepping back to make here a circle, there a dot, thickening a line to the wideness of a bridge timber, dragging out a line to the thinness of a spear shaft. At first there were only long lines, curves that seemed to follow no set pattern. Then slowly it all began to take on the shape of an immense man.

Daniel shaded his eyes and looked down. "Yes, it's a man, all right. Some saint, I think. O-Kita, what is it?"

O-Kita looked down at the running artist dragging his large inky broom over the tiles. He was now running over the figure's head as the broom began to outline hair, a great ear, a huge nose, breathing and alive. "It's the Buddist saint and patriarch, Daruma."

Daniel almost shouted with amazement. "Two hundred yards of painting! And done so quickly."

Sharaku said quietly, standing behind O-Kita, "And done so well. The saint is ready to walk off. He's a real man, with life in his limbs."

Daniel looked down at the drying lines of ink. "Yes, it's certainly alive. What an artist is our friend Hokusai!"

There was great cheering from roofs and balconies. The Shogun nodded approval.

Hokusai stood proudly, bowing, his robe, hands and face soiled with sooty ink. Then he leaned on his broom the way a samurai leans on his sword after a great battle. Behind him the giant figure of the saint dominated the courtyard and the castle; dominated the entire crowd who were shouting their pleasure at the great feat.

Sharaku said, "For this they should bury him honorably some day in the garden of Togakuji temple at Kita-Matsuyamacho."

"Don't be so gloomy, Sharaku," said Daniel. "O-Kita isn't very cheerful either today. The two of you tell each other some funny stories. I have an appointment now."

O-Kita bowed and Daniel pressed her arm through the

sleeve of her robe. He went down to the courtyard where the ink of the drawing had dried a beautiful jet black. He patted Hokusai's back as the artist, sipping a bowl of *sake*, grinned. Daniel said, "If you could roll this drawing up I would buy it."

"Yes, if I only could. Tomorrow the castle servants will wash it away with the horse brine and droppings, and one of the world's great drawings will be lost forever. Better maybe to design stiff *uchiwa* fans for the ladies. Drink with me."

"Some other time. I have my duties too."

Daniel crossed to the main palace where Lord Ito was waiting for him. They went down long halls to a room where the Shogun, looking tired and pale, was reclining on a pile of red silk mats.

Daniel bowed and took the Shogun's pulse. "Does Your Highness feel any pain?"

"There is a drawing, a plucking, at my wounds."

"That's the last of the stitching. You need a small operation. I want to pull out the last ones. Those I can't reach will do you no harm. They will be absorbed by the body in time."

The Shogun took a drink from an attendant and waved the servant out of earshot. "Lord Ito thinks you should work on me at his house, when it gets dark."

Daniel shrugged his shoulders. "It would be better if you rested more."

The Shogun said, "We shall, soon. I want to think now."

In the hall Lord Ito took Daniel's arm. "My friend, you must not leave your rooms today."

"Why the devil not?"

"We think Prince Kwammu Taira will make his move to get rid of the Shogun tonight. His party and his forces have been secretly moving into the city, bit by bit. Some of the court nobles are with him. Not too many, but it will bear watching."

"It's hard to believe in all this sunshine and beauty."

"As your friend I advise you: say nothing to anyone. To *anyone*, I repeat. *Anyone* can be an agent of Prince Taira."

Daniel looked at the slim young lord, who nervously chewed on his lips. "No, that can't be. One must trust other men. Who would betray the Shogun?"

"It is usual to use anyone for this sort of thing. Remember, they can only obey. They are nothing. Prince Taira is powerful here."

Daniel frowned and shook his head. "It's a rotten thing— to use people in this way."

"You must stay in your rooms. Whatever you hear, do not come out. If we move the Shogun back to my house for the new operation, I will have you brought there at twilight. There is some pain again, as you saw."

"He's a very brave man," Daniel said, as a long file of samurai in full armor began to crowd past him.

He walked to his rooms, gloomy and upset, aware of unusual activity about the castle. He glanced toward O-Kita's terrace. Men in the basketwork helmets of the police were patroling it.

Daniel went to look for Foxy; he wanted to be sure his pistols were primed and loaded in case there was really a palace revolt in progress. He felt a slight spinning, a distortion of focus, before his eyes.

He thought of O-Kita, and of a saying he had heard from a French doctor in Canton. "I love you less than tomorrow, but more than yesterday." The spinning did not go away, the focus continued to blur. He suddenly realized he was going to have a seizure within the next twelve hours. He supposed the excitement about the castle had re-awakened the forces inside him with more sharpness than usual, coming after the peaceful hiatus at Lord Ito's house.

Foxy watched Daniel staring at him with his dark eyes. Daniel said, "Stop looking at me. Is there any of the Holland gin left? Get it."

"There is one small bottle. You said you wanted it saved."

"Never mind that now. Get it out. I'm going out to drink it with a friend."

Foxy said softly, eyes down, "O-Kita . . . is not in her rooms. She went out with a litter someone sent for her."

Daniel rubbed his eyes. He had that uneasy floating sensation now, his feet seemed at least several inches off the floor. He swam through the air as if it were water and he a fish. Yes, a major seizure was coming, and coming very soon. He took the stone bottle from Foxy and filled a *sake* cup with gin. He swallowed the burning stuff at a gulp and shook his head to keep back the tears of reaction from the strong alcohol. The buzzing stopped and he sank his heels down onto the floor. But before he took a second drink it was all back. In uncontrollable rage he flung the *sake* cup into a corner and it broke into little shards of porcelain. He sat down on the floor and drank from the bottle in panic, but nothing could stop the steady march of lightness and unreality that preceded a seizure of his disease. It was not really unpleasant; he felt larger, above worldly things, able to think quicker; but the panic remained.

He sat staring numbly at the floor. He took out his journal and began to write slowly while Foxy cleaned up the fragments of the broken *sake* cup.

"I am here in a desperate isolation," he wrote, "among strangers. I don't belong here. I am not wanted. I must go on, anywhere but home. My whole picture of existence is dark. I am alone in a hostile, violent world. I can feel it about to break out all around me. O-Kita is all that keeps me anchored to the earth. I should be with her now. I don't want the world and its wars, its fame, or rewards.

"Am I writing now out of fear of my illness, which has one arm locked around my shoulder, and will soon grip me stronger than a lover across the throat, and lock its legs in a bear hug with my legs, and then throw me to the ground. It's getting dark outside. I feel, taste, touch the immutable hostility of the universe. My hands tremble . . . I can't write . . . It will be soon now. *Soon* . . ."

He closed the journal and sat, head on hands. Foxy came in and Daniel looked up. There was a purple twilight outside the windows. "Hasn't Lord Ito sent for me yet? I'm supposed to see the Shogun at his house."

"No, it's very still here, Heacock Sir. Suddenly very still."

Daniel listened. There was now no clanging of guards, no heavy step of samurai, no scurrying footfalls of servants.

"Never mind. I'm going to Lord Ito's house. It's important

that I see the Shogun now, not later, when, when . . . Never mind. You stay here. Protect O-Kita when she comes back. Things are happening. I'll be back soon."

Foxy watched the big man lurch through the low door, ducking his head as he went out. Foxy had been with Daniel through two major seizures on the Dutch trading island near Nagasaki. He knew the symptoms, and that he must not be alone at such a time, or among strangers. Foxy got a dark robe and hurried after Daniel.

Daniel walked down the lane in the night air thick with moths and the smell of cherry blossoms. He did not share the natives' love for cherry blossoms, and his New England conscience did not approve of raising trees just to blossom and not give fruit. There was a strange stillness, but he put this strangeness down to his approaching seizure. There only seemed to be fewer lights in the lanes and fewer people standing in doorways. Summer lightning, yellow-tongued and crisp, forked in the sky and the roll of thunder rang out from far off near the cone of the famous mountain. All he could think of was of one of Hokusai's prints of Fuji in a storm. But there was no storm coming; the air was dry and warm, and wind that did not cool ran around his feet, carrying silently in its invisible teeth the bits of torn paper and straw at the end of a busy street day.

Daniel had reached that state of lightheadedness where reality and imagination were one. He moved on, not feeling ground or seeing much but a kind of tunnel ahead of streets and garden walls. He turned in toward Lord Ito's house and he wanted only to see the Shogun and then lie down and get this seizure over with. He must not be caught out here alone when it came. He needed help to keep from harming himself when he fell.

There was a yellow battle lantern in Lord Ito's garden, and men with great bleeding cuts on their faces, and red-stained swords in their hands. Daniel felt no shock at this; it was part of the pattern now, he accepted everything. Even the soldiers parting and letting him pass. On the terrace before the house several samurai in full armor lay dead, many of them horribly cut by the sharp razor-edged swords used for close fighting. One man was pinned to the terrace by a spear through his head, but he had been dead for some time; the blood under him had turned black, Daniel clinically noticed.

As he entered the house he saw a retainer of Lord Ito cutting the throat of a wounded man. The man screamed and Daniel knew this was real and no vision. Shock came. He saw that a fearful battle had raged desperately through the gardens up the terrace and into the very rooms of the house. Dead samurai, undramatic lumps of flesh, lay in all corners, and the delicate walls of paper and wood were torn and splashed with red and there was already a slaughterhouse odor.

Daniel stumbled over a disconnected hand holding a sword and moved heavily into the room where he usually examined the Shogun. Great lanterns stood on a floor of mats trampled and soiled. The lanterns cast half-black, half-white shadows on several men in full battle armor, some wounded, all soiled by sweat and grime. They were, Daniel saw, the nobles who had examined him at the wrestling match.

Lord Ito came forward, a cut across one cheek, pale and taut under a fearful helmet of horns and ear flaps. The iron armor on his chest was dented and cut and he carried a sword that had been recently used. When he spoke it was not Daniel's friend at all, but a man hysterical with some rigid madness of combat. Daniel hazily wondered if Lord Ito was drugged or drunk.

Lord Ito's breath came from a taut throat. "You were not to be here. No."

"You didn't send for me. I thought you forgot."

"No. There was an attempt here on the life of the Shogun. The attempt is over."

"Was the Shogun hurt?"

"He was not here. We learned of this plan at the last minute and sent him to a castle of a faithful lord."

The nobles behind Lord Ito were making gasping sounds, their faces terrible to watch as they leaned on their bloody swords. Daniel's mouth was dry and his tongue seemed much too large for his mouth. He held on to a wall; the preliminary symptoms of a seizure were closing in on him. He held on grimly, his fingernails clawing at the wall.

"What . . . happens . . . now, Lord Ito?" He spoke with difficulty.

"It has all been done. Many are dead all over Edo. Here the best of Prince Taira's force died, or are dying. We too have lost many men. But the *goroyu*—the Shogun's council—remained loyal."

"I don't feel well, but if I can attend the wounded . . ."

"The badly wounded get quick mercy. I am sorry you came. We have captured Prince Taira at the castle and brought him here."

"Judgment on Prince Taira is being passed here?" Daniel asked, eyeing the grim nobles and samurai.

One of the wounded nobles said, "Justice is an abstract word. Death is not."

Lord Ito motioned to the wide opening into the next room.

Daniel leaned in the doorway and held a hand over the doorsill to keep from falling. Reality was fighting his seizure and losing.

On the floor of the inner room knelt Prince Kwammu Taira, his arms tied to his sides. With one bound hand he was twirling slowly and deliberately a heavy rosary, a set of Buddhist prayer beads. The old prince was dressed in a plain white kimono, and a white band of cloth was tied around his head in some ritual pattern. Lord Ito went into the room followed by a powerful samurai carrying a large sword.

Lord Ito nodded and the samurai untied the old prince's arms. The old man was unfrightened, his poise was untouched and his face calm.

Lord Ito lay a sword wrapped in white cloth before the kneeling figure. "For what you have done and planned there can be no mercy. But you are a prince. You know what to do. Do it."

Prince Taira said, "This is no time to think of human pettiness or worldly ambitions. There will be other Emperors to free at Kyoto."

"Prepare yourself, Prince Taira. With dignity, but hurry. There is much more to be done. Not everyone gets the mercy of preparing his own departure through the last *torii* gate."

"I thank you for the honor. I would like to die meditating but I am old and have already meditated too much." He bowed three times to the Buddhist altar in the room and picked up the sword. He wound the white cloth around the hilt and read the letters engraved on the blade: "To die with honor when one can no longer live with honor." With two hands he placed the sword below the ribs on the left side of his thin body.

"I ask forgiveness for all my ways that have been wrong, for all my sins and habits, my paltry amusements and my greedy way of life. I am aware I am unworthy of this good death. I know only that I have lived a long time and done too many things for pleasure, for vanity, and because I was a great prince and such are the ways of princes. *Namu myoko renge kyo*."

Daniel was aware of the great hammering heat under the low ceilings, and the odor of slaughter was closing in on him like an invisible vise, constricting his breath. He gasped and made a sound of struggle in his chest.

Prince Taira was praying in a low voice. Out loud he said, "One does many bad things. This last thing I felt was right. Burn *nusa* to it. It could have been you here now, Lord Ito, holding the sword, waiting for life to leave you through a sword cut."

"Yes, Prince Taira. I know that." Lord Ito looked at the giant samurai holding his sword. "I have granted you the extra stroke."

"For this last kindness I thank you."

Prince Taira muttered one more prayer. Daniel saw his arms flex, the body hump itself and a gasp of pain come out and the white robe was stained bright pink. The body shook as if in fever, the arms moved across and up, and the head fell forward. Daniel saw the lean stringy neck of a very old man. Lord Ito gestured and Daniel only saw the whirl of the samurai's sword in the air and the lean neck suddenly held no head.

Daniel turned away, mouth open, bands of pain across his head, an acid fire in his entrails. He found himself sucking up *sake* someone had handed him and Lord Ito was looking at him. "You are very ill."

"The sickness I told you of. It's on me."

"I will take you to the house of another *daimyo* where you will be safe."

"No, take me to the castle. My friends will care for me."

Lord Ito, grim as a skull, stared at him. "Heacock Sir, my friend, I must tell you something. O-Kita Mitsu has been arrested."

"What! Why?"

"She was an agent for Prince Taira. She reported to him all that she could learn of us and of you."

Daniel began to yell, beyond shame or control. "What the devil do I care! I don't care what she is! I tell you I need her!" Daniel grabbed Lord Ito by the sleeves of his robe. "You can't do this to her!"

Lord Ito covered Daniel's shaking hands with his own steady fingers. "It is unseemly to act this way over a geisha. I am your friend, and so I forgive you. I know you are an outsider, and not trained like us to control your emotions in public."

Daniel almost fell, and two nobles assisted him to stand. Lord Ito said quietly, "We will take you to her. Her fate, however, is in other hands."

Daniel was not at first aware of anything beyond the shock of the cold night air and the bouncing of a litter. Then there were steps, and the stink of long reeking corridors of stone, and the jail smell and the straw and dirt of a prison.

In a stone cell, in the light of torches held by cruel faces, O-Kita crouched in a soiled robe, chained at her waist and feet to a wall. Daniel was vaguely aware of her and of the seeping of water and the buzzing in his head. His eyes took a long time to focus in the dimness.

Two steps led down to the wall to which O-Kita was chained. She was staring at him, her hands held to her sobbing throat. Her mouth was open but she could not speak. He heard only low gasping sounds, and then a voice he could not believe was his own rasped out, "O-Kita!"

He tried to reach her as the shifting torches threw red and black patterns on the wall. The smoke made twisting curls of black soot in an atmosphere smelling of night pots and rotting straw.

The roof of the world parted as he touched her and he was stretched by agony twenty feet tall and a great steel trap shut over his head and he fell for what seemed a long time and the first unhuman scream of the seizure of his illness came from his knotted throat and echoed on the heavy stone walls and his mouth opened and foam came out and he howled again. He hit the rush-covered dirt of the floor and rolled over and began to choke, making animal sounds so dreadful that the prison guards moved back and a torch fell in terror in a shower of sparks. O-Kita recoiled from him in horror and disgust.

Only Lord Ito ran forward and hunted for his tongue, recalling that Daniel had told him of the danger of choking, and all Daniel remembered as he howled like a rabid wolf was the thin sad face of his friend as it expanded and contracted and the great black tunnel sucked Daniel down into the mercy of unconscious darkness . . .

In the void of nothing there was a red spark, and it bored a tiny flame into the brain. Then it spun itself out and the fleck of pain became big as a disc of gold and there was a fire burning to ash under his eyelids. And peace came. The calmness went on for a long time. His mind knocked on his eyelids for an exit as if they were doors and the man was aware of being very tired and very calm. He had found rest. Most likely he was dead now, and he smiled inwardly at the wonder and relaxing of death. What a fool to have feared it. There was no pain, no panic, no tensions. What did death look like? He opened his eyes, wary and amused, and he was in a beautiful golden world with dark green space and cloud patterns. And there was no sound. He contentedly closed his eyes to sleep, and was happy that death kept sleep sacred.

The dead awake from sleep just as the living do, Daniel discovered. And awake, he saw that the dead live in a world just like the Sistine Chapel. He was looking up at the great ceiling paintings by Michelangelo he had once seen in Rome.

He shouted, "No, No! I want the other place for the dead! I want to be with O-Kita!" No one answered.

The world of Michelangelo came leaping and twitching to life. The gods and bodies painted by the master flew around Daniel, cavorting in a rocky void with a thunder of purpose as Old Testament shapes broke out of lethargy into a sense of the inevitable.

God was dividing the Light from the Darkness, swirling in smooth action His wonders to perform. He created the Sun and the Moon. His angels rushed to follow His order. The beard of God was long and beautiful, and His hands were hands of work and creations.

Daniel said softly, "So I've returned in death to the New England Bible of Aunt Rose and not to the Nirvana of Buddha."

God divided the Waters from the Earth, and there was the Creation of Man. Adam naked on the rock of the new Earth, big-boned and tired with the process of being created and God's finger breathing life into the noble frame while His angels hide in His great cloak, wondering if perhaps he was making a mistake in giving this thing Life in His own image.

An auspicious beginning, Daniel felt sadly, and from the ribs of the sleeping Adam a woman appeared—a Woman with a great belly and big thighs, the mother of all races, a creature of sorrow and strength and, of course, weakness. She was not pretty, this Eve, but Michelangelo never painted a pretty woman in his life.

"Hokusai and Utamaro," Daniel said, "did more beautiful women."

Swiftly he saw the Fall of Man and The Expulsion, and so into the Great Flood that wiped out the sins of mankind—and wiped out Man, too, all except Noah.

Daniel shouted, "No, no. I don't belong here! The dead have a right to choose! Take away this Old Testament! I want Buddha, Kwannon, Amida. I'm finished with the world by King James, by Michelangelo. I've left it!" Still protesting, he again fell asleep, disturbed, contorted.

When he awoke he was looking up at celestial Buddhist pine trees and clouds from old Chinese scrolls. He repeated carefully and slowly words he had heard a Zen monk recite: "I have brushed out all things from my mind. I give up all desires, I discard all words, I am being carried into the unknown, touched by an unseen power. I have lost the boundaries of my physical body, I am standing in the center of the universe. Many, many people are coming toward me. All are the same man. All are myself! Why have I never known them? I once believed I was created, but now I know I was never created. I am creation. I am the universe."

Dead, and whoever he was now, he slept again, this time in peace and contentment.

18

"I swear by Apollo, the physician, and Aesculapius, and Health, and All-heal, and all the gods and goddesses, that, according to my ability and justment, I will keep this Oath and this stipulation . . ."

It seemed foolish to repeat the oath now that he was dead and lying on his back under the blue bowl of sky, pine trees and clouds in the Buddhist afterworld.

"I will follow that system of regimen, which, according to my ability and judgment, I consider for the benefit of my patients, and abstain from whatever is deleterious and mischievous. I will give no deadly medicine to any one if asked, nor suggest any such counsel . . . With purity and with holiness I will pass my life and practice my Art . . ."

He hadn't, he knew, always practiced with purity and holiness, but he had done his work with skill and with a feeling of compassion, and he had been rewarded, for now he was within the gates of this Heaven; it could only be Heaven with such great Japanese pine trees.

"Into whatever houses I enter, I will go into them for the benefit of the sick, and will abstain from every voluntary act of mischief and corruption; and, further, from the seduction of females . . ."

He tried to laugh and it came out clear and amused; seduction, he had found out while alive, was a myth. The female, pursued, always managed to catch the male. He thought of O-Kita, and there was pain in his head trying to recall an incident that took place in the other world, some danger that no longer mattered now that he was dead.

There was no wind in the pine trees, and the clouds did not move. There was panic in him; was he suspended, inanimate, in limbo, where nothing would stir in a million, million eons and was this Hell after all, where one could see but not touch— What the devil was Foxy doing here staring down at him?

"You are feeling better, Heacock Sir?" Foxy's voice came to him with surprising clarity.

Daniel asked, in tender concern, "Did something happen to you too, Foxy? We are sharing the same hereafter?"

"Here-after-what?" Foxy asked, holding a cup of something sweet to Daniel's lips. He drank, lifting his head, and he saw that the pine trees and clouds were painted all along a wall and a ceiling, and that he was on strange sleeping pads. The back of his head ached worse than ever. Foxy put down the cup.

"You cracked your head on the stone floor when you fell down."

"When was that?"

"Last night."

"Where am I now?"

"This was once Prince Taira's house. But he is dead. He has joined his honorable ancestors in a most honorable way." Foxy grinned and stabbed himself in the groin with a finger.

"Where is O-Kita?"

Foxy's face went bland and expressionless. "Oh yes. O-Kita. I will find out."

Daniel put out an arm and grabbed Foxy by the collar of his robe. "Don't get Oriental with me, Foxy. She was—I remember now—in prison . . . last night, wasn't it? Chained to the wall?"

"Yes."

"They must be mad to think she was an agent for Prince Taira. What kind of people are you, to treat a woman like that?"

"She has fully confessed," said Foxy, offering him the sweet drink again. Daniel took a long sip; the seizure and blow on his head had left him weak.

"Do you think it matters much that . . ." Daniel felt drugged and was aware now there was something in the drink that would put him back to sleep. "I don't . . ." he added, and he fell back on the sleeping pads.

When he came awake again it was afternoon . . . and Hokusai, looking very tired, was kneeling by his side fanning him slowly.

Daniel said, "Something terrible is going on."

The artist nodded. "I have been trying to awaken you."

"I was drugged."

"We must go to the castle and see Lord Ito."

Daniel turned and sat up, running fingers through his growing hair, his topknot undone.

"I don't know if I ever want to see him again. It's all become distasteful to me. This whole world of cherry blossoms and blood, cruelty and bowls of goldfish. Buddha smiling everywhere and people dying in fearful agony."

Hokusai said, "O-Kita has been condemned to death with all the other agents of the departed Prince Taira."

Daniel sat up straight and grabbed the artist's arm, halting the steady movement of the fan. "Help me to my feet, Hokusai. Has the Shogun gone mad as Nero?"

"No one knows what has happened. Nothing has been announced. There is a great silence at the castle. But many bodies are being burned and most of them carry their heads under their arms."

"What prison is O-Kita in?"

"She has been moved to the place from where no one comes out on his own feet. On the river by the big bridge."

Daniel, standing, held on to the wall and looked around as the once calming painting seemed to mock him. Leaning on Hokusai he walked out into the yellow afternoon sunlight. Daniel wondered how the rest of the world could remain so calm and indifferent in brocaded silk with tranquil faces . . .

At the castle, where golden pheasants with iridescent three-foot tails strutted, the guard had at first refused Daniel and Hokusai entrance, but Hokusai, his hands moving in quick gestures, had told some story, speaking so fast Daniel never could remember it. When they reached the captain of the guard it took at least a half an hour before they were shown into a small room hung in black and gold.

At one end of the room Lord Ito sat cross-legged at a low

table, brush in hand, writing with great speed on long sheets of paper bearing the Shogun's crest. He looked up at Daniel as the guards pushed Hokusai out of the room.

"You fell down hard, my friend. I am pleased that you are up and better."

"My head hit the stone floor."

"I have tried to make you comfortable. The Shogun has taken over Prince Taira's house. Use it."

"Where is O-Kita?"

Lord Ito put down his writing brush and put his arms into his sleeves. "In the proper hands."

"She's to be killed, I hear."

"It is a police matter. She was one of Prince Taira's agents. She reported to him on your doings, on everything she knew. She has, of course, confessed everything."

"I'm sure she did. Under torture!"

"It doesn't matter. She is guilty."

"I want to see the Shogun. He owes me a favor. A large one. A very large one. He would have been insane or dead in two months if I hadn't saved his life. And he had better see me or I'll spread the story of his illness and operation all over Edo. Or will you have me murdered too? You do and there will be an American squadron-of-war sailing into your damn harbors, blowing your paper civilization to hell."

Lord Ito looked down at the table. "When a man is angry over a woman he says things no one should hear. The enormity of his bad manners can not be admitted; I have heard nothing."

"You heard what I said and what I want. I'm going to the Shogun, and if his guards run their lances through me, just remember you've helped in your own petulant way to destroy your precious country. My death will bring a curse on you all."

Lord Ito seemed to sigh at the inherent failings of human relationship. "I still hear nothing that will end our friendship." He clapped his hands. "You are still my friend. I will do what can be done. If there is time. Sit down."

A young man in a black hemp robe came in. Lord Ito brushed letters quickly on a slip of paper, whispered in the ear of the young man, who bowed and went out with the paper. Lord Ito stood up and talked earnestly to Daniel. "I have no control over the police. The Shogun has given them full power. I have just asked them not to proceed with O-Kita until they hear from the Shogun. What has been done so far cannot be turned back like the skin on a plum. I do not know if the Shogun will grant you her life. Sometimes no understanding of love is possible to a man fighting for his own life."

Daniel did not look up. His despair had drowned his anger. "Do what you can. This means everything to me."

Lord Ito said, "As you say, the Shogun owes you something. He is generous, but he is a just man. He is also human. And he has lived in the shadow of this court rebellion, ill as he was, for some time. His anger is great at anyone, no matter how much a dupe, who became involved in it."

"Your women are slaves. You know they have no rights. Could she refuse to do what Prince Taira ordered?"

"Our codes are not your codes, nor our ways your ways. You will never know us well."

"I'm beginning to see that. Let me go to the Shogun with you."

"No, no. You would show your anger and your head would come off. Rest here. If you want anything clap your hands."

Lord Ito lifted his eyes up to Daniel's face. "My friend, your pain hurts me. But there are times in every life when the way is clearly marked and we cannot change it."

When Daniel was alone he sat down on the floor mats and buried his face in his arms. His surroundings for the first time seemed completely alien and hostile. He disliked this place.

Daniel, angry, fearful, abusive, restless, waited a long time. He waited a week. Every day he went to the castle. They brought him grapes, pears and persimmons but he couldn't eat. He paced, he sat, he examined the blank walls and ceiling. Despondency and fear for O-Kita etched images of horror on his mind. He remembered all his night-long experiences with O-Kita, aware now that memory hoards images that we do not fully value at the time—images of pleasure, of frenzied happiness.

At the end of a week the young man with the black hemp robe came bowing to see him. "Lord Ito begs for you to go to the house of Prince Taira at once and wait. He has at last arranged for you the release of a friend."

"It's been done?"

"I have said all Lord Ito told me to say. Go please now and wait."

He told Foxy to prepare a meal, to open fresh wine, and to be sure there was no noise from the servants when they came to the house that had belonged to Prince Taira. Apprehension and hope filled his mind.

It was dusk and lanterns were just being lit when Daniel heard the grunt of litter bearers as they set down palanquins from their aching shoulders. Daniel in a fresh robe stood in the doorway.

O-Kita came toward him in the dusk. She walked slowly, head down, between Hokusai and Sharaku. The two artists waited as she stepped forward into the light of the lamps. Daniel saw that she wore a dark veil over her face.

She said softly as she bowed to Daniel, "Send the servants away."

Daniel, mustering all his emotional resources, heard Foxy bark an order behind him and the lamps were put down on the ground. He came close to O-Kita. She lifted slowly and with both hands, as if it were a ceremony, the dark veil. The beauty of her face had been destroyed by sharp iron combing.

He heard her sob. The veil fell back into place. He took her in his arms, unable to tell if the sparks dancing in the night were horrors or fireflies. Below in the garden Hokusai and Sharaku stood silent and still. There was no breeze. Not a leaf stirred.

Incommunicable and silent rage filled Daniel. *"Irasshai—* please come in," he said.

Alone with her in the large room with the *shoji* screens pushed back so that they could smell and sense the garden, with no lamps lit, Daniel sat with O-Kita. He faced her, holding her hands in his. He could just make her out in the soft darkness; he could see the gleam of her teeth but none of the horror of her cruelly destroyed beauty.

She had accepted her mutilation more calmly than one should, Daniel felt. He wondered how well he had really known O-Kita. She had come out of her ordeal broken, but not fully destroyed. Some core of acceptance he could not understand seemed to have served as a calming influence. He controlled his great anger and his tragic pity with taut effort.

She said, "It is nothing to talk about. I am destroyed. But I promise, Danhil, I will not drown myself."

"I'll tell the Shogun of this. There will be some punishment. He must be made to understand the horror of this."

"That will not remove the scars, not heal smoothly my torn face. Besides, I think there is a sort of justice in this. I should not have fallen in love with you, Danhil. You are not of us. I dreamed too high and I lost my wings."

"Don't talk that way. We are together."

"No, Danhil. We aren't together. I'm not the person you thought you loved. And you're not my fairy-tale hero anymore. It's real now and not beautiful. I made you get the falling sickness."

"No, no . . . I've had it a long time."

"Let's not talk as if we could stay as we were. It's all changed."

He knew she was weeping, tears flowing down the torn flesh. He put out a hand in the dark and touched her skin, feeling the scabby harshness of the healing wounds. She moved her head away with an intake of breath. His hand followed her and caressed lightly the destroyed face.

"Danhil, Danhil," she said very low, and sank against him. He said nothing more and they sat through the night, his arms around her. He remembered her weeping, now in full release. He felt the ache and stiffness of holding her against him, and the tiredness that came down on him before dawn as sleep came to him in his painful position, to blot out the dreadful things that he could not yet believe.

He rolled away from fitful dreams with the sun in his face. In the distance he saw a scud of black clouds around the top of Fuji. He reached for O-Kita to reassure her in the full glare of sun.

There was no one on the mats by his side. He rubbed his face in wonder, stood up and walked about. He passed a mirror and looked in it. His blond hair had grown in like fuzz, and most of the black was gone from his topknot. He knew now he had been synthetically Japanese.

"Foxy," he called, one arm held over a door sill, leaning on a wall. "Foxy!"

No one came. Daniel, puzzled, went into the little room where the house shrine was. Hokusai sat there barelegged, drawing swiftly on gray paper a battle scene of mounted samurai slashing at each other over the necks and rumps of rearing horses, animals exposing their teeth and iron heels.

Hokusai looked up, restraint painted on his broad face. "Foxy will not come. He has run away. He can not face you this morning."

Daniel looked around, bewildered, on the rim of panic. "What the devil do you mean, run away? He can't face me?"

"O-Kita is gone."

"Gone?"

"Gone away with Sharaku. It's very simple, only you will not at first believe me. You and Sharaku both love her. He's loved her from the moment he met her."

"I knew that, but O-Kita wouldn't . . . I mean—"

"O-Kita returned his love. How much, how soon, we shall never know. She may have just teased him at first. A geisha knows how to tease with charm. Now that she is ruined by . . . well, what she is . . . the two of them, both feeling they are failures, have gone off together."

"This is mad . . . Everything in the last few days is mad."

"Of course—but what is normal?" asked the artist putting down the drawing and taking up Daniel's Holland gin. "Before Foxy ran off he gave me this last bottle of your special drink. He thought you would want it. I would like to try more of it with you."

Hokusai filled two *sake* cups and handed one to Daniel, who sank down beside the artist. "Where did they go? It's just a gesture, I tell you. My falling sickness horrified her. Her torture unbalanced her. Nothing has changed." He was clutching at straws, and he knew it.

Hokusai filled his mouth with gin and swallowed slowly. "I don't know where they went, and if I did it would be foolish to tell you. Sharaku has been badly scarred too; he feels rejected as an artist and makes no more prints. He is off to hunt up his theater friends. And O-Kita made no romantic gesture. Women are not like us. There is a reality in their passions that no man dares dream of. Do you think you could have ever made her happy when every time you looked at her she remembered how her beauty once held you? And does she want to twist the knife of memory inside herself of how it had been every time you made love with her, and she has to hide her face? Or that a dreadful falling sickness can come to you from your love? No."

Daniel, despondent in an envelope of fears, put down his gin untasted and held his head. "To go without a word."

"It is the way in this country to end things quickly. She was taught never to embarrass or to make ugly scenes. Her love was very great for you, but was it real? She saw in the last few days that it was a fine dream only. She saw this unreality destroyed her beauty, for if she hadn't met you, she'd still have a face. Admit it."

"That's true. Or half true. What will happen now?"

"She will make a new life with Sharaku. They can love in a more normal way. After a while does anyone really notice what a wife looks like? The face will heal. The scars will not be so red; they will be closer to what the skin once was. But of course it will always look like a plowed field. To Sharaku who loves her from the inside out it will not matter."

"What do you think my love was?"

The artist slowly poured himself another cup of gin. "Wonderful, but all pretty surface. From the outside in. Like your topknot, your fine robes designed for men built in other ways. A marvelous surface, and you are a fine man. Don't be angry at what I say. I am drunk of course. But I always speak the truth at these times."

"I can't accept anything you say.

"Accept again the true Heacock Sir, which O-Kita has returned to you." Hokusai pointed to a bundle in a yellow cloth in the corner. "She has also returned most of your gifts. You'll find out what when you open the bundle."

"No, you take it, do what you want with it."

Hokusai held up something between two stiff bits of thin wood. "This she also gave you. It's a woodcut print of her I once made."

Daniel gulped the gin. In his mind he could still hear O-Kita reciting:

GEISHA

"I feel emptiness
Grow on the mountain.
The flowers
The eyes of the world
Have all gone away."

19

What was the use now, Daniel Heacock thought, in circum-
venting death or evading family roots? With O-Kita there
had been hope. With her he had been seduced by passionately
lovely moments. But the enjoyment of the moments was lost
in memory and the time of crisis was over and he was left
numb and empty. He would drift now like a leaf on a river
painted by Hokusai.

The afternoon sun of Edo was casting long black shadows
when Lord Ito and his retinue arrived at the house once owned
by Prince Taira, carrying scrolls and artfully wrapped gifts.
The house servants bowed as the retinue entered.

Lord Ito found Daniel on the terrace looking out at the
city below the gardens. Daniel had cut off his topknot, and the
yellow fuzz again covered his head. He had discarded Japanese dress and he wore a wrinkled pair of heavy white canvas
pants that American sailors wore, a blue square-cut jacket
with brown New England bone buttons, and blunt-toed heavy
shoes that seemed to set the big man closer to the earth. He

seemed huge, taller than ever, and completely out of place in this dainty setting.

Lord Ito bowed, ignoring Daniel's icy stare.

"We come from the Shogun. You are now a samurai under the protection of the Tokugawa crest. This house and all its treasures have been given to you."

Daniel remained silent.

"And you will bring much honor to Edo as a physician and surgeon appointed to attend the Shogun, the court and the city."

Two black-robed men held out scrolls, but Daniel did not take them. Lord Ito inhaled and bowed again. "The Shogun makes one condition." He stepped closer and spoke low to Daniel alone. "The geisha O-Kita Mitsu, her life spared, is free to go where she wants, but his Royal Highness considers that it would not be seemly for her to be part of your splendid household now."

"These are the conditions of my honors?"

Lord Ito bowed again. Daniel laughed, neither agitated nor perturbed. The startled people looked up in polite wonder. Daniel shook his head. "O-Kita the geisha is gone. I know I am honored. But I will accept nothing from the Shogun except an escort to the coast, to Osaka, where I will take any ship to any other port where I can get transportation away from Japan."

"That is your only wish?" Lord Ito stood very straight, his voice under quiet control.

"I would like to leave in the morning."

Lord Ito wanted to say something soft and conciliatory, but in his cocoon of manners and breeding, in his pride, and because of his position he could say nothing of what he felt for this stranger who had been his friend, and had suffered deeply as a result. He bowed briskly and said, "Your escort will be ready at cockcrow."

Daniel turned back to the gardens and when he turned around again Lord Ito and his retinue were gone. He was aware of someone slipping up to him. It was Foxy carrying the journal and the ink case.

"Heacock Sir, I am back, miserable coward that I am. Would you perhaps like to write in the journal?"

"No. I'm through keeping a journal. You'll pack just what is needed for my trip, my medical cases—and only what I brought."

"I will come with you on your journeys."

"No, Foxy. I came to Japan four years ago with my medical cases, some clothes, and a silver watch. I leave with them. I want to go the way I came. So you see it hasn't cost me anything at all."

Foxy nodded, bowed and withdrew.

But Daniel, as Foxy had guessed, was tempted to write one last time in the journal:

JOURNAL OF DOCTOR DANIEL HEACOCK

"If I am fortunate, this journal will be lost in my travels. I don't want to reread what I have written in it. It was mostly vanity, and a desire to show myself how superior I was to these strange people. And there are too many passages where the thinness of my philosophy shows through, like the lining in a coat of inferior cloth.

"I think I am now humble enough to recognize the reality of things. I became deluded by beauty and art, and refused to admit that this place is like most corners of the earth. I didn't lose O-Kita; I never really had her.

"I am not angry. My rage is gone, or sleeping. I think clearly but bleakly; the only way to learn about the world is to love it at the risk of pain. But the price is too high, and I am not a whole man. I can hear the revels at the teahouse beginning for another night of senseless orgy. In the latticed doors the miserable courtesans stand, tainted trade goods. Shy men driven by lust walk by, their faces hidden under hats of basket rush. The doormen leer and hold out hands for tips. I once thought all this was romantic and beautiful. I see now what the poet meant when he spoke of the skull beneath the skin. Too bad we are not made entirely of unfeeling bone. They are lighting the *toro* lanterns now, symbols of the soul of the legendary courtesan Tanagiku. For the first time I see her as an actual living, suffering woman, not a pretty legend or a beautiful painting. Art is a liar."

Daniel put down the pen and closed the journal for the last time.

There was a crush of gaily dressed people on the outskirts of the city of Edo. A *mikoshi*, sacred car, covered with the emblems of the deity Hotsei—one of the seven gods of luck—was being carried around a Shinto shrine on the shoulders of devotees. The car was crowned by a crowing cock of gilded wood, and its fluted columns were strung with clanging bells and holy writing. The heavy *mikoshi* moved in bobbing slowness as people pushed against its bearers, trying to touch some section of its sacred sides. There was much noise, the smell of humanity, incense, sandalwood, and the odor of rice and bean cakes cooking in bubbling oil at roadside stands.

Daniel, with Hokusai by his side, pushed past the happy frenzy of worshippers and the young girls who were gesturing through the holy Shinto shrine dance. They reached the steps of an inn near the shrine.

Hokusai said, "What a walk from the city. Look. Some of these girl dancers say they can talk to the dead, or to the gods, and tell the future. Let's ask them about your future."

Daniel shook his head. He looked completely different in European attire, the artist saw. His friend had disappeared.

Daniel said, "No, it doesn't interest me. Where is the damned escort? They were supposed to have horses and baggage here at the first inn outside the city on the Tokaido road."

The artist sat down on the steps of the inn. "It's too crowded today to say a proper goodbye, Heacock Sir."

Daniel watched Foxy come down a lane followed by a dozen soldiers of his escort, porters and several riding horses. "You've been very kind, Hokusai. You are a very great artist and the future will show it. Greatness isn't something one meets often in a lifetime."

"Don't get so serious," said Hokusai. "It doesn't ever matter: the future. What has posterity ever done for *us*, eh? Now, if I had a coin, I'd buy us some cups of *sake* at this inn."

"I'll buy the *sake*," said Daniel as Foxy came up to him, wiping his face.

"So many crowds on the road, so many shrines celebrating festival day we had trouble getting through."

"Escort ready to leave?" Daniel asked, motioning to an inn waitress.

"As soon as you mount."

"Have a drink with us. Waitress, some of your best *sake.*"

The three men stood on the steps of the inn holding their filled cups level with their eyes. Hokusai said, *"Hito wa isa omoi yamu tomo*—others may forget you, but not I . . . very old drinking saying."

They sipped slowly and Foxy, sadly but with a smile, lifted his cup. *"Kaku shi moni arikeru mono wo*—we were together only a little time."

Daniel shook his head. "I have no words worthy of parting."

Hokusai, grinning, picking up a fresh cup of *sake,* rolled his eyes and said, "What are words? *Words* are men's daughters, but God's sons are *things.* And we have been many things, done many things, made many things for each other."

Daniel handed his empty cup to the bowing maid and threw a coin on the low table. Pressing first Foxy's shoulder, then Hokusai's, he walked briskly to the waiting escort in the inn's courtyard and mounted a horse. He waved once and rode off.

When Daniel reached the rise in the brown road that led on and around a bend to the west he turned in the saddle and looked back. Foxy sat on the inn steps, his face buried in his arms; Hokusai was standing feet apart, waving with both hands in the air. The dust raised by the stomping pilgrims rose like a golden pollen through which filtered the great cone of Fuji, placid and symmetrical in the distance. The escort toiled up toward him and Daniel beat his heavy leather heels into the horse's ribs and rode hard, the hoofs on the packed road echoing Foxy's parting words in his head . . . *we were together only a little time . . .*

Epilogue: Figures on a Scroll

1. THE TEAHOUSE KEEPER

Kyoto was a beautiful city, famous for its great stone *komainu* dogs, the Higashi-Hongan-ji temple, Okazaki park, picnics under Tsuten bridge, its gardens and its trees. For men of refinement, used to pleasures, there were many teahouses, of which the most admired was that of Madame Snow.

When she came to Kyoto years ago, to take over the place, it had been called the Teahouse of the Brocade Walls. Now it was known simply as Madame Snow's, and behind its *shoji* walls no *abaremono*, wild fellow, full of sweet potato flatulence, was ever permitted. The dignified guests were greeted by beautiful maids, who bowed and helped them off with their clogs and outer robes and escorted them into rooms filled with beautiful objects of art. The geishas at Madame Snow's were properly trained, very clever, and played exotic music with the easy skill of those who do not have to labor at their art. When later Madame Snow sent for the courtesans, the geishas disappeared with a smile, never looking at their tips. No matter how famous the courtesans, or how high their price, they

263

treated Madame Snow with a respect that they reserved only for their most highly born lovers.

Madame Snow herself was never much in evidence at the teahouse. A corps of ornately dressed and skillful servants saw that her orders and her desires were strictly carried out. She liked to sit meditating on the little porch overlooking the green hills. She sat surrounded by her bowls of goldfish, which she bred and traded with a skill that was admired by collectors and sellers of delicate fish life.

Madame Snow, even for her years, was a striking woman. One could still see in the fine bone structure under the badly scarred skin of her face what a beauty she must have been in her youth. She was known to be a stern mistress, but fair. When she took one of the younger girls into her room as a companion there was a kindness and a tenderness about her that made the girls wonder. She never spoke of her past or looked into a mirror at herself, but all the girls at Madame Snow's got *kagami*, mirrors of the finest white bronze. She would tell them, in a dry, unemotional voice, "The mirror is the soul of woman and when the mirror is dull the soul is unclean."

Madame Snow had many old-fashioned ideas about morality, the gods, and out-moded procedures of behavior. Many girls carried lumps from blows on their heads for not following to the last point of expected behavior the rules of ceremony and ritual that ran the teahouse.

"All significance in life is ritual," she always said.

Madame Snow rested now in the last of the day, a sunset dying in the west. The lords and the princes from the court of the Emperor, bored by their concubines, would come soon for their pleasures. There was more activity now at the jaded court. The fat merchants, who came humbly to the teahouse to spend their money among the impoverished lords, said, "There will soon be a change; the end of the Tokugawas is coming. Japan will be open to the world. You can't stop progress, and wages must be met."

The first litters were arriving in the teahouse garden. Tonight there were to be two parties and a great deal of passing of tips would result. None of it mattered much to Madame Snow. Her assistants, Cat San and Pony San, would take care of things properly. The court lords, despite their poverty, managed to come often, even if they had to sell their best jeweled and golden sword guards. There would be a big merchant from Edo tonight, and there would be male *otoko*, as well as female geishas and singers.

The merchant was entertaining an artist from Edo. Ichiryusai Hiroshige, who did fine enough landscapes in the new manner with much color and some skill. Madame Snow was curious about him. She had seen some of his work. But for her the old artists had been better. Utamaro, Shuncho, Masanobu, Koryusai, all of them fine men who had once drawn and painted her in her youth. Gone now. Hokusai was still said to be alive in Edo, most likely peddling red peppers again, but still drawing.

She got little news from Edo these days and it didn't matter. She rarely thought of her old life, or of a blond giant. Sometimes lately, not often but with increasing regularity, some foreign sea captains, driven ashore or shipwrecked near Kyoto, came to her teahouse before the Shogun's men ordered them away. They were huge bearded men, some with blue eyes and blond hair, but mostly tanned dark as leather. The girls were frightened of them. Madame Snow could talk to the seamen a few words in their own tongue and they would drink their *sake* and shout at each other: "She's a damn attractive biddy herself and some damn Yankee sea lawyer must 'ave crossed her compass, an' you kin bet on the trade winds on that."

Madame Snow sat on her porch feeding her goldfish. Cat came out to her, wallowing in fat, her heavy wrists ending in amazingly small hands making gestures of surprise. "Excuse me, Madame, but the merchant in the red silk asked for a full *tokkuri*, the large bottles of *sake* all at once. Unheard of!"

"Do as he wants."

"The artist Hiroshige has been talking of the new print-makers in Edo. Would you like to see him later?"

"If he wants to talk to me. It's not important. And be sure no one falls asleep in the *benjo* again. Lord Kitao went home all soiled last night."

Cat smothered a giggle and went out with a bow. Madame Snow shook her head. How wide and fat Cat was getting. Someone else would have to take over the teahouse when the time came. Not Cat.

The sun was all gone now, and the little lamps in the houses and in the O-Hara temple were going on. It was a wet spring after a very cold and snowy winter. What did all the parading of seasons matter? Sometimes in the morning after ordinary dreams she would look back to the past. All life, she had learned, was an act of salvage and to catch even one moment of significance in it one had to be very lucky. She had had luck. What lay ahead interested her very little. "What is to happen," she said out loud to her pet goldfish, Otani, "will never make up for the past, good or bad."

Now in the early darkness of night she meditated. "When I see one of those seamen with the power in his arms to lift the biggest geisha off the mats with one hand I again feel the past was once real and I pray, I thank with all my heart. Did we harm anyone? Could it have been different? It was after all only a fairy tale retold, like the bits of compressed prepared dust one throws in water during the festival of the nativity of Buddha and huge flowers appear as the dust becomes swollen with moisture. But in the morning it has all dissolved and become dust again."

A man was bowing to Madame Snow from the doorway. Cat stood behind him and said, "The artist Hiroshige comes to pay his respects."

The man tried to bow again and she saw he was already drunk. He was lean and his eyes were serious eyes, but he was unsteady on his feet.

He sat down facing Madame Snow and she said, "Not many artists come here from Edo."

"I've been walking along the Tokaido. I wanted to paint some theater posters and scenery on the way for some money, and I ran into Yukio, the rice dealer. He gives fine parties."

"Are the artists in Edo still making a great many woodcuts?"

"Too many *ukiyo-e* as usual. Too loud and wildly drawn."

"It is a great art."

"No longer, no longer. Men like Kunisada and the rest, they grind out prints like rice paste. And the publishers are low fellows. The great days are all over, believe me."

"They said the same thing when Kiyonaga and Shuncho were in their prime."

"You knew them, Madame Snow?"

She gave away no personal information. "They were there when I was young. What do they think now of Hokusai?"

"Hokusai?" The artist pouted and rubbed his unshaved chin. "I haven't seen him around for a long time. He hasn't held up well, you know. I don't think anyone will remember him for long."

Madame Snow smiled. "And Sharaku? Someone once told me he was the most original and greatest of all the printmakers, and would be the most famous."

The artist took the bowl of tea Cat handed him. He shook his head. "Sharaku? No, I can't say I remember ever hearing of him."

"He did large heads of actors in a different style."

"Oh." Hiroshige slowly sipped the tea, his hands trembling. "Oh, there was a boy—an actor or something of the sort—used that name once. Ugly things he did. I seem to remember a few. Worthless stuff. Oh, now I know who he was. Went off with some *shirokubi*, a whiteneck, an unlicensed prostitute. They drank and dissipated themselves to death, or he was eaten by a shark. I heard something of the sort. Anyway, it was a sordid thing. Could I have some clams-and-rice? I fear I have drunk too much. I find clams-and-rice help me."

"Of course. We are honored to have you drunk here and in our poor house. Cat, take care of the artist's wants."

268

She did not bow as Hiroshige rose. She looked up. "This Sharaku—he was a bad artist?"

Hiroshige belched. "Worse. An amateur."

When she was alone again Madame Snow lit the two floor lanterns on the porch and stood leaning on the railing, still handsome and slim in her simple robe. What things happen in the world! People say cruel or stupid words without thought. Her own sense of evil these days was not connected with any personal identity. She understood the cruel irrationality of human life. She was alone in time. Her last values, all that remained to her, were courage and loyalty . . . and she had a small weakness for beauty. Life was part holy, she thought, and not fully cruel.

The two teahouse parties were very active. She heard the singing and dancing falling away into a growl of laughter; then there were shrill female cries of "*shibaraku*, stop a minute," and whispered remarks and the whinny of some joke that brought laughter from the *bimbo kuge*, pauper nobles. The little goldfish floated on the bottoms of their bowls, stirring only a feathery fin as they slept with their eyes open. Somewhere along the Tokaido road little pack horses with bells around their short necks were moving under the great black pines toward the wild mountains of Ikigawa and Gokoyama.

In her room, plain except for a row of Noh masks on one wall and a small dwarf pine tree in a shallow blue tray, Madame Snow sat on her sleeping mat. From a hidden drawer she took out a small hand-sewn book of thin paper. It was her only weakness, this writing of secret poems. Not even Cat knew of it. Wetting her best brush, she wrote rapidly, whispering the words as they flew into her mind:

> "O Edo
> In the night
> Through the hall of memory
> I come away
> To you
> Secretly."

2. THE OLD ARTIST

"I understand the very innermost secrets of nature, the things that are the substance of animals, flowers, birds and insects. . . ."

The old man wrote with raw weathered fingers in the white brutality of a fearful winter. He sat in the windy ruin of the cold temple of Skin-shu, a building long since beyond repair, its windows gone, the roof partly fallen in. Here gathered miserable shivering vagabonds and dismissed servants, runaway apprentices, outlaws and priests that no respectable shrine would have. They bent over small pots of charcoal when they could afford it, in bitter cold, when even the water in the drinking cups froze. They lived torpid, desperate lives wrapped in rugs, eating whatever morsels they could beg or steal, or buy for the smallest copper coins they could make in the few miserable jobs they could pick up carrying a load, assisting a gambler to fleece a victim or a woman to prostitute herself in an alley. The old man writing was wrapped in his tattered sack and his several thin summer robes of different colors. He leaned forward to catch what heat was left in the last gray fragment of charcoal and saw that the little fire pot was dead. He put his brush to the ink stone and then went on writing.

"When I am painting birds I feel they can fly away from my paper. So vivid and skillfully are they painted . . ."

He was better off than most other artists he had known, and he had done more. He had even married twice, and that thought gave a wry twist to his toothless mouth. Marriage was like a tiger; exciting to look at, but who wants to own it? He chuckled. Yes, he had tried to live like one born under the *manji*, the sign of a long and happy life. Of course there had been tragedy and many troubles. But the pleasures of drawing and painting, what could come close to them? He sighed and ached for a sip of *sake*, but he was penniless in this wreck of a temple, in the dead of winter, when the hungry foxes sharpened their teeth on stones, and feet of birds of prey froze to their perch.

"From the age of six I had a mania for drawing the forms of things. When I was fifty I had published an infinity of designs."

All that mattered now was that he still painted and drew. The other results of his life had amounted to nothing. Omiyo, the daughter of his first marriage to that woman who was such a bad painter, had given him a grandson, and that grandson had ruined him again and again. A clever boy, he had to admit, but touched by *oni*, evil spirits—always in debt, gambling, a great one for the geishas and the courtesans. He had lost, because of this boy, his house, his portfolios of drawings —everything he had went to pay the grandson's debts. Ah, well, young hot blood. The grandfather had been no saint in his time. No, certainly not.

"But all I have produced before the age of seventy is not worth taking into account. At seventy-five I learned a little about the structure of nature; of animals, plants, trees, birds, fish and insects."

And Oyei, daughter of his second marriage; she was divorced now from the painter Nanchaku Tomei. Now she herself was a fine artist; Oyei painted women better than he did himself. When some pious fat merchant got her to paint him a silk lantern for a temple, the buyer liked it so much he kept it himself and gave the temple a poor paper one. She had even painted him, with a wrinkled face, a chin broad as a jug bottom, big ears and thin remains of grayish hair at the temples.

It was going to be a murderous cold night. In his youth, hot blood had kept him warm.

He and Fuji were all that remained of his youth. He could see the mountain in the clear freezing air, through a crack in the wall where an earthquake had opened an unwanted door into the old temple. A fine mountain standing there over Edo, its sides white with snow, topped by a bitter blue sky of ice. The trees below were bent over, asking for mercy from the cruel wind, and the people huddled into their padded robes, thick cloth tied around their heads, walking quickly as the cold bit to the bone and the little smoke that came up from the straw roofs was torn to bits as soon as the wind caught it in its teeth.

"When I am eighty I shall have made true progress. At ninety I shall penetrate the mystery of things."

And his best things so far had been Fuji. No one could ever look at that mountain and not think of him. He was the artist who had done the famous "Thirty-Six Views Of Fuji" (he had done forty-six, to be exact). What marvelous things he had done in woodcut prints! The great print of "Fuji Seen From Kanagawa," called now "The Great Wave." The huge white finger of the sea crests rising to fill out the menacing storm sky and the small boats scudding before the wind in the thundering blue caves of tumbling water. Men clinging to their wooden sea toys, and in the distance, resting in dignity, Fuji itself, calmly indifferent to the dangers and brevity of existence. A great work. It seemed to warm him a bit just to think of it.

"At a hundred I shall have reached a marvelous stage. At a hundred and ten everything I do, a line, a dot, will live as never before . . ."

Yet tomorrow he would have to earn his frugal bowl of rice once again, find a warmer place to roost, produce something to keep the money lenders from throwing his grandson into jail. Who could he turn to? Everyone he knew was gone. Lord Ito had been amused by the artists, but Lord Ito was dead a long time; had died of the coughing lung sickness as his wife had died before him, spitting up blood, a young man, stern and serious, serving the Shogun to the end. A Shogun still played listlessly with his caged women and issued scrolls signed with his running signature, forbidding contact with the strangers from outside and their strange knowledge. But things were changing faster than ever. The foreign books, the exciting ideas of the outer world were being smuggled in; every student had a forbidden text, every serious person was mastering some of the sciences and crafts that were changing the outside world. The merchants, traders, and artisans had won.

"To all those who will live as long as I do, I promise to show how I keep my word."

He looked up at a tattered print of a map pasted to the temple wall. It had been done by the famous cartographer, Nagakubo Seikisui of Mito, and showed the globe of the world and its great land masses, the names of cities. He was too old now ever to see Amsterdam, New York, London, Madrid, Moscow, and the places to the north marked merely "the people of darkness." He would have liked to buy drinks for the artists there, searching as he was for the great line, the ultimate form. Yes, buy them all a drink of that gin that Heacock Sir had loved. How long ago was that? Not one word had come back from Heacock Sir after he left Japan. All the others were dead, he supposed; as dead as his fellow artists Utamaro, Toyukuni, Buncho, Kiyonoga, a hundred others. And Sharaku? Forgotten now; you rarely came across one of his fine prints of actors, even in the second-hand shops. What had happened to him and O-Kita? People go away and are rubbed out by time, by space, by memory. They live only when a friend keeps their name on his lips. O-Kita. He wished he could have afforded to have kept the collection of prints done of her by the artists. He had sold the entire collection one Year of the Hare when the grandson was sick, and the Chinese doctor had needed ground unicorn horn and mandrake root to cure his closed-up throat. Even his own prints of O-Kita had been sold. All he had plenty of was memory. He wrapped his rags tighter on his thin body as the bitter cold wind grew in fury inside the ruined temple and brushed down

drifting snow onto the paper he was writing. He must finish
before the ink froze in the biting winter air.

*"I write this in old age—he who used to call himself Hokusai,
but today signs himself The-Old-Man-Mad-About-Drawing."*

3. THE OUTCAST

There were more white men coming to China, and to
Peking, one of its busiest cities. They were both traders and
missionaries, but mostly traders, for there was a demand in
Europe for the blue ceramics, and the tea of China, and even
some of the furniture. And there was a very small market for
the native drugs with which medical men in Europe were
timidly beginning to experiment. The white men, and a few
of their women and children, lived just outside the native city
in low, flat houses with gardens around them, attended by a
great many lazy and thieving servants.

For fever and major illnesses the white people were treated
by a thin young German with hard brown eyes and a heavy
guttural accent, Herr Doktor Sigmund Muller, who knew
enough to use the Peruvian bark for fever and to look seriously
Teutonic and scientific when he was puzzled and to stare at
his big silver watch when he felt a pulse. The small Christian
burying ground was growing larger; even a few sailors off
the American clippers loading at Canton were offered the
courtesy of six feet of ground if they died in Peking. When
Doctor Muller, who was writing a thick dull book on native

herbs, went inland to hunt for specimens once or twice a year, the white people dreaded the idea of an emergency which would mean sending for Doc Kan-Pei—"Drain-The-Cup." No one invited Doc for tea, or to the Christmas dinners or the lily-scented Easter services.

"He's gone native, you know," the hostesses would say to each other. "He's been here for years and years and says dreadful things about us."

"When a white man sinks in Asia . . . there's no bottom."

But when a child was desperately ill and the German was away, a servant would be sent into the native quarter. He would usually return with Doc Kan-Pei, an old man in soiled white linen wearing flopping native slippers. What sparse hair he still retained was white and long on the back of his head. His tall body was hunched down over a generous paunch. Doc Kan-Pei always smelled of the native city and of rice wine—and there were those who detected, they said, something else: he was on the smoke. As the British consul said whenever the subject came up, "I mean it's common knowledge, you know, he smokes the *yeng-tsiang*."

"Why don't you deport him?"

"The truth is, the old rotter is American. Besides, at least he is a fairly skilled medical man, and that swine Doctor Muller doesn't care if we all live or die as long as his blasted herb collecting goes on."

Doc Kan-Pei didn't care if he was paid or not. He came in his loose soiled linen suit, tossed his rough-woven palm straw hat to the floor and listened to chests, thumped backs, or looked into eyes or mouths. And usually he said, "Feed her a little more," or "Whiskey by the tumbler isn't the best thing to begin the day with," or "There isn't anything to do. Just make the patient as comfortable as you can. It can't last much longer."

Doc Kan-Pei smoked thin reeking cheroots and never used an ashtray. He had clear blue eyes that would stare at you for a moment; then he'd reach for his dilapidated hat and put it on his almost bald head and shuffle off with an old man's gait toward the native city, toward whatever life he led there. He wasn't standoffish, just indifferent. He'd take a drink at the trading compounds, or smoke a cigar with a sea captain. But he wasn't chummy, didn't seem to need the companionship of his own kind.

The truth was, he despised the usual brand of white men in China, except for some odd fish of a collector hunting ancient Tao-tsu paintings or a T'ang grave figure. He was very clever at examining a ceramic of a tiger spirit from one of the tombs at the old capitol at Loyang. Fingering with pleasure the glazed surface of the tiger or a grave figure, Doc Kan-Pei would say, "Yes, yes. That's the real thing. But you have to be careful. They're very clever at faking them, you know. This one? The real T'ang. Seventh century, all right; very early. No, I don't collect anything. Not any more. Don't buy any Han bronzes around here. The man who makes them is a very good friend of mine. They'd fool anybody."

The disreputable old man loved the city, and knew every part of it. He moved all over, speaking Chinese, Japanese, Tartar, a score of dialects. He had native patients everywhere, and for the women he used a small ivory carving of a nude girl, and the shy women would point to it to show him where it hurt.

Doc Kan-Pei lived alone with a series of young servants—all of whom he called *Yen-tzu*, Swallow—in a small room over the shop of a silk merchant. He had very few expenses beyond the cost of smoke. He would walk home in the late afternoon and everyone knew him, the sellers of larks and thrushes, preserves, and puppies.

The city was always alive, and almost everyone was poor. They wore blue canvas and padded cotton, and lived mostly, it seemed, in the streets. They ate there and curled up there at night, using the curb as pillows.

Doc Kan-Pei would stop with one of the native families in the middle of the street, squatting and waiting for bowls of bamboo soup, or two little meat balls, or noodles, or water chestnuts, or seed cake, or fragment of melon. They would all eat and pay for it with little coppers.

Doc Kan-Pei did not drink as much as most of the white men. And he drank native stuff. There were no vintage years in China, no grape country, no popular and expensive wines. The wines were made of rice and corn. They had taste and bouquet to Doc.

The wine was hot or very warm, heated in a pot of porcelain or pewter. It was drunk hot, Doc Kan-Pei said, because that brings out its flavor. Some of the rice wines were fortified with pomegranate and lotus and, of course, bamboo leaves.

In his room over the silk shop Doc Kan-Pei had very few personal belongings. Only some old books, their leather bindings eaten by house ants, and a small Japanese chest of leather that was once bright red, from which he took everything he seemed to need. He would recline on his native bed in the dark little room, the one window closed to the city below, and take out from his chest the tools he needed for the smoke. The servant had retired for the night into some far corner of the house and Doc Kan-Pei was alone and content. He skillfully handled the *yeng-tsiang* pipes of orange wood. The pill, *gow hop*, was rolled from a ball of opium. Small balls, rolled between thumb and first finger. Then he put them on the *yen-hauch* needle and placed it in the blue flame coming up from the perforated glass globes of the *ken-ten* lamp.

The opium cooked and was removed with a *tsha* knife and placed in the pipe. The smoker took three big puffs of the cooling opium. Then a few more . . . The rest was pleasant dreams . . .

The old hands like Doc Kan-Pei never smoked more than a pipe or two at a time. They smoked three or four times a week and kept it up for years. Most white men didn't last long. They overdid it, started too late and ended up wrecks.

When the first puff of smoke would fill Doc Kan-Pei's lungs he would look up at the wall over the native bed, look up at a woodcut print now faded by sun and darkened by lamp smoke and cooking fires and stained by the rain that came through the ceiling. He would look at Hokusai's picture of the beautiful geisha O-Kita, and the last thing he always saw before the smoke shut out the world was the inscription she had written on it when she had left it as a parting gift. The delicate brush strokes were still fairly legible: "*Kenko to fukuin wo machimas*—I always await good tidings of your health and achievements. . . ."